MY MOTHER'S SPIRIT

By

Dolores Eostenuni Stanfield

PublishAmerica
Baltimore

© 2004 by Dolores Eostenuni Stanfield.
All rights reserved. No part of this book may be reproduced, stored in a retrieval system or transmitted in any form or by any means without the prior written permission of the publishers, except by a reviewer who may quote brief passages in a review to be printed in a newspaper, magazine or journal.

First printing

ISBN: 1-4137-3431-6
PUBLISHED BY PUBLISHAMERICA, LLLP
www.publishamerica.com
Baltimore

Printed in the United States of America

Acknowledgments

In honor and praise to my mother, Mary Sawatis.

I give thanks to my friends, and dearest of them all, Earl Fletcher, who inspired me to write my story.

Irene Lasater, my writing instructor, read my first draft and gave me encouragement. She gave up her time and worked with me until my story took shape.

My daughter, Mary, a published writer, made sure I had all the necessary tools: computer, printer, and writer's manuals, at my fingertips.

Laura Eckert helped with editing and Meg Park tamed my computer.

My husband, Raymond, took over household chores, shielded my calls, and never complained.

MY MOTHER'S FUNERAL
Saint Regis Mohawk Indian Reservation
1934

My mother's useless death deprived me of a mother's love at the age of three. Mary Sawatis Stanfield passed into the spirit world on a numbing, ice-cold morning November 21, 1934. Her unborn baby, conceived seven months before could have had a chance to be born, survived if the priest had not interfered. Instead, she took her baby with her to join her own two angels: the daughters she had just buried, Muriel, age seven and Agnes, barely five.

Muriel, the pluckiest of us three, came down with typhoid fever that September. Everyone expected she'd bounce back in a few days. She died the first Friday of November. They buried her the following Monday. Indians, spiritually sensitive to signs and rhymes of age-old beliefs, predicted two more would die that month.

Muriel walked with a limp, her left leg being two inches shorter, and punier than the other. Relatives claimed that she was born crippled. Grandmother Agnes replied, "Nonsense! The kid had Infantile Paralysis." Muriel, brown and perky, her dark eyes sparkled. Resembling my mother the most, she became my father's favorite. Moments after her birth, cradling her in his arms and admiring her plump little red face, he crooned, "My little buddy." From then on every one called her Buddy.

Two weeks later, Agnes, a pale and frail little blond, died of pneumonia. Angelic, a breath of sweetness here on earth, then she was gone. For three days after Agnes's funeral, my mother lay on Agnes's bed hugging Agnes's little pillow, weeping quietly refusing to hear my grandmother scolding her.

"Stop feeling sorry for yourself and get out here to take care of this little girl who needs you," reminding her that she still had me to care for, with only my cousin Florence, fifteen, to help.

On two occasions, a few days after Agnes's funeral, a friend, Jo-ba-num watched my mother as she approached the riverbank not far from his fish house. She stood there staring off into space. After a few minutes, she turned and walked away. He kept vigil after that. The shoreline of the St. Lawrence River was crusted with thin sheets of ice in spite of the swift currents. Three days later he saw her again, wearing only a short-sleeved cotton dress. He watched her as she came to the riverbank looking down as though she were looking for a path less rocky. As she inched closer to the water's edge, he suddenly appeared at her side. He took off his coat and draped it over her shoulders. He gently led her away from there, and walked her home. She stepped inside and no one noticed.

The houseful of mourners stayed for days after little Agnes's funeral. They sat drinking and commiserating with my grandmother.

The next evening, my mother, still wearing a light cotton dress, came in from taking the frozen laundry off the line.

"Put a sweater on. What's the matter with you?" my grandmother yelled. "You'd think you were deliberately trying to catch your death of pneumonia."

My mother ignored her. She had learned a long time ago how useless it was to argue with grandma, especially when grandma was drinking.

My grandmother, Agnes Jacobs, had just sold her International Hotel, and she had all the money. She had moved us all to a grand house she had built for herself on the Canadian side. My mother didn't have much choice. My father, a white man, without a job and at the height of the Great Depression, chose to live on our reserve with my mother. Occasionally he'd hitchhike to New York City, haunt the old familiar gyms and his hangouts, looking for work. Finding nothing, he'd soon return. Once a respected and proud New York state trooper, he was now jobless and broke. He sat drinking with grandma. He didn't notice how my mother was growing more despondent.

Before her two little girls died, my mother enjoyed sitting on his lap laughing at his jokes. He liked to tease her about being plump. "Mary," he'd say, "you are built like a brick outhouse and not a brick out of place." Then she'd laugh.

Soft spoken, her Mohawk name, Ga'wen;na'no-lon (Mohawk meaning holy voice) suited her and her warm smile portrayed her gentleness. She moved unhurriedly with graceful ease. Her gentle gaze softened even the hardest of hearts. But now after the deaths of her two babies, she avoided him and hardly spoke to anyone.

The night before she died, my mother came into the kitchen and asked where my father had gone.

My grandmother answered.,"He's gone to find more refreshments for our guests."

My mother labored a sigh. "These people have been here for days. Are they ever going to leave?"

MY MOTHER'S SPIRIT

"You just hold your tongue," my grandmother scolded my mother in front of them. "They're my friends. You can't ask them to leave. What's gotten into you? You haven't been yourself with all this sadness burying our two little girls. We can't seem to take care of the babies we got, keeping them healthy and alive and here you are, big and pregnant again. Go on, go to bed." Annoyed, grandmother gestured a wave for her to be gone. Then she added, "Do you want me to send Stan upstairs when he gets back?"

"I don't care anymore," my mother sighed. "I'm so sick of all of you, always drunk. I'm going upstairs and I'm never coming down again." Holding up her swollen belly, she wearily climbed the stairs.

The drunks included my father, my grandmother and her old cronies, Uncle Jack and his drinking buddies, rejoiced over all the free beer. They paid no attention to her until it was too late.

Our reserve didn't have a doctor. The health nurse might have been able to save my mother if only someone had bothered to fetch her soon enough.

Just then, my father returned with the beer and asked, "Where's Mary?"

Pretending concern, grandmother answered, "The poor woman's exhausted, so I sent her to bed." Then eagerly, she instructed Uncle Jack, "Pour the drinks. Drink up everyone." They raised their drinks to my grandmother and those who were sobering up managed to get drunk all over again.

Hours later, when my father went upstairs to check, he found my mother burning with fever. Barely able to raise her head, she made one final request—that he hold her once more before she died.

He gathered her up in his arms, cradled her against him, and sat by their bed in the yellow glow of the kerosene lamp turned down low. He felt her body struggling as she labored for her breath. He lowered her back down onto the bed and pulled the quilts around her. He ran downstairs to fetch the health nurse. Grandmother, sobering up, shook uncle Jack and ordered him to get the priest. She left the few remaining guests asleep in their chairs or wherever they had passed out.

Unfortunately, the health nurse and the priest arrived at the same time. In reverence for the aging Father Bourget, she stepped aside and let him climb the stairs. She followed him. My father and my grandmother sat at the kitchen table and waited. The nurse voiced her immediate diagnoses and asked that a doctor be summoned at once. The priest, ignoring the nurse, presided by my mother and administered to her the last rites. My mother died, taking her baby with her.

Florence told me how people talked about my mother's tragic death for many months saying that if only the doctor had been called sooner. He might have been able to save my mother, or at least he could have saved the unborn baby by cesarean.

"Your father wanted a son so bad," Florence said.

My father cursed the Catholic Church to his dying day.

HOW MY MOTHER'S SPIRIT SCARED GRANDMA

Florence told me what really happened after they buried my mother. While family, relatives, and close friends attended the funeral Mass and trekked to the cemetery, Florence stayed to look after me along with the good women who stayed behind to clean, put the furniture back in order, and prepare a meal with huge pots of good Indian hash. As always, the good women knew how comforting a good hot meat would be for those who returned to the house after my mother's funeral.

Everyone in St. Regis liked my mother and almost everyone came to pay respects and to eat the meal. After a decent interval of quiet conversation and mumbled words of sympathy, the good people including Aunt Helen, left. My grandmother and her cronies, my father, Uncle Jack and his friends remained, sitting at the table bemoaning their sadness and yearning for something stronger to deaden their sorrow.

"As if your grandmother and her poor wretches needed an excuse to start drinking again," Florence continued. "Grandma bought enough beer and whiskey to drown out a whole regiment of state troopers and the Royal Canadian Mounted Police. The two state troopers stationed a few miles from our house on the American side were useless, having no jurisdiction on the Canadian side. Our one Canadian mounty stationed on the reserve made himself scarce that day."

Florence told me how she kept me hidden upstairs so the drunks wouldn't scare me. "They all, including your father, drank way into the night. They got so drunk the women found the trek to the outhouse was too much bother. They squatted right outside by the back door. The men didn't bother stumbling to the outhouse either; they stepped out the kitchen door and aimed over the door stoop. They weren't too loud in the beginning, trying to be solemn and respectful. As the liquor took hold, their thick guttural voices grew slurred and sticky. Soon, their words made no sense at all, repeating the same things over and over. Then Emma Beano and Jake Phelps got to singing. Their songs of mourning sounded more like wailing. The wailing grew louder and louder as the others joined in until they either were too tired or they had run out of songs or were starting to sober up. They grew quieter, and then your grandmother started crying. Your father sounded disgusted and told her to shut up. He accused grandma, saying that it was she who pushed Mary into her grave with her mean tongue, never paying her a kind word. 'You and your priest,' he snarled. 'You old hypocrite, now you're expecting us to feel sorry for you?'

"Your grandmother could sear the souls of angels with her insults, especially when she was drinking. She shouted back at him, calling him a has-been. 'Even the state police kicked you out,' she yelled, waving her fist at him. 'You couldn't even support your own family. And now that Mary's gone, you can't live on this reserve any longer. Get out of my house!' She tottered over to the door and held it open for him."

"Uncle Jack jumped between them, defending his brother-in-law. 'Hey! You can't talk to Stan that way.'

"'You shut up,' yelled Grandma. 'You're no good either—Katsi'nonwakeras—a bedbug, sucking my blood, stealing from me. You think I don't know what's been going on? I want you the hell out of my house, too. Go on, get the hell out of here, both of you.'

"Your father and Uncle Jack staggered out. Grandmother slammed the door behind them.

"That's when the rumbling started. Grandma heard it first. 'Who the hell is stomping around upstairs?' she hollered. 'Sounds like it's coming from the attic and into Mary's room.' The rumbling sounded louder and louder until it felt like the whole house shook. Outside, the fierce, wild November winds hurled against the house with hurricane force rattling the windowpanes. The rumbling roar reverberated over their heads until the drunks woke up. In a stupor, bewildered and bedeviled, they sat up...scared witless.

"'Go up and see who in hell is making all that noise upstairs,' Grandma ordered to no one in particular. No one moved. They were all so damn superstitious. Afraid of the dead."

"'Utkumsarawksa, (Mohawk expression: the crazy devil) Useless, all of you,' she muttered, and started for the stairs. She made it up two steps before deciding it was too much effort. She sat down again.

"'Someone's walking around up above,' mumbled old Emma Beano, sitting next to her.

"All of a sudden, maybe for the first time in her life, Grandma sounded scared. 'Oh my God! It's Mary's spirit? She's come back to haunt me.' Those who were sober enough to sense her fear reached the same conclusion. They scrambled to their feet and aroused the others, shaking them, until all stumbled towards the door and disappeared into the howling mad night.

MY MOTHER'S SPIRIT

"The rumbling and banging sounds coming from the attic that horrible night were only the ferocious winds getting up under the eaves, forcing the metal lining of the roof to vibrate against the rafters. Not only did the pounding sounds like heavy footsteps, scare the bejesus out of the mourners, it scared the devil out of grandma.

"For many nights, she sat brooding alone at the kitchen table, deserted by her friends. Friends—when she made lots of money, providing good food and good times, they were willing to do her bidding. Running her hotel and speakeasy had been very profitable. It also caused the ruination of many lives, including your father's. After this frightful episode, she started to turn her life around. She made a solemn promise to your mother's spirit that she'd never take another drink."

Florence's story convinced me that it must have been my mother's spirit who appeared to my grandmother that night. My grandmother's promise bettered my chances for survival. She, then truly became my "Tota." (The affectionate name for a grandparent.) I loved the grandmother I came to know. Florence knew her as a drunk, mean and spiteful.

"Florence," I asked. "Why did you hate my grandma so much? She was your grandma too. Surely, she must have loved you at one time."

"You'd hate her too if she treated you as she did me from the very first time she saw me. She told my mother, my father must have been the ogre who lived in the cellar at the convent. Grandmother never forgave my mother for not telling her who my father was."

"Who *IS* your real father? I've always been curious myself. You're so smart and good at figuring how to make money. It's been rumored that your father must have been a Jew."

"Never mind who my father was. Grandma sent me to live with Great Uncle Mitchell cause your grandmother couldn't stand the sight of me and didn't want me around. But, she always liked you and was good to you, even though she used to call you Nuisance. That's why I never said anything. I didn't want you hating her too."

"Didn't you like living with Great Uncle Mitchell?"

"I had nothing to say about it. He's the only one who'd take me in after our grandmother threw my mother and me out. She told my mother she might as well marry the worst bum in town because no man would want her after having me. My mother married Pete who beat her and didn't want me either. Great Uncle Mitchell said I'd make a good farm hand when I got older. Then, when I broke out with chicken pox and got all scabby, he sent me back to live with grandma. Grandma sneered and told every one I needed to be de-loused. She got some kerosene and soaked my hair in it. Then she told Uncle Jack to shave my head so I wouldn't get lousy again. He tried his best not to make me look bad. Your father laughed and said I looked like a long-handled, worn-out broom with my hair chopped off and being so skinny. Your mother liked me and told him to leave me alone. I tried taking care of you from the time you were three. But I got pregnant at eighteen and that time grandma threw me out for good."

Brightening up, I said, "Florence, I remember that time my father coming home in the middle of the night and taking us away in his car. His car broke down on the middle of the road and he was flat on his back underneath trying to fix it. The next day we were in some cabin, just you and I. While we were sitting under a tree a bird flew over and dropped poop on your shirt pocket. And you said, 'How do you like that? Even the birds are shitting on me.' We laughed. It's the last time I remember seeing my dad for many years."

"Do you remember all that? You were barely five and I was seven months pregnant. Your father wanted to take us both away from the reserve. But when your grandma found out you were missing, she called the state police and you know what they did to him. We have our grandmother to thank for that."

Florence claimed that it was our grandmother's fault my father was sent to the state penitentiary for so many years. I couldn't understand how my grandmother could have been so cruel until many years later.

MY GRANDMOTHER
Agnes Jacobs As A Young Girl

I saw my Tota as a scrawny wrinkled old woman who hobbled with a cane, especially when her arthritis hurt her so. Miserable and mean, she cursed the universe. But most of the time she acted as though she liked me and I felt happy about her. I liked looking at the photos of her in the picture album on the buffet. Tota looked young and pleasant like Aunt Helen.

My Aunt Helen resembled my grandmother. They were both small, fair skinned, and had that confidant look with just a hint of a smile. Aunt Helen kept quietly busy and never complained. By contrast, Tota liked to argue, had to mutter the last word, even if it was to herself. Some days I'd get tired of listening to Tota and I'd find an excuse to visit Aunt Helen. I went to her house one morning and saw her peacefully stitching on her quilt. This was rare. I sat and watched. After a while, I asked, "Aunt Helen, tell me about Tota. When did she get so miserable?" This is the story she told me about my grandmother.

The Mitchell Jacobs family eked out a living by farming down Snye, an island on the St. Lawrence River. In the early 1860's, a young Irish immigrant rowed up one day, fell in love with the shy young daughter named Sarah. He liked living with the Mohawks and stayed a few years. He knew farming and how to make babies. Three children were born to them, Mitchell, Paul and Agnes. Agnes's two older brothers, Mitchell and Paul became good and aggressive farmers. By the time Agnes came into the world, in 1879, squalling, demanding and showing her Irish temper, the young Irishman had disappeared as mysteriously as he had come. Years later no one even remembered his name.

Mean and ornery for a girl of twelve, Agnes delighted in annoying her brothers. She'd stone the outhouse whenever she spotted her brother, Mitchell, going inside. Or she'd hide behind the barn door and sneak up behind Paul as he prepared to do the milking. She stopped only after he pitched a pitchfork full of cow muck and threw it at her bare legs and bare feet. Scowling mad, she stomped off, and rinsed her feet in the horse's water trough. She balked at helping to prepare splints for her mother's baskets nor would she sit long enough to braid the sweet grass for the baskets. Bored with weeding her patch in the garden, she'd take off for the woods and hide until almost dark. To bring tranquility to the farm, Agnes' mother sent her to the nearby convent in Hogansburg. She hated it and called the nuns God's penguins. Just for spite and to show the penguins she was no dumb Indian, she learned how to read and write better than most people on the reserve.

By sixteen, she had her eye on the willowy dark skinned Indian boy who delivered bags of potatoes to the convent. Tom, a full-blooded Mohawk from St. Regis Island, and the youngest of the five Sawatis brothers, enjoyed the special attention she heaped on him, sharing with him sweets that the nuns had baked. Then she lured him behind the woodshed, puffed up her skirts, kicked off her bloomers and seduced him. Wiry and spunky, she lived up to the rumor about the Irishman who washed up on shore one day and fathered a wild haired she-devil.

When Tom told his four brothers he planned to bring Agnes to live with them, they threatened to banish him from the family farm. "There's already a Jacobs family at the other end of the Island," argued the oldest brother.

"We don't want her claiming a part of our farm. Why do you want to take up with that half-breed?" Spat out the second brother.

Tom, seventeen, explained in his slow quiet voice, "We will marry as soon as the ice jams break loose after the first thaw." His oldest brother not moved by Tom's offer, replied, "She is a woman of too many words. She's been heard to say, she's half Irish of royal land owners. She's got her eye on all this farmland."

"Too bossy for your own good, Tom," advised another. "She'll run you ragged doing women's work."

Buoyed by Agnes's insistence, Tom persevered.

The Sawatis family, angry with him for not following ancestral traditions, marrying a girl more to their liking, sectioned off two scraggy acres far north of the island.

Agnes stared defiantly at Father Bourget when he visited her on St. Regis Island, to warn her of the consequences for cohabiting with her young man before marriage. Agnes scoffed, "Why should I listen to a man wearing a dress? Go tell it to your penguins."

Tom and Agnes fixed up a lean-to on the edge of their two acres, not fit for farming. But, their acreage had standing timber of black ash. Having watched her mother, Agnes knew how to prepare her splints and soon learned the art of baskets making. They eked out a living with Tom felling trees, pounding, stripping and preparing the skeins of splints for basket weaving. Between weaving baskets, and growing vegetables, three children were born to them in six years, Helen, Mary, and Jack. Jack, age two and not walking yet, tended to be slow. He chose to be born when Agnes was home alone. She went into labor and had to bring him out herself.

Agnes agreed that Tom would take the baskets to the trading post or the general store on the mainland to barter for her baskets. Crossing over on the frozen narrowest channels of the St. Lawrence River in the wintertime was bad enough. It was even more dangerous crossing the river in the warmer months after the ice broke up. In summer, it took great strength to row across the river at times bucking high waves and strong currents.

Tom welcomed the daunting task eagerly, if only to get away from Agnes's demands on his time for chores he thought should be hers: chopping firewood, hauling water for drinking and after he had to do all the pounding and stripping of the ash logs. He looked forward to hiding an extra fifty cents for himself so that he might treat his friends to a few bottles of home brew. His monthly trek to the trading posts became his means of socializing. With money in his pocket and fire in his belly, lingering here and there, his over night stays soon stretched to three days. Each time he returned, he had less staples and less money, bemoaning the high prices of flour, sugar, matches, and kerosene for the lamps.

Suspicious, Agnes threatened to go with him next time. "I'll take the children to my cousin's farm and I'll do my own trading." Tom promised he'd try to do better. And he did for a few months. When he was gone for three days his excuses were the same.

"Mr. Mc Kenna isn't paying what you told me to ask for your baskets, says they're not as nice as you use to make them. Says, too, the tourists coming through the village are not buying as many baskets for souvenirs."

In a dilemma, not wanting to impose on the Jacobs cousins, to watch her children if she were to do her own trading. She'd have to find some other way to make a better living. "Damn you, Tom! I'm selling this land to my cousins. I'll buy us a place on the mainland and you're not coming."

"Why'd the Jacobs want it? There's nothing but scrub brush grow here."

"Paul wants to add to his acreage. I've drawn paper. I know the law. You don't." She had him buffaloed.

"We warned you this is what she wanted all along. She can't do no such thing. John Sawatis is one of the old chiefs on this island and we got influence with the tribal council," his oldest brother replied when Tom told them what Agnes had just said.

Emboldened by what his brothers told him, Tom returned with the smell of whiskey, been gone four days and hardly any supplies: a sack of flour, matches, and no sugar, sugar spoils the kids, he says, and no money left over.

Agnes's Irish temper reared up. She grabbed the tomahawk and chased him into the woods yelling, "If you dare to come back, I'll chop off your wilted bejum." Tom ran back to his old homestead, where he felt safe among his brothers. Determined to make it on her own, she continued making baskets. In winter, she bundled the three children, stuffed her six dozen baskets into three big cotton bags, piling them all on the home made sled, and pulled the load across the one-mile path over the frozen river. In summer, she rowed across, with her children huddled together on the back seat of the boat and the bags of baskets stowed in front. With her feet braced against the footrest, facing her children, she pulled on the heavy oars and rowed with all her might. A day, less windy, and the waters less turbulent, was a good day to cross over. She bartered for her own baskets at two general stores until she got her asking price. She managed to get three dollars for her six dozens baskets. She preferred to buy her splints, bought her supplies, and still managed to pocket a dollar.

Agnes accepted and did not question the burlap bags of vegetables: potatoes, onions, and carrots, deposited outside her door. She gladly took the rashers of pork and made salt pork. But she would not let Tom inside the house, nor would she listen to any of the Sawatis brother's, suggestions to make it easier on her and move back to the mainland. They'd even help her they said.

"I'm no fool," she retorted, "You just want your two acres back." She continued making baskets for four more years. Then the Mohawks on the American side declared that the Mohawks on the Canadian side could no longer bring baskets or items of trade to the state side for sale. Some of the crafty Canadians (or British Indians as they were called back then), defied customs by smuggling their wares by boat, rowing up the St. Regis River into the white settlement, Hogansburg, in the stealth of night. Proving too much, even for Agnes, she put her plans into action. Agnes dressed her youngest, Jack, four by then, and carried him to the Sawatis farm. She ordered the Sawatis brothers: "Raise Tom's son for me and you can have your land back."

She packed her few belongings, took her two daughters, Helen, eight, and Mary, six, and crossed the St. Lawrence River for the last time. They walked the three miles to the convent. She looked the Mother Superior in the eye and told her to take good care of her daughters…or else.

MY MOTHER'S SPIRIT

"Just do what these penguins tell you," she whispered to Helen. "And look after your sister. I will visit when I can and before you know it, I'll be back to get you."

Mary and Helen joined the throng of young girls already enrolled there.

Until the 1940s Canada and the United States had a program for de-Indianizing all school age children in North America. Girls where boarded in Catholic convents. Boys were sent to manual training schools. Once enrolled, they were deloused and boys were forced to have their hair cut. All children were forbidden to speak their native language or practice any of their native customs and traditions.

As demoralizing as this program proved to be to Native Americans, it provided the safest place for Agnes's daughters, for the time being, until she could get a fresh start. Hitching rides on the back of buckboards, sleeping in barns, and walking along dirt roads, Agnes made it to Ottawa, Ontario before the icy fingers of winter gripped the city. She appeared at the back door of the King George hotel and began her new life as a scullery maid.

A hard worker, she quickly moved up as head housekeeper. Proud of her accomplishments, she readily, posed for photographs in her new finery. Hardly Indian looking, in her fancy wide brimmed hat, tight skirt, showing off her slim figure down to fine leather high button shoes defining her slender ankles and tiny feet. She looked more Irish with her head high, posing like she owned the great hotel behind her.

Agnes shared an attic room in the hotel with her best friend, Rose. One day Agnes climbed the four flights of stairs lugging a huge flat package. Rose asked, "What are you doing with such a large picture of an American general?"

Agnes explained, "It's a portrait of General Pershing. I saw him in a news reel and someday I'm going to marry someone just like him."

By 1920 with her newly acquired skills in running a hotel, she bought a huge wooden building straddling the Northern New York and Canadian border on the St. Regis Mohawk Indian Reservation and called it the International Hotel. With prohibition in full swing in the states her hotel would soon become a thriving speakeasy. "Buying and selling bootleg whiskey is going to make me wealthy way into my old age," she declared.

She donned her big fancy hat of black satin, feathers and flowers. Her shoes tweaked of expensive leather. She returned in style, in her own truck loaded with furniture and with her portrait of General Pershing beside her.

THE INTERNATIONAL HOTEL
1920

According to a compilation of *Mohawk Indian History* by Salli Benedict for the Akwesasne Library and Museum, as early as 1861, a hotel was built on the Mohawk Reserve by American authorities. It was leased to a white man, Ben Woods. In the late 1890s, Princess White Deer, billed as the first dancer and entertainer of Indian descent, acquired the building and had an addition built onto the hotel—a theater, where she performed.

My grandmother, Agnes Jacobs bought the hotel in 1920 and called it the International Hotel. Many others knew it as the busiest little speakeasy this side of the American border. The huge structure straddled the border between Quebec and New York State. A metal rod staked in the cellar defined the borderline.

Prohibition in the states was in full force, so my grandmother kept all the cases of beer and whisky stacked on the Canadian side. Whenever she got word the state troopers were headed towards the border riding their black mounts, she'd throw out all the drunks and she'd make sure the only ones remaining were very sober.

State troopers chased bootleggers on horseback and the bootleggers drove big fancy Packards. At night, "rumrunners" hired by Agnes rowed their cargo of whiskey, and home brewed beer, packed in burlap bags, down the St. Lawrence River from Canada and up the St. Regis River, to a hidden footpath leading right to the hotel. Agnes surrounded herself with people willing to do her bidding. Except Mary, her oldest daughter, by then, seventeen, who refused to be involved in such activities.

Mary chose to stay at the convent with the nuns.

"Over my dead body," Agnes cursed, when Mary hesitantly told her mother she wanted to be a nun. "What in hell do you know about life except what those penguins' been telling you? A bride of Christ, my ass."

Urged by the Mother Superior, Mary agreed to come home for a month's visit before she became a novitiate.

One day, two state troopers appeared at the back door of the hotel. Agnes had no warning. "Where in hell did you come from?" she demanded of the tall officer who walked in without knocking. Mad as hell, standing chest high to him, she looked up and glared. He stood grinning at her, which made her even angrier. His easy manner unsettled her. She was used to being in command. "Where's your search warrant?" she snapped.

"This is just a friendly visit." He stepped back, his right hand extended. "Name is Rod Stanfield...call me Stan."

Agnes looked at his wide grin, his prominent nose and his stiff brimmed hat. She refused his hand. He took off his hat, smoothed his curly blonde hair, and kept grinning. He looked around. "Nice place you have here."

She pursed her mouth and didn't answer. She suspected his partner was lurking about, looking over the premises.

Agnes again, demanded, "Where's your search warrant? If this is only a friendly visit, why didn't that other officer come inside with you?"

"Now, Mrs. Jacobs, this is not a raid. We just want to get better acquainted."

Agnes noted, that he did look splendid in his uniform as he stood looking down at her, his blue eyes mocking her. "The name's Agnes," she replied briskly. "Then, why are you appearing at my back door?"

Ignoring her question, he continued trying to disarm her with casual conversation. "Entertain much? I've heard a lot about this place."

"This is a hotel," she replied. "Why do you ask? Need a room for the night?"

"I'm tempted, but not tonight. Some other time, maybe. Tell me about this portrait you have hanging here. Interesting."

"It's General Pershing. I saw him once, liked him, so I bought his photograph and had it framed. Why do you ask?"

" Black Jack Pershing. I served under him in the Army."

"General Pershing led a command with the allied forces in France during the war," Agnes replied smartly, cocking her head to one side, pleased with herself.

Mary watched from behind the half opened doorway. She had never seen her mother acting so saucy.

"Who's the pretty young girl I see behind that door?" Officer Stanfield asked, looking towards the doorway.

Agnes stiffened, "She's my daughter, home for a visit from the convent. She's going to be a nun." She frowned, and clapped her hands. "There's work to be done," she said dismissively, and then adding, "Come anytime if it's just a friendly visit you want."

"Thanks for the invitation. I'll be back. You can bet on it," he replied. He stopped, hat in hand, as if reluctant to leave, then he hesitantly moved towards the door and joined his partner outside.

Agnes followed him and stood by the door as Officer Stanfield put his hat on and remounted his horse. He gave her a slight nod and then rode off. Agnes leaned against the porch railing feeling drained.

ADVENTURESOME AND RECKLESS

Roderick James Stanfield had a propensity for trouble from an early age. Born in 1897, a middle child, with two older siblings and two younger, he tended to amuse himself and no one paid much attention. Daring and mischievous, his antics knew no bounds. His father, James Lewis, a machinist on bridges over the Hackensack River married Sophie Stell and they lived in Staten Island with their five children. James Lewis spent little time with his family and left child rearing to his wife. At age fifty, Sophia died suddenly. Her sister, Philomena and her husband, Capp, having no children of their own, agreed to take Sophie's three youngest. Rod was fifteen, Jerome eleven, and Muriel eight. Rod soon proved to be more than they had bargained for.

A rascal with a happy disposition and a mop of tight blond curls and laughing blue eyes, Rod darted here and there, upsetting apple carts, knocking over vendors on busy street corners, and climbing over fences. Good natured and slippery, he didn't abide by rules. He liked sweets, particularly chocolates, and didn't share with others. In order to save some for his siblings, Aunt Phil had to hide her box of chocolates in the oven of the cook stove in the summer kitchen. One summer day, Rod came home shivering after swimming all day and lit the stove to warm himself. The melted chocolates made such a mess the maid spent a whole day on her hands and knees scrubbing the stove and the kitchen floor. His dislike for schooling upset Aunt Phil. (When the truant officer knocked at the front door Rod would sneak out the back.) Aunt Phil soon had her fill of him and sent him to live with his maternal grandmother, Granny Stell.

He adored his grandmother, a wise and loving little woman. Squinting, her eyes clouded with milky blue cataracts, she listened to him. He thought surely she'd give in when he sweet-talked her into buying him a motorcycle. She bought him a toy motorcycle to hold in his hand. A year later when his Granny died, he lied about his age and joined the Navy. Aunt Phil lamented, and Uncle Capp, a state assembly man, arranged a discharge for her wayward nephew.

With a penchant for adventure, he re-enlisted in 1916 at Fort Bliss, joined the 11th Cavalry, and went galloping after Pancho Villa in Mexico with

DOLORES EOSTENUNI STANFIELD

Black Jack Pershing. In 1917, shortly after the United States entered World War I, Rod was wounded and suffered shrapnel wounds across his back during the successful battle at Saint-Mihiel, France. After his discharge in 1924, Rod joined the New York State Police and became a member of the elite corps of the legendary Black Horse Chapter. He was stationed in Malone, New York. He and his partner, Rod Langevin, rode their sleek black horses and chased bootleggers along the Canadian border up the St. Lawrence River from Dundee, Quebec to Hogansburg, New York and as far south as the Adirondacks. They made many surprise visits to the International Hotel and the busiest little speakeasy on the United States and the Canadian border.

Stanfield wasn't interested in Agnes nor was he particularly interested in her speakeasy. He resolved to see that girl who had been peeking from behind the door at the International Hotel.

GIVING IN

After that first encounter with the winsome trooper, Agnes Jacobs, for the first time, eyed her daughter, Mary, as a possible rival.

Two weeks later the troopers were back again. These surprise visits unnerved Agnes. She determined her scouts were either sleeping on the job or were being bribed. Always wanting to be in control, she found herself at a disadvantage. She felt Officer Stanfield's steady gaze sizing her up. Then he grinned and she relaxed. Her eyes lit up. Agnes, determined, open and feisty, shot back with a hint of a smile. Until she discovered how these two troopers were slipping through, she'd have to play coy.

Agnes also made sure Mary remained in the background, giving her plenty of chores to do. "Stop your mooning and get busy," she'd snap at Mary. "After getting all the dishes sorted, make sure the dining room is in order." She barked her orders to others in general. "We've got important friends coming all the way from New York City for our famous fish dinners. Mary! Hurry up with these chores and get your brother to help you. Then get the hell out of here. Go to the fish shack and make sure Jo-ba-num saves us enough fish." Agnes demanded strict attention from everyone including Mary. Mary, dutifully and quietly, did as her mother ordered. Agnes would do everything she could to keep Mary out of sight.

"Who is coming for dinner?" Stanfield asked.

Agnes replied curtly, "Customers. I told you. This is a hotel. I have friends and customers from all over." Wanting to keep her in conversation, he persisted, "Tell me about this hotel?"

"Now Officer, I don't want trouble. I've got important and frequent guests from New York City. It wouldn't do for you and your partner to be hanging around. Just what is it you want?" A sudden tautness twisted between her shoulder blades. She winced, but masked her pain and stepped forward, challenging, "A warrant!" Her hand out, demanding, "search and be done with it." She stood straight, solidly planting her feet, her gaze turned bleak and hard.

"Please call me Stan," he reminded her. A faint crease built around his lips. His usual gleam in the eye returned. Mary, timidly, poked her dark head in and shyly asked her mother for more instructions. Mary's liquid brown eyes and melodic voice captivated him. Bewitched, he watched her every move with a gentle disarming smile until he caught her taking a quick sidelong glance at him. He gave her a sly wink. And that's all it took. Mary was smitten and didn't return to the convent. Within the year Stan resigned as a state trooper.

Stan showed up again unannounced. In casual talk, he confided in Agnes. "I think I've fallen in love with your daughter." Taken aback, Agnes stammered, "You're to old for her. She's ignorant of worldly men like you and I aim to keep her that way. For her own good. I'm her mother, I ought to know what's good for her."

He grinned and agreed with Agnes. "You're right. I'll give Mary all the time she needs." The more Agnes objected, the more agreeable he became until she gave in. He became a frequent visitor pitching in with the work. Stan was especially kind to Mary's fourteen year old, brother, Jack, which pleased Mary.

Agnes almost caved in, heartsick and disappointed over losing Stan to Mary. Determined, she bucked up. She couldn't help but admire the way he helped run her business. He charmed the help and all the guests, everybody like him, including her own son Jack, the oaf, who quickly became one of Stan's minions. Stan's presence electrified Agnes. If that's what it took to keep him around, so be it, she invited him to live with her and her children. Stan's new career as a bootlegger took off. He became a rumrunner with the rest of the Indians.

My cousin, Florence told me many years later. "Stan and Mary were so much in love. Blissfully happy, every chance she got, Mary would sit on Stan's lap and they'd hug and kiss like two love birds—until Agnes entered the room grumbling, 'Damn! At it again, time wasters like kids. There's too much work to be done around here for you two to be sitting around smooching all the time.' Mary would jump up, patting her hair and straightening her skirt. Stan would keep on grinning, so pleased with himself."

A year after Stan moved in, Mary gave birth to baby girl. Stan named her Muriel, after his youngest sister. He beamed cradling Muriel in his arms, crooning. "My little buddy."

Agnes resented the disturbances caused by such a wee person, grumbling. "I never knew a kid could be so much bother." It annoyed her especially when everyone around made a big fuss about Muriel being lame. Agnes called her "Bandy."

"It's God's way of punishing me because we are not married," Mary, laboring under pangs of guilt, lamented over and over.

"Stop your sniveling," Agnes retorted. "God had nothing to do with it. The kid was born with Infantile Paralysis. If I were you, I wouldn't have any more kids."

Two years later, another girl was born, a fragile blond child and sickly. Mary named her Agnes, thinking, her mother would be pleased. Instead, Agnes sneered, "Breeding like rabbits. Hmph!"

Mary, tired from keeping up with Buddy, now two, who learned to propel herself forward in spite of a stunted leg—and trying to nurse a sickly baby—she began ignoring Stan, keeping her distance. Every time he jutted his face up to her, puckered up wanting a kiss, Mary would bat her dark eyes, and tell him, "I don't want anything to do with you anymore unless we get married." She moved into the bedroom with her babies and wouldn't let him in.

Stan gave in. They were married in the rectory of the Catholic Church that October 1930. Julia, Agnes' best friend and hotel cook, witnessed the union. Jack, barely eighteen, and proud to be included, stood up for his brother-in-law. Agnes, bitter, refused to go to the ceremony. "That's no way to get married," she scoffed. "It's no different than sneaking off somewhere and squatting to piss."

According to Mohawk law, now that they were married, Mary gave up her rights as an Indian. Stan, certain that Agnes wouldn't be able to run the hotel by herself, told Mary, "I'll persuade your mother to sell this place. She and your brother can move in her new house she's just had built on the Canadian side. She can afford to retire. We'll move to New York City, where, I know, I'll get a job."

"Go ahead, go to New York City, see if I care," Agnes shouted when he suggested that she sell her hotel. "I'm not selling this place. You'll be crawling back. You'll see. Agnes squared her shoulders and cocked her head in defiance. "Go to hell," she added.

Stan and Mary went to New York alone. They hired Helen, Mary's older sister, to take care of Buddy and little Agnes.

"We'll be back for the girls in less than a month," he promised, "as soon as we get settled and find a job."

The Depression was on, and there were no jobs anywhere. Once a young boxer with promise, lithe and light on his feet, he had sparred with the best fighters, Gene Tunney and others. He was turned away, labeled a 'has been.' He had lost his quick and powerful punch. Tired and dispirited, after six months, he found nothing worthwhile.

DOLORES EOSTENUNI STANFIELD

Mary hated the city. Heart sick with worry for her little girls, and seven months pregnant, in desperation, she went to the Salvation Army and asked for their help. They gave her a one-way bus ticket home.

No sooner did Mary get off the bus than her mother started in on her. "I knew you'd be back. Look at you, pregnant again. For a girl who wanted to be a nun, you certainly haven't kept your legs crossed." She hurled every insult she could think of until there was nothing more hurtful she could come up with. "You're to blame for Stan leaving here. Now get out of my sight."

"What am I going to do?" Mary cried, sitting in the kitchen with Julia the cook. Julia, with her ample bosomed, hugged Mary, comforting her the best she could. She poured her a bowl of corn soup.

"You mustn't let her upset you. It's the drink, you know, that's poisoning your mother," Julia said. "I wish Agnes would give up this horrible business before it ruins us all. We should all pray that she sobers up and comes to her senses."

Just then, Agnes stuck her head in the kitchen, smiling sanctimoniously, "Mary, stop that blubbering and go get your kids. The sooner you get back to a routine the faster you can start earning your keep."

So needy for her mother's encouragement, at that hint of a smile from Agnes, Mary perked up. She stepped lightly down the path to her sister's house to fetch her little girls.

Two months later Stan shuffled home, weary and broke. Walking over three hundred miles, the soles of his shoes had completely worn away.

Seeing Mary and Stan, so happy they were together again, annoyed Agnes. Every time she walked by them, she'd mutter, "You two make me sick."

A few days after my father came home, my mother went into labor with me. My mother writhed in pain for most of the day all the while the health nurse reassuring them Mary was doing nicely. My father came out into the hall soaked in anxiety.

"The baby doesn't want to be born," he cried.

"For crying out loud, take Mary to the hospital in Cornwall," Agnes yelled. "What in hell is the matter with everybody around here."

The next day, March 2nd, 1931, Mary gave a final push and I slid out onto the birthing table in the maternity ward of Hotel Dieu (House of God) in Cornwall, Ontario. I became another subject to be counted for the Canadian census with Richard Bedford Bennett as the Prime Minister of Canada…but to the hospital staff, I was just another baby girl born to a Mohawk Indian.

MY MOTHER'S SPIRIT

My mother wanted to name me Mary Dolores. My grandmother scoffed, "What kind of a name is that to give to a wee babe—after The Seven Sorrows of Mary? How depressing!"

Julia caroled, "Let's call her Eostenuni (joy or happy in Mohawk). She's such a little joy." I was baptized Mary Dolores Eostenuni Joy Stanfield. My grandmother called me Nuisance.

"Get Nuisance out of here," she hollered at my mother when I started crawling and pulling my self up by the legs of furniture. "Keep her out of the parlor." Her so-called guests were the customers who did their drinking in the parlor. A surprise raid in that parlor in the spring of 1933 bought an end to my grandmother's infamous speakeasy.

Late that evening on a balmy month of May, when the guests were partying and whooping it up, a motorboat carrying six or seven federal officers, purred softly into a cove. Within seconds, the feds with their tommy-guns forced their way in. Jack and my father climbed out of a back window and got away.

The raid alarmed my grandmother. She got rid of the booze, fired her lazy scouts and rumrunners and went into retirement. She sold the hotel to Big-Six Sawatis, a nephew of my grandfather, Tom Sawatis.

My grandmother moved us all to the grand house she had built on the Canadian side. Even Julia, our cook, came with us. My mother had three of us to care for—Buddy, by then, age six, Agnes, four, and me, two. My grandmother allowed my cousin Florence, fourteen, to stay and help.

"They were all depending on me," my grandmother told me years later. "Hmph! Useless, all of them! My fancy house with the best of everything and nothing worked: no plumbing, nor electricity. I bought four pieces of property and built four houses on them, figuring I'd rent them to support myself in my old age. With everybody so damned poor no one could afford to pay rent. When my money ran out, so did my friends."

"What happened to my father after my mother died?" I asked.

"With your mother gone, he couldn't stay on the reserve. He went back to New York City, leaving you here with me."

"Florence told me you kicked him and Uncle Jack out right after my mother's funeral. Two years later he came after me and took her too; to help care for me. But you tipped off the state police."

"Don't believe everything she tells you. She thinks, she knows everything."

"Did he really get arrested for bootlegging?"

DOLORES EOSTENUNI STANFIELD

"Rumor has it, he went back to New York City and got mixed up with racketeers. When the law caught up with him, he was sentenced to fifteen years and sent to Dannemora State Prison. I'd say, as a former trooper, he should have known better. Your father's disregard for authority finally did him in."

I felt sad for Tota—deserted by her friends, broke and with me to take care of. Tota kept her promise to my mother and struggled to keep us going. She kept up appearances and never let on how poor we were.

Father Jacobs, Tota's cousin, talked her into going back to church, dragging me along. I thought she over did it, going to early Mass every morning, and twice on Sundays—at ten o'clock and again at two for Vespers. She sent me to Father Jacobs' catechism classes every summer. By age six, I knew all my Mohawk prayers. She bribed Father with one of her prized quilts so he'd let me make my First Holy Communion a year before the rest of my class. To make sure I made my Confirmation by age nine, she even bribed the bishop with another one of her quilts.

"She sings like an angel," she told Mrs. Thomas, the children's choir director.

I ached to join the children's choir only because once a month, after choir practice, Father Jacobs treated the choir to ice cream and cake.

One day I learned why we had no food in the house, I over heard Tota telling her friend, Mr. Phillips, why she went broke.

"I gave out mortgages with a handshake and thumbprints on useless paper. I paid top dollar for the lots I bought in the village and paid cash to the builders. I was too free with my money, believing that I'd ride the wave of easy money as long as the booze kept flowing down the river to my hotel." Mr. Phillips shook his head, then got up and left.

Tota told me how her friends left her, one by one. Julia was the first to leave a few months before my mother died. Bent over from cooking all those years, she waddled up the road with her satchel to live with relatives on the American side. Since she was my godmother, Tota allowed me to visit Julia often. Julia always poured me a bowl of Indian corn soup.

As was our custom on New Years Day, all us kids would visit our godparents and humbly kneel before them asking for their blessing. Usually, your godparent would give you a small gift. Julia always gave me a handful of hard candies.

After receiving Julia's blessing, I'd stay and visit for a while. One day I asked, "Julia, what's depression? Tota says we're poor because we're in a

MY MOTHER'S SPIRIT

depression."

"Depression or sadness, it means the same thing. Your grandmother is depressed because she spent all her money. Powerless without money, she no longer can make people do want she wants. Your mother was depressed because your grandmother was so mean. She prayed that your grandmother would get out of the hotel business. Her prayers were answered. Your grandmother sold the hotel and life quieted down. There were no jobs for anybody. I felt sad for all those who were so dependent on your grandmother."

"Do you feel sad for Tota?"

"Yes, for you and your father too. If only he had not been so adventuresome and reckless. It's not right the state sent him to prison for such a long time. A good man, your father was too. You're only seven, and you won't know him while you're growing up...it's all so very sad." Julia's dark eyes misted and dabbed at them with her hankie. "I don't know what's to become of you when..."

"It's okay," I said. "My mother's spirit is watching over me."

NO NEED TO FEEL SAD
A conversation with Julia

Julia and I sat in front of her window overlooking the cemetery where my mother and two sisters were buried. Small wooden crosses, off to the left, some painted white, some faded, some not painted at all, stood in rows. Most of the graves were unkempt. Stalks of weeds, withered brown, protruded around a few larger headstones. The pretentious dark gray gravestones, family names chiseled at top denoted family plots; they whispered wealth of long ago. Tota had no such plot. Sentimentality served no purpose for her.

The two small wooden crosses marking my two sisters' graves stood in line with many others with no names…small mounds, forlorn and forgotten. There used to be a small stone for my mother, not far from the small wooden crosses. It no longer stood at the head of her grave. Three years ago, the river, had frozen thick and solid. During the spring thaw, ice jams of the huge blocks of ice bulldozed their way down the river onto the cemetery grounds, knocking over many of the headstones and pushing them into a heap. No one cared enough to repair or replace the stones. At one time, Florence had pointed to where she thought my mother's grave had been, but she wasn't sure. At the edge of the cemetery, the narrow brown St. Regis River flowed, meandering slowly by on its way towards the point, where it melded into the mighty St. Lawrence. The dismal sight of the cemetery's dank brown earth blending with the river below suggested a melancholy aura. The sadness in Julia's face, as she sat looking down weaving her basket, prompted me to ask, "Are you feeling sad?" She nodded and kept on weaving.

"Why are you sad?" I asked Julia. "I'm not sad…just awful hungry sometimes. But then I know Tota will sell or barter for some of her stuff and we'll have food in the house again. She gets rent money once a month from the (White) Indian Agent who rents one of our houses. He pays us fifteen dollars a month. As soon as we get the rent money we hurry over to Hemlock's grocery store to pay our grocery bill. Mr. Hemlock always gives me a jawbreaker and a bubble gum ball. But our groceries don't last long. Then we got to get trusted again."

Julia sat quietly by, listening as she continued braiding sweet grass. Only her short stubby brown fingers moved…they were just a-flying. After a

MY MOTHER'S SPIRIT

while, she said softly, "I feel sad because your mother's gone. A girl needs her mother. Your grandmother is finding it harder to get around with her arthritis."

"One of these days, your daughter, Marie will come and get me and she will be my mother. Remember? From the time my mother and Marie were living at the Convent. They were very good friends. My cousin, Florence, told me that just weeks before my mother died, she asked Marie to take care of me if anything ever happened to her. And Marie promised."

"Yes! But, Marie has her troubles too. She has to keep working to make a living. Sometimes I worry about my daughter. She tells me that she works as a model. But still, working in such a big city…I just don't know."

"Everybody in St. Regis knows who Marie Martin is—a famous model," I emphasized. My eyes focused on the framed picture of Marie on Julia's buffet. Tall, and poised, with high cheekbones, and her long straight ebony hair combed tightly away from her smooth satiny skin, she had that dark Indian beauty, I admired. Marie even reminded me of a movie star, the way she held her long tapered fingers, so gracefully relaxed. She appeared to live the life of ease. I copied her stance, posing every time I walked in front of a mirror.

"Tota said her boyfriend's a racketeer. What's a racketeer?" I asked.

"I don't know. I wish your grandmother would mind her own business and not repeat all the gossip she hears," Julia sighed heavily. She heaved her heavy round body out of her chair and limped to the door. "It's time you went home."

Why should Julia be sad for me, I wondered as I walked home. My Tota and I lived in the nicest house in the whole village. There were times when I awoke and felt real hungry—starved—I'd find a crust of bread in the cupboard, the heel of a loaf of bread, pushed way back, unnoticed for days until I had need of it. With a cup of water from our water pail I'd feel full, satisfied, and go back to bed contented. That's nothing to be sad about, I thought. For our supper the night before we had had a bowl of hot macaroni with a gob of fresh butter melting into it, making it nice and juicy. With a little salt and pepper, even rich people would like it as much as I did. Tota saw to it we had milk to drink.

One time, she traded her big plush red settee for a heifer from her brother, Great Uncle Mitchell. He had a big farm on Yellow Island with cows, horses, pigs and chickens. I remember the fun I had the day we ferried the red sofa to the farm and brought back the brown Jersey heifer.

DOLORES EOSTENUNI STANFIELD

Aunt Helen's husband Uncle Pete (everybody called him Kwa-ne-li) owned a crude wooden boat with a powerful motor. It looked more like a scow. He made his living taxiing people across the two rivers. Sometimes, he'd take a boatload of lacrosse players to Cornwall. Every Sunday he ferried churchgoers from the islands to and from the church on the mainland. His leathery brown pock-marred face was weathered and darkened even more by the constant cold winds and the relentless burning sun. He was a big raw-boned man, built solid and stocky. He grinned when pleased but only rarely. I saw him in a good mood just once when a friend came to visit him.

The friend fiddled some Irish jigs and Kwa-ne-li jigged on his toes. He was as light on his feet as a feather blowing above a gently breeze. Then he taught Freeman and me how to jig and we learned it fast. Rounding our shoulders, hunched in like a ball, we kicked our toes out and tapped to the beat sounded by the clapping of hands. We called it Indian jigging.

But Tota lorded over Uncle Pete as if he were her lackey, as if he should be grateful to her for allowing him to marry my Aunt Helen. He didn't dare refuse Tota when she ordered him to ferry us to Yellow Island that day, lest she get testy with him and mouth off. The less he riled her goat, the better they got along.

Uncle Pete heaved the settee onto his broad back, carried it to the wharf and whammed it into his boat without a word. Tota's bony hands clutched my arm as if she feared I would bolt for the boat. She stepped gingerly with mincing steps, favoring her aching arthritic hip, sputtering, "Don't you get grease on it, you clumsy ox." He paid no attention to her. I swung my legs over the side of the boat and jumped in. One look at Tota and Uncle Pete scooped up her skinny carcass, lifted her into the boat, and set her down onto her sofa. He cranked up the motor, drowning her out, and steered his scow down the St. Regis to the St. Lawrence. As soon as his boat hit the swifter water at the wide mouth to the St. Lawrence, he opened up full throttle and the boat lunged forward and left a foot-high wake. I looked out far and beyond and felt the fresh water mist caressing my face. Expanding my chest, I took in deep breaths of the moist breezes and felt invigorated. Tota looked pleased, as if she enjoyed the ride too.

As soon as uncle Pete put her down on dry ground, Tota braced for an argument with her brother. "I'm making sure Mitchell doesn't give me some old cow for my expensive divan," she sputtered, with a determined look. "And for you," she said, staring into uncle Pete's face, "I'll see to it, that you get a good side of beef." Less forceful now, she mumbled, "Mitchell would trade with the devil if he thought he stood a good chance of winning."

Uncle Mitchell, dressed in his drab gray overalls and black rubber boots, greeted us with a sly smile. A faint glimmer of jest played at the corners of his eyes, his gray bushy mustache twitched. Rotund, with heavy jowls, and jolly, he said, "What! You want me best heifer for this old faded settee? You can see it's old—no telling how many drunks been sleeping on it."

"The young heifer or I'm taking the sofa back with me."

"Okay! Leave it. Take the Jersey. You drive a hard bargain."

But, I could tell he was pleased, when he winked at me and invited us to stay for dinner. He even gave me a burlap bag half-full of hazelnuts. I had a hard time dragging the bag, so he grabbed the bag and tossed it into the boat for me. "You should feed this little girl. She's as scrawny as a hobo's dog."

"I'm trying to," Tota scowled. "Why do you think you got my beautiful red velvet sofa?"

We spent a good part of the day visiting. His daughter-in-law, Aunt Elizabeth, cooked us dinner of fried pork chops, milk gravy and boiled potatoes. For dessert, Uncle Mitchell went out into his garden and selected two ripe muskmelons. He took his jack knife from his side pocket, wiped the blade on his overall, cut both melons in half and cleaned out the orange seedy goop right there. Then he handed me the halves to take back to the table. I bit into the deep orange flesh in big bites, slurping it's delicious juices, some of it running down the sides of my mouth, until nothing was left except a thin strip of rind.

Getting Jersey into the boat took some doing. Uncle Pete formed a walkway of an old barn board from the landing to the boat. Uncle Mitchell took Jersey by the noose and led her up the gangplank. She balked, her big brown eyes bulged. He gave her a big slap on her behind and she scuttled up and onto the back seat of the scow. Her legs buckled and I thought they'd snap in two but they didn't. She remained standing. Uncle Peter tied her muzzle close to the rim of the scow so she hardly had room to move her head sideways.

Tota and I walked up the wharf. Tota grabbed onto me and managed to step into the front of the boat. We waved goodbye and Uncle Pete started the motor. It purred nice and easy, rippling the waters rhythmically until we got to the middle of the narrow Snye River. I could see the spire of our Catholic Church far off like a beacon on the mainland. Then he opened full throttle and we sped, skimming and bucking waves like a zephyr.

Approaching the shore, he slowed the motor turned the scow around and backed into the shallow cove and the boat drifted right up to the pier. I scrambled out of the boat and onto the wharf. Uncle Pete had to lifted Tota from the boat and placed her upright onto the wharf. Then he yanked at Jersey's muzzle and she hobbled up the wooden bench seat of the scow and out into the soft muddy landing.

Jersey joined all the other cows in the communal pasture up the hill. After she had her calf she gave us plenty of milk. Uncle Pete took care of the particulars in keeping Jersey productive, and took his share of the milk. When Uncle Jack came home for a few days from whatever job he got fired from last, often from some logging camp, Tota would send him up the hill to do the milking.

"Might as well earn your keep while you're here," she'd say sarcastically. Uncle Jack, easygoing and exceptionally tolerant of Tota's derisive attacks, would take me with him. His rounded shoulders made him look shorter and smaller than he actually was. Always in need of a haircut, his big shaggy mop of dark brown hair overpowered his soft features. He resembled my mother and had the same pleasant disposition. He'd playfully aim one of Jersey's teats and squirt a stream of milk toward my mouth and the stream would hit me in the face instead.

When the three of us sat down to supper, Uncle Jack would take his knife and shape my mound of mashed potatoes into a square little house with a roof and a chimney on top. I enjoyed demolishing my mashed potato house. Tota never let Uncle Jack stay more than three days and then he'd have to go.

"Tota," I asked. "Why does everybody call Uncle Jack Katsi'nonwa'keras (Mohawk for bedbug)? He doesn't look like a bedbug."

"Because, he's lazy and would rather stay in bed all day instead of working. He lived on the island with his uncles. They spoiled him and never showed him how to work, never sent him to school. As he got older he traveled with his father from one logging camp to another. Your grandfather, Tom, never learned how to read nor write either."

"But I like my Uncle Jack. He's good to me."

"He's a bum just like his father. He'll never amount to anything."

When Jersey got too old for milking, we had her for stew. Then, we were hungry again. A friend here and there kept us from downright starving. Mr. Hemlock continued trusting us for groceries. Jo-ba-num would throw me a fish, all de-scaled, cleaned and gutted if I were playing around the shore when he came in with a good boatload of fish. He'd say, "Here, catch! Take this home to your grandmother." At times, he'd skin a muskrat from his traps and

MY MOTHER'S SPIRIT

give us the carcass. Tota would roast it and it tasted just like chicken, all dark meat, moist, sweet, and tender. Mmmm good! There was nothing as good as our muskrat chicken.

Summer days on the reserve were the happiest. At age seven, I had no compunction disobeying Tota's, "Now don't you go out of this yard and don't you go near the river." Shaking my head solemnly, I'd say, "No I won't." As soon as she looked away, down the road to the river's edge I'd go. Knowing I'd get a switching when I got home didn't keep me from going were I wanted.

The mooring where Uncle Pete kept his motorized scow provided a perfect spot for frolicking in the warm water. Clear of reeds and seaweed, the boat landing created a soft muddy beach, perfect for wading and catching polliwogs and minnows. Brown as berries from hours in the sun, we kids either darted under the water quickly or moved stealthily, ready to scoop up a handful of minnows. No grownups ever needed to come watch from shore, or ruined our concentration by yelling, "Don't do this and don't do that." Yet I never heard of a kid drowning while swimming.

My friend, Jo-ba-num, had his fish house nearby. It's where the white folks came to buy fish. I enjoyed watching them traipsing, fancy like, down the path to his fish box to pick out the fish they wanted. Pale beside Jo-ba-num, eyeing him, they grew quiet. They'd stand there watching him clean it, not saying a word. Only the million flies of all sizes whizzed about the blood clots and fish guts. Then he'd wrap their fish in newspapers and they'd be all smiles for the fresh fish, a good bargain, and walk happily back to their fancy cars.

I'd visit with him for a while, until the sun-kissed waters lapping at my feet beckoned. Then I'd be off again chasing the magic of a thousand diamonds sparkling on the rivers edge. The summer I was seven was when I learned to swim.

Often, trusting souls who had come from the neighboring islands for errands left their oars in their rowboat. To us kids playing nearby, the boats were ours for the taking. We'd push the boat into the water, jump in and we were water bound for deep waters. This one time, my cousin Freeman, strong for a boy of seven, rowed, and our boat cut through the placid waters and we joined the bigger and better swimmers out at the sand bar. The older kids preferred to swim out to the big old abandoned sand-dredging scow in the middle of the St. Regis River. As soon as we reached the sandbar, Freeman and I jumped out into the shallow water, enjoying the clean sandy bottom.

Freeman tied the boat to the scow so as to make sure we had a way to get back to shore before we splashed about, reaching down for handfuls of the clean sand, delighting in watching it wash from between our fingers. The older kids cannon-balled on the other side of the scow where it was deeper, daring one another, higher and higher up and jumping from the iron beams of the scow, until they were too tired to swim. Then they rowed back in our boat leaving Freeman and me behind. All of a sudden we became aware of the silence

"Listen," Freeman cautioned me. "They've all gone with the boat."

"What are we going to do?" I whispered, as if afraid of puncturing the silence with words. I stood shivering, waiting for Freeman to think of something. Fearlessly, his dark eyes sparkled and his mischievous grin returned. Then he pursed his lips as if he knew exactly what we had to do. Boldly, he climbed down into the deeper side of the river and plunged into the water. I followed him doing exactly the same. Barely keeping our faces above water, we dog-paddled for all we were worth until we reached shore and our feet hit solid ground. We flopped to the ground huffing and puffing, relieved. We had made it. From then on, like a couple of otters, we got better and better.

Another time I stowed away on Uncle Pete's boat when I heard that he had to ferry a load of lacrosse players to Cornwall for a game against the Canucks. I crawled under a pile of canvas and curled up in a ball and stayed under there until I heard the steady roar of the boat's motor slowing to a soft purring sound. I could hear the slapping sound of the water against the bottom of the boat. Knowing we had docked, I crawled out expecting to catch Uncle Pete's furry.

"Hey! Look at this kid," yelled one of the players.

"It's Agnes's granddaughter," Uncle Pete answered. His swarthy face loomed within inches of mine and stared darkly. "You're in for a good licking. You know that, don't you?" I stared back at him, defiantly, letting him know he needn't warm me because I didn't care.

"Ah! Let her be. We'll keep an eye on her," Dick Seymour spoke up. He had married one of my cousins and I knew him. I followed them into their box inside the arena and sat in between two of the players. They jokingly called out to others that I was their mascot. They took turns buying me ice cream bars until I couldn't eat any more. I had so much fun that day, I refused to think about the trouble I'd be in when I got home.

As soon as we returned and the players had disembarked, Uncle Pete took me by the wrist and delivered me right to our door. Triumphantly, he announced to Tota, "She hid in my boat and I couldn't afford to double back just to bring her home."

I cowered, pleading, as she reached for her willow stick, "Please don't hit me, I promise, I won't do it again." I leaped for the corner behind the big dining room table, figuring Tota couldn't catch me. Angrily, her face darkened, determined to teach me a lesson, she pushed the table against the wall and cornered me. She reached across, whacking me again and again on my back and shoulders. I bent over, hiding my face into my chest as best as I could, with only my arms for cover, and yelled loud enough to satisfy her that I had learned my lesson. Smarting, the welts puffed up red on my arms. But I knew I deserved the licking because she told me that I did and I believed her. Tota dealt with me as she saw fit and my prolonged sniffling afterward did me no good. She disliked whiners and listened to none of my foolishness.

WINTER DUDS

Twenty below zero winds blew across the St. Lawrence and froze the river rock solid twenty-four inches deep, except in the very deep channels. The narrower St. Regis River flowing into the St. Lawrence froze first—a thick solid mass. Well-packed wide paths on the frozen rivers provided fast traveling by horse and sleigh, and best of all: rinks for skating. To some, winters were long, bleak and hard, unless you were a kid like us. Dressed warmly, thanks to Tota and Aunt Helen, my winters were almost as much fun as summers. My heavy dark khaki wool army coat and my Canadian Maple Leaf brand brown PAC boots with rubber bottoms and leather tops, hand-me-downs from my Aunt Helen, were government issues. Tota knitted everything else: the red wool hat, scarf, mittens, skirt and sweater—even the long, brown woolen stockings that hooked to my long johns.

In the fall, the Indian Agent, Mr. McNoughten, announced a shipment of wool coats and boots from the Canadian government. Aunt Helen made sure she was first in line to get the right sizes for her six kids, Freeman, Ronald, Agnes and Mary (the four at home) and her older boys, Jimmy and Bobby (away at the Ojibwa School for Boys). I got the coat and boots one of the boys had outgrown.

"Why can't I get in line for a new coat and boots?" I groused, watching everyone lined up for the new handouts.

"You're not eligible for any handouts from the government."

"Why not? I'm a kid and I get just as cold as anyone else."

"You are not Indian. Your father didn't do you any favors when he agreed to marry your mother," Tota explained, almost as if she were joking. What she said made no sense. "Your mother gave up her rights as an Indian when she married your father. You're a white man's child according to the Canadian government. You are not entitled to Indian aid. If she had not married him, you would have been illegitimate, but you'd be Indian."

"Why is that? I live here with you. You're all Indians. If I was born here and my mother's Indian, then I must be Indian."

"Not according to Mohawk Council. It allows you to live here with me only because you're a kid with nowhere else to go. I asked social services in Malone (New York) for aid. The American officials told me you're Canadian and they couldn't help you.

"Like a man—or a girl in my case—with out a country. The Canadians say I'm American. The Americans say I'm Canadian. The Indians say I'm white because my father married my mother. Then I must not have any rights anywhere?"

"Maybe not. But you've got warm winter duds and that's all that matters…at least for now."

THE LOSS OF INNOCENCE

Hurriedly, I bundled up, eager to play outside on a beautiful sunny day. "Now, don't you leave this yard," Tota warned me.

" No! I won't," I mumbled, going out the door. Outside, the sun's rays bouncing off the clean snow was so bright I had to squint in order to watch the colorful wings of a thousand fairies as they danced on their white magic carpet. Soon, bored with chasing dancing fairies, I trudged around the huge evergreen tree in our snow-covered yard, craning my neck, looking up. The tall pine touched the sky. Surely, today I would spot that blasted owl up on one of the branches winking down at me. As long as I could remember, Tota had been telling me to be quiet when I went to bed or that darn owl would hear me and steal my voice for its own. I was almost sure I had heard it hooting some nights when I couldn't go to sleep. Tota said the owl was really saying, "Who Who Who…Whose voice will I take?" Some days, though, I had my doubts…was that owl like Santa Claus and the Easter Bunny? Would Tota tell me a make-believe story? Today, I'd look until I could see the owl. A few times around that tree and my neck got sore.

Not yet eight, I was forbidden to cross over on the ice to Snye, but I kept eyeing the road that led across the frozen river. Well-packed and wide enough for a team of horses, it didn't seem dangerous to me. I'd seen lots of people crossing on it many times. My cousin, Archie, my age, lived on the island. He had the prettiest dolls I had ever seen. They had real porcelain faces with hair of spun gold and blue glass eyes that closed when you laid the dolls down and opened back up again when you raised their heads.

The only doll I ever had was homemade from Tota's old brown cotton stocking. She'd stuffed the stocking with cotton for the head and body and had sewn arms and legs. It was a boy doll with no face. I'd take him by his stubby arms, stand him on my knees, and bounce him up and down just as I had seen mothers bouncing real babies. I'd sing to him: "Jo- Jo- Jo-Jo-ba-num."

"Why do you call your doll Jo-ba-num?" Tota asked me one day.

"I named him after my friend Jo-ba-num. I think he's a nice man, that's why."

Then Tota had to go tell Jo-ba-num about my naming my doll after him.

MY MOTHER'S SPIRIT

He started calling me "Ista" (Mohawk for mother). Every time he saw me, he'd say, "Hello, Ista."

"Oh! Stop that. I'm not your mother," I'd scoff, batting my eyes, mildly annoyed. Jo-ba-num would laugh. Short, round and stooped shouldered, always cheerful, I liked his teasing me and I liked his round smiling face and his brown button eyes.

As much as I loved my boy-doll, Jo-ba-num wasn't anywhere near as pretty as Archie's dolls. I reasoned that Tota would probably never take me to Archie's house, with her arthritis hurting her all the time. I'd never get to play with Archie's dolls again.

Bundled up nice and warm, I could run over to Archie's house and be back before Tota noticed I was gone. When she looked out the window, I was throwing myself on my back in the snow, flailing my arms up and down, making angels. As soon as her face disappeared I hightailed it down the road, running as fast as my legs could carry me across the ice, a little less than a mile, to Archie's house.

"My goodness! Eostenuni!" Aunt Martha exclaimed, surprised to see me. "You're all out of breath. Does your Tota know you're here?"

"Yes," I lied, taking my hat and coat off. Aunt Martha was really my mother's second cousin. Here on the reserve, we called all our friends and relatives "aunt" or "uncle" if they were about the same age as our mummas or bubbas. We called all our elders "raksotha" for grandfather and "aksotha" for grandmother. Or, if we really liked the grandpa's and grandmas, we'd call them Tota.

Aunt Martha gave me a bowl of hot corn soup and let me stay for a while. I got right down to business dressing and undressing the two dolls. Archie preferred the doll baby that had no hair but cried "mama" when it was tipped just right. All too soon, Aunt Martha appeared with my hat and coat and told me it was time to go.

"You'd best be getting home. I don't think your Tota knows you're here. Mind you, you stay on the path and don't even dare to stop until you get home, or I will never let you come again. Do you understand?"

"Yes I do," I nodded solemnly.

Midway across the ice I saw Jake Gibo hulking towards me. A big bulky man, I didn't like him. He and his wife Bertha lived across the street from us. She was nice. I liked her. She often gave me homemade hard ginger candy pieces. I'd pop one into my mouth and suck on it till it dissolved. But I felt uneasy whenever he was around. I often caught him leering at me.

"What are you doing on the middle of the river?" he sneered accusingly and stood smack in the middle in front of me. I'd seen right away, he wasn't going to let me pass. He shoved his big fat belly into me.

"Tota told me I could go to Archie's house," I answered boldly, with false courage. "She lets me go whenever I want and we play with his dolls."

"I don't think so," he wheezed. "I heard her calling you. You like playing with your friend's dolls? Here, I've got a doll you can play with."

My eyes followed his hand as he unzipped his pants and I saw him take out his maleness. I knew I was in trouble from what Tota had told me about a person's privates. He shouldn't be showing me his thing. I stood frozen on the spot.

He grabbed my arm, "touch it," he said, coaxing. "Touch it. I'll give you this bag of candy."

"No! I don't want too," I squirmed. He would not let go of me.

"I'll tell your grandma you were on the ice."

Hesitantly, I reach out with my mittened hand and touched it, quick-like withdrawing my hand.

"Take your mitten off. Go ahead and stroke it nice," he ordered. He yanked me closer.

I took off my mitten and held his hardened member. He clamped his paw over my hand and yanked it up and down fast. Then, his member spewed out a milky white fluid. He squeezed it with one hand, stuck it back into the opening and zipped up his pants.

"Now I don't want you to tell anybody about this. If you do, Bertha will be mad at you. She'll think you are bad and won't give you any more candy. Go on home. I won't tell your grandma you were on the ice and you won't get a licking."

I knew from catechism class what I had just done was a sin. I felt bad. As soon as I got home, I told Tota, "Jake made me do a terrible thing." I told her about my meeting him on the ice.

Tota stared at me long and hard, scrutinizing my face. I stood there worried, ready to cry, afraid, not knowing what was going to happen next. Finally, she grasped my shoulder, looking deep into my eyes. "You're right in telling me what happened," she said. Then she went quiet again. "Wash up and get ready for supper." She seemed deep in thought, as if she had a lot on her mind. When Uncle Pete came in with a pail of milk, she motioned to him to step out into the summer kitchen. They talked out there for quite some time. When she came back in, Uncle Pete had gone home. She acted as if nothing

MY MOTHER'S SPIRIT

had happened.

I never saw Jake again. No one knew where he went or why. A few months later Bertha moved back to Caugnawage.

The only one I ever told about what Jake made me do, other than Tota, was Father Jacobs, in the confessional on Saturday afternoon.

I knew all about "impure thoughts" from catechism class. Father Jacobs had rehearsed with us plenty of times how to confess our impure thoughts.

"How many times did you touch yourself there?" he'd ask sternly.

"Ten times, Father." If I wanted to really impress him, I said fifty times. I spent a lot of time thinking up some really good ones.

"For a good absolution, say three Hail Marys and one Our Father. Now say a good Act Of Contrition and try not to do it again."

No matter how many sins I confessed, or how bad I made them sound, the penance was always the same. Three Hail Marys and one Our Father. Once when I was confessing my sins, Frankie Hart, on the other side of Father in the next confessional, overheard me. He told all the kids what I had confessed and teased me until I wanted to die right there on the spot. After that, I learned how to really whisper.

When I confessed a real big sin that I did not make up, "I touched a man's privates." Father Jacobs questioned me.

"How did it happen?" I whispered how I had run away and told him what Jake made me do. Father Jacobs said it was not my fault and I had not sinned. He said the man was a bad person possessed of a sickness.

"He really could have hurt you. If you had minded your grandmother and not run away this would not have happened. Lying to your grandmother, disobeying her and running away are venial sins. Your many venial sins will soon roll into one big mortal sin when you no longer honor, love and respect you grandmother. Then you will have broken God's Commandment. Do you really want to do that?"

"No, Father."

"Mind your grandmother from now on. For your penance say the rosary with your grandmother every evening before bedtime and say a prayer to your mother, Mary, and thank her for watching over you."

"Yes, Father. Thank you, Father." I left the confessional feeling good, light hearted and pure.

INDIANS AND DOGS NOT ALLOWED

Tota taught me my letters as a way to amuse me, way before I could remember. By age seven, when Freeman and I started school as first graders, to learn English, I could read and write my name. Our front hallway leading to the living room had two bookcases filled with leather-bound books of all colors: reds, greens, and browns, old, faded and musty. These books I looked at many times. Some had pictures, and most of them had scribbling all over, artwork done by me before I knew better. All of the books had their front and last blank pages torn out. To find a blank page or a page without too much writing on it excited me so, that I would tear it out and use it for practicing my letters or for drawing pictures. We couldn't afford paper. Tota had enjoyed reading before her eyes grew dim and had bought the books when she worked at the King George Hotel. She told me stories about Jason and the Golden Fleece, about the Roman Gladiator, and how the Christians held religious services in catacombs lest they be fed to the lions. The big dictionary sat by itself on the roll top desk. She had to use a magnifying glass to read the words. As I got older, she made me look up the words. She liked to keep informed as to what was going on in the world by reading old newspapers the Indian Agent, Mister McNoughton, had saved for her.

That February, upon Tota's receiving our rent money, we dressed warmly in preparation for the drive to Cornwall to do some shopping: stuff we couldn't buy at Hemlock's grocery store, such as new underwear, and shoes for me.

Uncle Pete harnessed his old white horse, Whitey. Uncle Pete said he had rescued Whitey from the glue factory on account of he was blind and considered useless. Whitey pulled all of us in the wooden oblong-boxed sled filled with hay, as fast as any sleek, well-groomed steed. He trotted nicely along the path hugging close to shore and crossed over on the narrowest frozen channels of the St. Lawrence. Tota sat up front with Uncle Pete. Freeman and I snuggled in back under the old buffalo robe, cozy as two little bunnies in a rabbit's den.

Soon, Whitey had us up and over the riverbank and down the street to the livery stable. Uncle Pete jumped off and helped Tota down, tossed a quarter to the stable boy for a stall and Whitey's reward—a bucket of oats, water, and

MY MOTHER'S SPIRIT

a well-earned rest.

Freeman and I scurried on ahead, anxious to get out of the cold, yet eagerly trying to see everything, our heads swiveling in every direction, almost tripping over one another. We passed many big buildings, in our excitement almost running, getting way ahead of Uncle Pete and Tota. Tota kept her head down shielding her face from the icy cold air and hanging on to Uncle Pete's arm...they bumped into me. I had stopped abruptly to read the sign in front of the big brick hotel. INDIANS AND DOGS NOT ALLOWED. "Tota! What does that mean? How come we're not allowed in there?"

"Never mind, keep moving." She motioned for me to keep going until we came to the Chinese Restaurant. We pushed in the door, gasping for the warmth and the smells of hot food. A beaming roly-poly China man greeted us. We followed closely behind, eyeing his one pigtail hanging down his rounded back and his little black silk beanie. Cheerfully, he showed us to our booth. Freeman and I scrambled into it, grabbing the white starched cotton napkins and tucking them inside our collars for bibs. We slurped our bowls of steaming hot vegetable soup. For an extra treat, the jolly man, smiling widely, gave us dishes of delicious kumquats—tiny baby oranges—in a thick sweet syrup, and hot tea in tiny little cups with no handles. Freeman and I smiled at everyone around us. Even Tota relaxed and lost her scowl. Uncle Pete ate as if he were by himself. Yet the sign back there still bothered me.

"Tota! Can we go into that hotel if we don't have a dog with us?"

"No! We are not allowed in there, because we are Indians."

"But we are allowed in this restaurant," I persisted impatiently.

"That hotel has a saloon. White people are not allowed to sell alcohol to Indians. Some Indians get drunk and cause trouble. The proprietors can't tell a good Indian from a bad one. We all look alike to them. It's easier if they don't allow any of us. They feel safer that way. You can't blame them, can you?"

I had to agree. "I guess not," I stopped asking questions.

"O'ksa! O'ksa! (Hurry, Hurry)" Uncle Pete hurried us along. He made money, taxiing people in his sled, and he couldn't charge us. If he had, right away, Tota would have started ranting a whole litany of favors she had bestowed upon him since he married her daughter. Uncle Pete preferred silence to Tota's criticisms.

We returned home soon enough, and Tota ordered Freeman to help us with our packages. Impish and boisterous, her nagging didn't bother Freeman. He couldn't read as well as I, and the sign that upset me so had meant nothing to him. His dark eyes darted for anything amusing, so he could be off exploring a new curiosity. Not at all bossy like me, he wore his mischievous little grin like a suit of armor.

It angered me. "Freeman," I said, "it's time you learned how to read better. I'm going to teach you."

He followed me into the living room not at all concerned, flung his cap off to the corner of the room, and threw himself on the couch. "Okay!"

WHITEY'S LAST WINTER

Whitey, though blind, worked hard to earn his oats. For the few years that Uncle Pete owned him, he pulled, plowed, and hauled all kinds of loads: people, water, ice, and even a homemade snowplow. Not long after he pulled us along on our buying trip to Cornwall, he accidentally backed into an opening on the ice and died.

Uncle Pete had himself a nice little business peddling blocks of ice. He hired two men to saw square twelve-by-twelve chunks of ice out of the frozen St. Regis River, leaving a dangerous, huge square opening in the middle of it. He then piled the blocks onto a flatbed sled. Whitey did the rest, pulling the heavy load. Uncle Pete delivered most of it to Mr. Hemlock's store and supplied those who had iceboxes in the village. Tota and I owned an ice chest, except ours stayed empty most of the time. Uncle Pete stored the leftover blocks in his icehouse—a shed by the river filled with sawdust. The chunks of ice covered with mounds of sawdust stayed frozen into spring.

I felt so bad for Whitey that day. On my way to Aunt Helen's house to visit Bobby, who had been sent home from the Ojibwa School, I spotted three men down on the frozen river waving and shouting to one another. Curious, I ran down to see what the commotion was about. Whitey had fallen into the opening, and his huge eyes were filled with fear. He struggled, trying to keep his head above water. Uncle Pete and the men were trying to lift Whitey with ropes. I edged closer for a better look. Uncle Pete saw me, and swung his arm waving me away. I ignored him. His one hand groped for his belt buckle. Knowing he whipped his kids with a belt, I wasn't about to give him a chance to whip me. I turned and ran back to their house. Before I reached the front step, I heard a gunshot and I knew poor Whitey, was a goner. Trusting his handler, the poor blind horse, following commands, had backed into the huge opening.

I knew how scared Whitey must have been. The same thing had almost happened to me a week before. It's a good thing Uncle Pete didn't see me. He probably would have shot me too.

TALES, TRUTHS AND WITCH CRAFTS
(The Story of Blazing Bones)

The powerful high winds from the north ferociously blew across at the point where the smaller rivers emptied into the St. Lawrence. In winter that wide area froze solid, deep, and stayed free of snow, slick, and clear as glass. Nature had perfected a skating rink and we didn't ever need to shovel it. That was the place we all went, to slide, skate and play tag. On a Saturday or Sunday afternoon it would be teeming with kids of all ages frolicking in the winter sun.

One bright Sunday afternoon, Tota let me go dog sledding with my friend Annie George. We were the same age but she seemed wiser, and Tota swelled up with admiration every time Annie showed up at our front door. Annie behaved older, and was resourceful and capable beyond her years. With serious intent, she had harnessed and trained her big brown dog, Ohkwari (Mohawk for bear), to pull her sled. I doubted if Tota knew we were headed for the skating area but that's where we went.

A whole lot of kids were all ready there. Some had skates. Those of us who didn't have skates made our own, by crunching empty canned-milk cans, stomping real hard with our booted foot in the center of the can so the edges curled up and clamped tight to the boot. We made one for each foot. It felt awkward but it worked good enough for sliding and that's all that mattered.

I slid around with all the kids having fun until my mouth felt parched and I had to pee. I looked around and didn't see Annie anywhere. So I started walking home. I spotted a round water hole near the bank where someone had chopped through the ice to scoop up pails of water. Every house near the river had an ice hole. It was the only way to get water in the village. I got down on all fours to take a big slurp of the icy water. I crouched down, and my icy mittens slipped into the hole and my whole head and shoulders disappeared into the icy water. Sputtering and groping wildly I was able to lift my head back out and grasped the rim of the hole with my soggy mittened hands, and gasping for air. Annie came running, pulled me onto her sled, yelled at Ohkwari and he took off. She ran along side until we got home, and helped me inside.

She and Tota pealed the wet clothes off of me and Tota wrapped me in a

MY MOTHER'S SPIRIT

warm blanket. "You don't have the sense of a pea hen," Tota scolded me, calling me stupid, and embarrassing me in front of Annie. Tota mumbled curses all the while she was fixing us a cup of French coffee (a half cup of hot coffee and filled it to the brim with hot milk). Annie quickly drank hers and left.

In spite of Tota scolding me for not knowing any better, she must have gotten scared for me too. She forgot to give me a licking for trying such a dangerous stunt. She had made me promise to stay away from ice holes after Whitey fell in. That night, as I prepared to go to sleep, bunking on the small couch in the corner of our front living room close to the wood stove (Tota slept on the longer couch on the other side of the room), she told me the story of Blazing Bones. It put the fear of spooks forever into the inner parts of my brain. I took it as a true story because I knew the woman it happened to, Lizz Jocco. She had no nose.

Lizz and her six-months-old baby, Sammy lived on St. Regis Island. One day she crossed over on the ice to visit friends. She stayed until dusk, and then hurried to get home before dark. She paid no mind to the creature, Blazing Bones, who lived underneath the ice.

Blazing Bones liked to stick his bony skull out of ice holes at dusk when people weren't apt to see him. He was a skeleton with a red ball of fire burning in the center of his chest for a heart. His heart sent rays of red fire out of his eye sockets. He attacked his prey by melting and lapping the flesh off their bones. He licked away until nothing was left but a pile of bones. He saved the bones for spare parts and took them with him to his secret abode. In the morning, there'd be no sign of his prey except pieces of clothing piled wherever he lapped them to death.

Lizz hurried along home carrying Sammy in her arms. Half way across the ice, she felt a ray of heat striking her from behind. She turned to look and saw Blazing Bones climbing out of his hole ready to give chase. She ran as fast as she could, clutching Sammy tightly to her bosom. She felt the heat and knew Blazing Bones was gaining on her. She dropped her scarf hoping to distract him. He stopped long enough to look it over, and then took off after her again. She dropped her mittens, then her coat, and her skirt, one by one. Just as he was about to catch her, she heard her people hollering at her from shore cheering her on. They cried out to throw Sammy to them. She gave one powerful thrust, hurling Sammy through the air and into the arms of his Uncle Joe. The people let out a loud cheer. Liz looked back just as Blazing Bones directed a powerful ball of fire at her. It hit her squarely in the front melting her nose right off her face. To this day Lizz wears a heavy veil covering her face.

The next day over at Aunt Helen's house, I told the story to Freeman. He cocked his head to one side, looked at me skeptically as if I didn't know what I was talking about.

"Lizz Jocco ain't got no nose because a pig bit it off. Everybody knows that," he informed me knowingly.

I asked Aunt Helen if it were so. She smiled and asked, "What do you think really happened?" I said I'd rather believe Tota. Her story made more sense.

That winter, my ten-year-old cousin, Bobby, came home from the Ojibwa School. His plump round face radiated good cheer, he giggled easily, and we enjoyed playing with him. He taught us how to play checkers. Aunt Helen made us a checkerboard by painting red and black squares on a flat piece of plywood. For checkers, she sawed off slices from a broom handle and painted half of them black and the other half red. If we behaved and didn't get Bobby excited, she'd make us popcorn by putting popping corn in a heavy black iron skillet with a cover and shaking it over the kerosene burner. Bobby had us playing checkers all afternoon and we could never beat him.

Bobby often had a spell, and would fall down shaking terribly for a few seconds. It frightened us at first to see him convulsing on the floor. Sometimes after a violent prolonged shaking, he'd fall into a deep sleep. Other times, his spells lasted a few seconds and he'd come to, embarrassed and disoriented. After watching how Aunt Helen handled him gently wiping the spittle from his mouth, we became as adept and were equally protective of him. One day in summer when he and I were picking raspberries for Mr. Hopps, Bobby had a spell and fell to the ground. His face rubbed into the soft brown earth and he got a mouthful of dirt. I wiped out the dirt with the hem of my dress and held his head on my lap until he roused, and I helped him home.

Mrs. Hart from across the street said she knew who put a spell on him and she knew how to cure him. "The next time he has a spell," she told us, "take two long wide strips of black satin and wrap them around your hands. When he froths at the mouth, grab the froth with your hands, and yank it out. Then wad it up and bury it somewhere where no one is apt to ever disturb it and he'll never have any more fits."

"It's the most ridiculous thing I've ever heard," Tota scoffed when she heard what the old lady had told us. "Bobby has epilepsy. That's why the Ojibwa School sent him home."

MY MOTHER'S SPIRIT

Tota usually had a good logical explanation for everything—except the time they found our next—door neighbor dead on her kitchen floor. It looked like she had been beaten to death.

Kwa-ha-ron-nis (Mohawk for Hanging Out Clothes) was Tota's age. She lived in a log cabin across from us and kept to herself. Round bodied, short and spry, she wore her gray hair in two braids hanging down her shoulders. She was always pleasant, and I enjoyed visiting with her. She treated me as a grown up and her friend. I called her Akhsotha (formal Mohawk word for grandmother). The older women resented Kwa-ha-ron-nis and tended to avoid her. Her smooth round brown face was wrinkle-free and smooth as a baby's bottom. Even Tota didn't converse with her much. Yet she knew I went to visit Akhsotha often, and didn't tell me not to.

Akhsotha had a spring to her step and didn't hesitate to show me her cookie jar on the top shelf of her cupboard. That's where she kept her money. Akhsotha took out the dime for the ten pieces of chalk I had for her. "Oh good! Ten pieces of chalk will do me just fine for the month," she said, chuckling.

"Does it really help your digestion?" I asked. "I told Miss Cassa, our teacher, why I wanted the end pieces of chalk. She gave me an odd look and told me, I should tell you to see the health nurse for your runs. She thinks, eating chalk is going to make you a lot sicker."

"My goodness! You didn't tell your teacher all that, did you?" She laughed heartily. "Now these old gossips will have something else to talk about."

"I know," I volunteered sympathetically. "Mrs. Hart said you're a witch. You can change yourself into a pig. That's why your face is as smooth as pig's behind. You go rooting around in people's gardens at night. The only ones who can catch you are older teenage boys, whose voices are just beginning to change."

"Well, I'll be! They say all that? Don't you believe a word of it. It's all superstitious rot."

"I don't," I replied earnestly.

Later that spring, someone found her bloody and bruised body on her kitchen floor, as if she were kicked to death. At the time, farmers were plowing and putting in their gardens. Mr. Hopps found a remnant of a woman's sweater. Most people believed it belonged to the old lady who lived in the log cabin who kept to herself. The rumor spread quickly, how some teenage boys had cornered a pig rooting around in Mr. Hopps' garden. They kicked at it and left it for dead. People said Kwa-ha-lon-nias must have managed to crawl home, where she collapsed and died.

Tota offered no opinion who murdered Kwa-ha-lon-nis, when I asked her. Tota shrugged her shoulders and said, "To':ka' (I don't know)."

After a while I stopped dwelling on it and I went about my daily chores.

Freeman came every day and helped me. We struggled to carry the slop pail to the outhouse, and dumped it out into the hole. Tota reminded us our job wasn't done until we had scrubbed the pail and lid clean with a brush, hot soap-sudsy water and Lysol. Afterwards, we dumped the wash water in the garden and stood the lid and pail upside down outside the back door in the sun to dry. Tota poured fresh hot water in the basin and made us scrub our hands with Life Boy Soap. But I could never talk Freeman into helping me wash the glass globes on kerosene lamps and he wouldn't help me wash dishes.

"That's a girl's job," he'd say as he grabbed his hat and went home. I knew he'd come back the next day...he always did. Aunt Helen saw to it.

There was one more job I had to do before I could go out to play. I hated it more than anything: dusting Tota's fancy furniture. I'd have to get on my hands and knees in order to reach underneath the table legs and get at the ornate carvings and curly-cues on the legs and backs of the dining room chairs. General Pershing was the last to get dusted. I had to climb on the sofa to reach his portrait. Once he was done, out the door I went.

OUR ONE CELL JAILHOUSE
Minnie Mustard and Louie Ham

Our village had a one room jailhouse almost across from the Catholic Church. It had two small windows, one on each sides of the building. The jail cell with steel bars was located in one corner. The Jailhouse had a front door and a back door, with a path leading to the outhouse, a one-holer. It was the only painted outhouse in the village—white like the jailhouse. Louie Ham and Minnie Mustard manned the jailhouse. I liked Minnie because she hugged me every time she saw me. But Louie scared me with his gruff voice.

One day I needed to tell Minnie something and ran over to the jail. "What do you want?" Louie growled as I stuck my head inside the door. A big man with a barrel of a chest, his thundering voice "could scare the devil himself," as Tota would say.

Timidly, I squeaked, "I'm looking for Minnie."

"She's over at the house," he said, motioning with his head to the left, meaning next door.

I scooted over there and knocked.

Minnie yelled, "Come in!" (Nobody ever comes to the door like white people do, when you knock around here. Indians don't bother to lock their house during the day. When they hear a knock they holler, telling you to come in.)

"Oh, Eostenuni!" Minnie exclaimed happily, giving me a big hug. I forgot what I had come to ask. No one ever hugged me like Minnie did. Sometimes, I pretended Minnie was my mother. Her plump brown arms were like my mother's I knew, from a memory I had of my mother bringing in the laundry one time in her short sleeve dress. Minnie looked to me the same age as my mother would have been if she were alive.

"Come over here and see what I got," she said happily, leading me into the bedroom. I saw a crib in the corner of the room. A tiny little baby all wrapped up in a white flannel blanket lay sleeping.

"Where did you get it? Whose baby is it?"

"It's my sister's baby. She's scared to take care of it because the baby's sick. Would you like to hold her? I call her Rose Bud. She's a delicate little rose bud but one day she'll grow up to be a beautiful rose."

"Yes!" I nodded, positioning myself in the rocker by the bed, ready to hold the baby. Minnie placed the little bundle in my arms and I rocked little Rose Bud. I gazed at her sad little face. She looked pale and her eyes, although closed, were far apart. Her little nose flattened against her thin face as if she were in pain as she slept. I thought babies were supposed to be squirming, red, fat and jolly looking.

"Doesn't she ever open her eyes? What color are her eyes? Does she ever cry? How come you don't have babies of your own?"

"She's a good baby, sleeps most of the time. Now, I have you and Rose Bud."

Thereafter, I went every day to help Minnie take care of Rose Bud, bathing and feeding her. But, Rose Bud, at six months, didn't coo, gurgle, or smile.

Two weeks later, Tota and I were getting ready for church. I heard the church bells toll their slow death call to Mass...the funeral for little Rose Bud.

I stood solemnly by Tota's side as Father Jacobs sprinkled holy water around the small white casket. Two men, one on each side, carried the casket, in slow motion, from the front of the church to the entrance. Minnie followed close behind and relatives and friends followed her. She looked straight ahead, sad but not crying, and softly touched my arm as she walked by me.

After the burial, Minnie and I walked home from the cemetery holding hands. She said she felt tired and wanted to lie down. "You'd best be getting home," she said softly. We hugged each other goodbye. I went home to take off my good dress and forgot about Rose Bud.

That afternoon Minnie went after Louie with a butcher knife. A crowd quickly gathered in front of the jailhouse. By the time I cut through the crowd she was pinned to the ground by Mr. Evans our RCMP (Royal Canadian Mounted Police). Minnie was holding her left arm upward, as if to keep the deep three-inch gash ripped open on her forearm from hurting. I gasped at the raw flesh showing and bleeding. "Oh, Minnie!" I cried out, staring at her wounded arm in horror and disbelief. She looked up at me, reassuring.

"Don't be scared, it's okay. It doesn't hurt much. I'll be all right."

I saw the shining cold steel encircling Minnie's wrist. Looking up, I saw the Mountie putting on the handcuffs. He put his hands under her arms, lifted her plump body upright on to her feet and led her into the jail cell. He sent for the health nurse to sew her up.

"I don't know what came over her," Louie explained to Mr. Evans. "All of a sudden she came after me with this big knife. I tried taking the knife from her hand. She must have gashed her arm open by accident. Probably had too much to drink."

"The liar," someone whispered.

"Who saw what happened?" Mr. Evans asked. No one answered.

"I heard them arguing in front of their house," Tota spoke up. "Whatever it was that got Minnie so angry to come after him like that, must have been something. We've been neighbors for years. People called them Minnie Mustard and Louie Ham because she doted on him. Why! Minnie is a good woman—too loud, sometimes, but kind. I doubt she even drank."

I could never figure out how Louie and my good friend Jo-ba-num could possibly be brothers, but someone told me they were. Louie, swarthy, and always serious, looked like a man to be feared. His sharp stare felt as if it could slice me in half. I avoided him. He was not at all like my friend, Jo-ba-num, who was always grinning and saying, "Hello, Ista, my little mother."

Most often, Jo-ba-num could be seen around his fish house mending his nets, getting them ready for casting. When he was cleaning fish for the white folks, he'd throw some fillet fish aside. As soon as the whites were gone, he'd wrap the fillets up in old newspapers and tell me, "Here little mother, take these home to your grandmother."

No one could fry fish like my Tota. She'd roll the fillet pieces in a mixture of flour and cornmeal, throw them into the pan with the bubbling hot fat until they sizzled into a golden brown color…with some bread and butter, they made a feast fit for a king. Tota often said if it weren't for Jo-ba-num giving us fish and muskrat, I'd have gotten rickets a long time ago.

Why couldn't Minnie have loved Jo-ba-num instead of Louie? I worried not knowing what would become of her. I prayed that Minnie wouldn't move too far away so I could visit her sometimes.

I asked Tota, "Why did Minnie have to go to jail? She's the one that got stabbed."

"For an eight year old, you ask too many questions. I wish you didn't have to live in this hell-hole. It's the men who run this village. The government tells Tribal Council what should be done, and the council jumps—so as to keep getting government funding. It used to be, before the whites took over, long ago, it was the clan mothers who told the men what to do. Maybe so, a long time ago, but not today."

"What's to become of Minnie?"

"To'ka, you'd better get at your chores."

DOLORES EOSTENUNI STANFIELD

A few months later Mr. McNoughton got rid of the jail cell and I never saw Minnie again. The council rented the jailhouse to Lababut (Bullhead—that's what everyone called him) and his wife Wal-e-sose (Josephine) and their son, Junior. Junior, my age, looked like his father, short with broad shoulders and no neck. Josephine, a tall woman and strong, looked slightly crossed-eyed. Her head tilted slightly to the left when she looked at you.

"I think Wal-e-sose is a bit peculiar," said Tota.

"But she's not. She just looks that way. I like her. She's helping Junior and me make metal ornaments to put on our Christmas tree next winter. We flatten out tin cans and she cuts them into narrow slivers with tin scissors. She punches a hole at one end of each sliver and sticks a red ribbon through it ready to be hung on the tree. It shimmers and spirals, like tinsel. Next, she's going to show us how to make crepe paper roses. After we're done we all eat bologna sandwiches." Their house smelled homey and Wal-e-sose's bologna sandwiches were so good.

A few years later, construction began for the new jailhouse. The top floor would house the RCMP and his family. The first floor would serve as an office for the Indian Agent. The one cell jail was to be located in one corner of the basement.

IN SELF DEFENSE

By age nine, conceited, I had determined to be an opera singer when I grew up. The one piece of furniture I didn't want Tota to barter away was our victorola. I liked listening to records by Carusso. I'd put his record on the turntable, and crank the handle winding him up. Caruso's voice coming from off the old records sounded nasal, shaky, and scratchy. I'd sing along with him, puffing out my chest in front of the mirror, posing like the diva I'd be one day. Then, I'd listen to Nelson Eddy and sing along with Jeanette MacDonald. Every time I passed by a mirror, I'd check my stance, hold my head at an angle, puckering my mouth and looking doleful—the way I envisioned Jeanette MacDonald must look singing her romantic duets. Tota came along and caught me at it one day.

"I don't know what I'm going to do with her. She's always posing in front of a mirror." Tota apologized for my conceit whenever we had a visitor.

Lucy Hart, two years older and a foot taller, saw to it her way to keep me from getting too conceited. She'd beat me up every change she got. Whenever I had a satisfied expression or looked too smug after being complimented by our teacher, Miss Cassa, Lucy would hide, then ambush me on my way home from school. If I had told anyone, I would have been known as a snitch or teacher's pet. That would have been even worse; no one would have had anything to do with me. I disliked Lucy. She was pasty faced for an Indian with a broad forehead and steely gray eyes close together, and her nose flattened in a perpetual sneer. I wanted to smack her thin lips right off her narrow chin. I held off lest she really pounded me up good.

One time, Uncle Jack came home for a visit while I was in school. As he often did, he waited behind the door to jump out and surprise me when I came home. When I didn't show up at the usual time, he walked towards the school looking for me.

He found me sitting on the schoolhouse steps afraid to go home. The leer on Lucy's face in class had warned me I was in for it. As long as Miss Cassa was inside I felt safe. As soon as I saw Uncle Jack, I took a flying leap towards him.

Hand in hand, we started for home. We spied Lucy behind a tree as we turned the corner. He put himself between Lucy and me. She hurled a good-sized limb at us. Like a boomerang the limb arced around his body and hit me on my right eyebrow. She took off running as fast as she could. With her long legs, she leaped over a fence and into her house.

Washing the blood off my face and taping a bandage to my cut, Uncle Jack emphasized, "Listen. You can't let her terrorize you like that. You've got to fight back. Show her you're not afraid. Quick and deadly, aim for her nose. She won't know what hit her."

"Okay," I whimpered not quite convinced.

Meanwhile, Tota went across the road to have a talk with Lucy's mother.

"She probably deserved it. Always prancing around, thinking she's so much better than the rest of the kids," toothless, bony old Mrs. Hart replied sarcastically.

"Very well then," warned Tota. "We'll take matters into our own hands. You'd better tell your 'wild Indian' to keep her distance."

For days, I went around scrunching my face into a ferocious mug, punching the over-stuffed chair with my fists, hitting as hard as I could.

Tota wrote a letter to an old friend of hers from their old bootlegging days. She arranged to get me a purebred German shepherd. I named him Pal.

Uncle Jack stayed long enough to help me get used to Pal. After a few days, when school let out, Pal would be lying by the schoolhouse door waiting for me. Lucy kept her distance.

Before the month was over, Pal disappeared. A week later he appeared at the back door with his head bashed in. Tota doctored him as best she could. Eventually his head healed. A week later, Tota heard that it was Uncle Pete who had sold him to a breeding kennel in Cornwall. Pal had managed to get away and find his way home. I didn't have Pal's protection for very long. Two months later, I went outside one morning to give him fresh water, and found him dead, lying there with his tongue hanging out. I ran crying to Jo-ba-num, asking him to take a look at Pal.

"Why! Someone has poisoned him. See how his legs are all stiff and his stomach is sucked in?"

"How could anyone be so cruel?" I asked in disbelief. Jo-ba-num shook his head sadly. We had a good idea who did it but we couldn't prove it. Besides, what good would it do? No one cared around here—especially for a dead dog.

After Pal died, Lucy reappeared and continued to bully me. I pretended to ignore her until she stuck her snaky face in front of me, taunting me. A sudden fury welled up inside me and I hauled off and smacked her in the mouth. I

MY MOTHER'S SPIRIT

struggled to get both of my arms around her neck, and with all my might I swung her body to one side and knocked her off balance. She thumped to the ground on her back. I gave her a quick kick in the ribs, turned, and ran home as fast as I could. I got inside and breathlessly told Tota what I had just done.

"Good for you," she replied assuredly. "It's about time you showed some gumption. Your father would be proud of you."

The next day, I spotted Lucy up ahead on the way to school. She eyed me with a menacing look. I returned her stare, carrying a billy-club Tota had given me. She fell in with a group of kids, looking back every so often, leering. After school, I ventured out, prepared but nervous. She didn't appear.

Surprised by my newfound determination, for the heck of it, I grabbed Freeman by his suspenders and flipped him. "Cut it out!" he yelled. Getting back up and dusting himself off, he gave me a nasty look, and walk away from me. He ignored me and didn't want anything to do with me. He chummed with his buddies. Amazed at how easily I could throw him any time I felt like it, I kept it up. A few days later, he had had enough. When I went to throw him, he braced himself and grabbed me, knocking me to the ground. It knocked the wind out of me and I saw stars. Dumbfounded by his sudden strength, I didn't try it again. Nor did I attempt to try it on others. Best of all, though, Lucy left me alone from then on.

THE BIG MOVE TO THE LONGHOUSE

It seemed, no sooner did we get over one hurdle, along would come another hurdle—much like ocean waves coming at us, knocking us down one after another. Tota could hardly keep us treading water to keep from going under.

We learned we'd have to move if we were to keep the Canadian Government for a tenant. Once bouncy and ready for a good argument, Tota accepted this news without comment. "Damn it all to hell," I sputtered when I heard the news. "I like this house we're living in." I considered this house my palace.

Up to now the Canadian Government had not invested much on behalf of the Mohawks on the reserve. Welfare programs didn't exist. We had a two-room schoolhouse and two teachers. A Mounted Police officer (RCMP) and his family lived in a government house. Our Indian Agent, Mr. McNoughton and his family, now, also lived in a government house. The addition in the back housed our health nurse and the makeshift clinic. The doctor from Cornwall spent half a day once or twice a month at the clinic. There was a steady turnover of teachers, nurses and RMCPs; none of them stayed longer than they had contracted for. The RMCP who stayed the longest was Mr. Evans. He had a son, Robbie, my age. Robbie's mother called us sah-vah-ges—savages. She allowed Robbie to play only with me because I was fair, blond, and half white. Next to us Indians, he looked pale, sickly and moody.

The Canadian Customs officer, Mr. Cassa, was a white man. He and his wife were the only ones who stayed on for years—right up until Mr. Cassa retired. A few days before they were to leave, they invited Tota and me for tea. Mrs. Cassa gave me a gold necklace. It had seven little hearts on a chain and each heart had a letter on it spelling my name: D-O-L-O-R-E-S. Although I had never owned anything so beautiful, I didn't feel like wearing it—not even for Sunday's Mass. Kids might think I was showing off. During the next few days, while busy moving, I misplaced it and never found it.

The government rented the building the Cassa's lived in from Tota. The front room served as an office. The long building, painted yellow with brown trim (as all her three houses were) looked like a barn with its gambrel roof. The building stood in the forefront and center of St. Regis, the first official

MY MOTHER'S SPIRIT

looking building one saw upon entering our village.

I pouted for days after Mr. Cassa suggested that we move into that house. Ours was nicer, newer, and fancier with highly polished floors. But Mr. Cassa knew how we depended on the rent money. He persuaded Tota to rent our nice house to a the much younger Customs Agent, Mr. Bona, and his young wife.

Tota took Mr. Cassa's advice. Tota bartered more furniture, dishes, and quilts to pay for the move. We made the big move in one day. Uncle Pete borrowed a big wagon and a team of horses. It took many trips, but by evening we were in our longhouse.

A year later we lost our well-paying tenants anyway. The next couple that rented our nice house didn't pay the rent. "Deadbeats," Tota called them.

It was a good thing my friend, Mabel, my age, lived across the street. She invited me into her house for lunch sometimes if we were playing jacks and she was winning. Sometimes I let her win on purpose, especially when I was very hungry. One day, just because her mother, Mrs. Thompson, our choir director, told everybody I could sing the solo part of the hymn we were practicing, Mabel got so mad at me that she stuck her nose up in the air and kept her eyes closed, so she wouldn't have to look at me. The next day, she sat on her front steps with a box of Ritz crackers and offered some to her friend Annabelle, but would not offer me any. Then other kids stopped by to play. She shared with the others, all the while holding the box far away from me. Drooling and craving even one cracker, I joined in their game of "statues" as if I didn't have a care in the world and watched from the corner of my eye as she and the others finished off the whole box. The only reason I joined the choir in the first place was for the ice cream and cake Father Jacobs gave us once a month and once again at the end of the summer.

Living at the long house and hating it, I groused about doing my chores. "Why do I have to dust the furniture out here in the back room? No one ever comes in here to sit down. And this picture of a sour puss old general, no one knows who it is, except you."

"Do a specially good job today," Tota replied brightly. She was in an exceptionally good mood. "We have some old friends, white folks, from the good old days, coming for a fish dinner. Go over and tell your Aunt I need her help. Then go and tell Jo-ba-num to save me some good sized pike."

I caught her enthusiasm and felt the excitement in the air. Even Freeman came with his mother to help.

DOLORES EOSTENUNI STANFIELD

That day, getting ready for Tota's guests, Freeman and I worked together like old times, sweeping and mopping the floor of the outhouse and putting out a roll of toilet paper. Toilet paper was expensive; we hid the old Sears and Roebuck catalog that we ordinarily used instead. Freeman hauled the slop pail for me just as he used to.

We went to the store for canned peas, store-bought sliced white bread, and a pound of butter. Jo-ba-num cleaned and filleted fresh fish. I helped Aunt Helen set the table with a starched white tablecloth and good china from the old hotel days.

The guests had arrived, and were cavorting all over, joking with Tota. They were drinking glasses of champagne. Tota declined. (She had kept her promise to my mother and no longer drank.) The guests' fancy two-toned brown coupe with white-rimmed tires was parked out front. The car's rumble seat provided the perfect place for Freeman and me to show off until we were called inside to help.

I carried the small boat shaped dishes of warmed peas into the dining room. The guests were acting silly, as if drunk. A man and woman lay entwined around one another on the couch, kissing. A lady with blond curly hair sat on a man's lap, kissing him. I snickered at his gray spats. He looked messy with lipstick all over his face, his hair all mussed up, his tie off, and his shirt half unbuttoned, showing off his white undershirt. Such antics!

"Psst!" Aunt Helen caught my attention. "Stop staring. Put this plate of bread on the table." Staring and gaping, I missed the plate and all the sliced bread fell on the floor. Quickly, she scooped it up, and piled it right back on the plate, and placed it on the middle of the table. "What they don't know won't hurt them."

We all made out that day. Jo-ba-num sold a lot of fish. Aunt Helen got her apron pockets full of American dollars. Tota paid our grocery bill in full. Freeman and I each got a shiny fifty-cent piece. "A little hanky-panky now and then certainly pays off," Aunt Helen chortled. "What's hanky-panky?" I wanted to know. "Never you mind," she answered. "You'll find out soon enough."

"Hanky-panky and up to no good. It all means the same," Tota said.

The next time I heard that expression was a few days later, when I overheard Tota and her friend, Mister Phillips, talking about our neighbor, dapper Mr. Jona. He and his family lived across from us. "I think there's hanky-panky going on across the line," Tota said to our visitor, lowering her voice so I won't hear.

MY MOTHER'S SPIRIT

"You don't say," replied Mr. Phillips, "And there's his poor wife sick in bed with TB and all those kids to fend for themselves."

I spent a lot of time over at the Jona house with Ellen, my age, her four brothers and her niece, Barbra, age three. Tota didn't mind, as long as I told her and didn't stay too long or wander off elsewhere. The only two pieces of furniture in the living room were a beaten up old piano with most of the ivory keys missing and one wooden rocking chair by the curtainless window. The noises echoed off the bare walls. Sometimes, when Mrs. Jona felt well enough to come down stairs, she sat in that rocking chair. She was so thin and frail, it's a wonder she could climb stairs at all. Her hair, matted, looked as if it hadn't been washed in a long time. She stayed upstairs in bed most of the time. She'd holler down when we banged on the out of tune piano. Hubie, the oldest and noisiest, took charge of meal preparations. He opened the canned milk and mixed it with equal parts of water. He made us lard sandwiches—two slices of bread slathered with lard, with sugar sprinkled on the lard. They invited me to join them. The sandwiches were delicious, especially if we didn't have anything to eat at our house. Sometimes, for breakfast, I'd go over and we all had bowls of corn flakes with the watered down canned milk.

By the end of that summer the health nurse arranged to have Mrs. Jona admitted to a sanitarium and the kids were farmed out among relatives. I went to bed many nights wishing I had a slice of bread with some lard on it.

Shortly after I stopped going over to the Jona house, I got a big boil on my chin. Tota put poultices on it, but it wouldn't go away and it hurt just to touch it. "You probably got it from one of the Jona kids," Tota huffed and whisked me off to see the nurse, taking one of her prettiest dishes from the china cabinet. "Please accept this rainbow candy dish for your help," she said to Miss Barr, the health nurse.

"I'm sent here to help the people, especially the children. I'll take the candy dish, only because it's beautiful. But don't feel you have to bring me something whenever you need help. Now, let's take a look at that boil."

Miss Barr took some alcohol, and lanced and drained the boil. It hurt like the devil but only for a minute and, with a big bandage, I was fine. Miss Barr told Tota my enlarged tonsils needed to be removed.

She's not on the tribal rolls. Her father's white and I don't know how I will pay for it," Tota explained.

"I don't know anything about that. All I know is they need to come out. There are other children on the list for tonsillectomies. I'll see to it she's on that list. Don't worry about a thing."

DOLORES EOSTENUNI STANFIELD

A week later, six of us kids were driven by bus to the Hotel Dieu—the hospital where I was born—to have our tonsils out. I woke up in the middle of the night in a strange hushed gray ward that smelled of antiseptic and liniment. My throat felt raw and I couldn't swallow. I whimpered a bit. A sister in her white habit floated in and smoothed my hair. I thought it was an angel and I fell back to sleep. The next morning we were given a dish of ice cream.

In moving around, I had stained the sheet the tiniest bit: I must not have wiped myself properly. Greatly embarrassed, I kept the top sheet over the brown spot. A robust nun, Sister Angela, came swooping into the room and grabbed the sheets off the bed. She made no mention of the stain. She was truly an angel.

Later, I told Tota how kind Sister was to me. "She didn't look at all like a penguin. How come you call nuns penguins?" Tota scowled and pretended not to hear me.

The best part of getting my tonsils out was getting all the extra attention. Tota let me curl up on the sofa in the parlor. To my great surprise, Florence came all the way from Syracuse to see me, bringing ice cream and six cans of Campbell's chicken noodle and rice soups.

Florence was long legged and slim, with a rounded bosom and small waist. I hardly noticed her pockmarked complexion under the peaches and cream blend of makeup she wore. She ignored Tota's sarcastic remarks.

"If your neckline was any lower, your teats would fall out."

Florence wore a shiny navy blue dress with white polka dots. It showed off her figure nicely. I leaned closer and whispered, "When I grow up, I want to look just like you."

We snuggled on the couch and sang songs from a magazine with nothing but words to all the popular songs: "I've Got Spurs that Jingle, Jangle, Jingle," "Don't Sit Under the Apple Tree," and "Red River Valley" She knew every song in the book.

All of a sudden Florence jumped up from the couch. "I've gotta go. I've got a date with Angus."

"Stay and have supper with me," I pleaded. "We'll have more soup."

Just then, Tota walked in. "You still think he's going to marry you?" Florence ignored her. Florence bent down and kissed the top of my head. Then she marched out with her head high, looking straight ahead.

"There she goes, sashaying out of here as if she owned the world," Tota

MY MOTHER'S SPIRIT

sneered. I couldn't understand why Tota was so mean to Florence.

I had to pee and scooted into the outhouse. When I came back in, I said, "Tota! There are drops of blood on the floor of the outhouse."

"Some dog with a wounded paw probably went in there." Then I heard her say, as if to herself, "At least she's not pregnant again."

"Who's not pregnant again?"

"Never mind. Sometimes you hear too much."

As soon as my throat healed, eager to tell about my operation, I went across to Mabel's house. She, Annabel and Cezzi were sitting on the cement steps. Not impressed, they got up and went inside. Mabel closed the door behind her, clearly indicating I wasn't invited.

"To hell with them," Tota said. "Someday you'll be a famous singer and they'll be begging for your attention. Why don't you go help your aunt entertain Bobby?"

"Okay!" I stopped along the way to visit Josephine, to see if she needed help with any more of her paper roses and if maybe she would invite me to share a bologna sandwich. Her paper roses were so perfect they looked real. Some of the women said, "Isn't it odd that she makes such pretty flowers when she's so crossed eyed." I thought it was probably God's way of rewarding her for putting up with all their meanness

Josephine was making roses for the procession. On that last Sunday in June, the village held the procession honoring Saint John the Baptist and the Blessing of the Rivers (it was considerate safe to swim after that day), and the boys and girls also made their first Holy Communion and Confirmation that day. Many ladies were making crepe paper roses of every color working at great speed to complete all the roses that would be needed to decorate mini-alters erected at four places throughout the village.

Father Jacobs said, as always, "I want it to start on time this year." And, as always we started on Indian Time—that is, whenever all the people showed up. I doubted if anyone in the village owned a watch. The only way we showed up for Mass on time was because one of the Brothers rang the church bells to summon everyone to church.

The alter boys in their red cassocks and white blouses solemnly led the procession, with the tallest one in the middle carrying the crucifix. Stout and stately, Father Jacobs followed, wearing his white alb. The choir walked behind, singing hymns and saying the rosary in unison (in Mohawk). The parishioners shuffled along following the St. Lawrence River. At least the refreshing cool breezes from the river revived the faithful in the midday sun. The procession began at the church. The route formed a square, passing the first, second, third, and fourth alter, then ending back to the church. The procession stopped at each alter for prayers and each alter was adorned with flowers, all very colorful, but Josephine's was the most beautiful.

LOSING MY BEST FRIEND

I'll never forget the day I caused my cousin Freeman so much pain. I learned losing a friend created a hunger deeper and more painful than a hunger in the belly. Freeman and I were best friends. We were always together, until I let my smug sense of righteousness get in the way. After I lost his friendship, I felt so empty and missed him terribly.

When he came with Aunt Helen to help in our successful fish fry and we worked so well together, I thought he had forgiven me. I invited him to come with Tota and me for a shopping trip to Massena. Tota had hired Mary Mitchell to take us in her black Buick. "We'll spend our fifty cents and share a banana split at Woolworth's," I said.

"Why'd I want to go anywhere with you for? Just so you can boss me around and make trouble?" He sniffed, swung his head away, jutting his chin upwards. He pressed his lips together and crossed his arms in front of him.

Freeman hadn't forgiven me (I doubted he ever would) for all the pain I had caused him last winter when he stole my five pennies.

Coming home from church one Sunday morning, Tota and I saw small footprints in the fresh fallen snow leading to the back door. Freeman's blue mitten was inside the door and the red cap to my glass bear-shaped honey jar bank lay on the counter. My pennies were gone. I lit out of there and headed for Freeman's house. I burst in yelling, "He stole my money!" Freeman ran upstairs and hid under the bed. Aunt Helen ran after him. Short, agile and quick, she bent down and dragged him out and marched him downstairs.

Sobbing, he pleaded, "Please don't give me a licking. I'll pay it aback." She grabbed him by the hand and forced his five fingers to the top of the hot wood stove. Instantly, she let go of him. His agonizing screams etched into my brain and I sobbed with him.

"I'm so sorry," I kept repeating over and over. I huddled with him outside with my arm around him. He held his blistered fingertips in the snow and sobbed for the longest time. After a while, he went back inside and I came home so ashamed of myself. That winter he earned money, shoveling snow, and paid it all back one penny at a time.

I had no idea how he suffered until one day Tota poured hot skunk oil in my ear. I had earaches ever since I could remember. She'd heat a teaspoon of skunk's oil by holding it over a lit candle and pour it in my ear and my ear would stop aching. This one time, she must have heated it too much. I screamed as the hot oil hit the inside of my ear. I cried for days until my ear stopped hurting. I knew it hurt Tota almost as much the way she bit her lower lip and grimaced. I've been deaf in my right ear ever since. I concentrate and listen harder. Tota says I hear much that I shouldn't.

    Wincing, every time I thought of the pain I cause my best friend stopped me cold from being a busybody snitch. There after, whenever I was tempted to tattle on anyone, I remembered how Freeman's blistered fingertips must have hurt him. I doubted if Freeman believed how sorry I felt. I tried for a good many years to regain his friendship. I finally succeed after we were adults.

SURVIVAL BECAME A CHALLENGE

Tota would send me to Hemlock's store to get free spare ribs for our dog. "But, we don't have a dog."
"He doesn't know that. Just go ask him"
We had an account with him and, just for the asking, Mr. Hemlock would give us free spare ribs. He would trim off the meat from the ribs and throw the bones into a sack, for me to take home. When he was in a good mood he left more meat on them. Tota would roast the ribs and sometimes she boiled them to make soup. Cooked either way; they were delicious. "The closer to the bone, the sweeter the meat," she'd say and I'd agree, smacking my lips and gnawing the bone until it shone like porcelain.

Construction of the government building was completed by end of summer. We lost our tenants, our source of income. Mr. Hemlock no longer trusted us and gave out no more free spare ribs. Tota and I lived mostly on potatoes, macaroni, and corn. Then Aunt Helen got word that Uncle Mitchell would be butchering a hog soon.

Great Uncle Mitchell butchered his hogs in the fall. Aunt Helen had a great recipe for blood sausage and Uncle Mitchell needed all the good sausage makers he could find. She'd get a share of the pork and sausage for her labors. Freeman and I were allowed to come along to watch and to give Tota a rest. We were both eight and full of mischief. Aunt Helen got us up early that September morning. Tireless and dauntless, she rowed down the St. Lawrence to Yellow Island. The ride over proved easy enough as she rowed effortlessly going with the current. Freeman and I dangled our hands into the clear green water and then flicked our fingers sprinkling each other in the face. She rowed steadily and rhythmically paying no attention.

Preparations for the butchering were under way. A roaring fire raged skyward under a big old iron oil drum of boiling water. The drum slanted slightly. "That's to make it easier for the pig to be thrust into the boiling water head first and hauled back out again. Now stand back away from that fire," warned Uncle Mitchell. We wanted to be close to the action so we could see.

The pig was hog-tied and held down by two men. The third man stuck a big butcher knife into the pig's throat. The pig gave a pitiful squeal of pain. Freeman and I ran into the house up the stairs, and hid under the bed. We could still hear the hog squealing. We stayed under there until the squealing stopped. Then we came out to watch from the window. The men let the hog loose. It tried to get up, ran a few feet and fell down. The men stuck the knife back into its throat and bled it some more, while another man held a pail under its throat, catching the blood until the hog died. Then they lifted it by its hooves and heaved its body into the boiling water, head first, in and out, in and out.

"Why did they keep putting the dead hog in and out of the boiling water?" we asked.

Aunt Helen explained, "It's done this way to loosen the hog's bristles." I winced, feeling sorry for the lifeless pig.

The women worked for two days, boiling the hog's intestines and boiling pans of blood, until the blood thickened into blood pudding. " Pudding?" I exclaimed, making a face.

"Ugh!" said Freeman. "Pithyew," spitting on the ground. The blood pudding was mixed with spices, and stuffed into the boiled intestines. The women cooked it and gave us a taste. "Mmmm, good!" we agreed, forgetting our distaste moments ago. We ate the blood sausage with fried potatoes and asked for more.

After milking, we watched John, the farmhand, bring pails full of milk into the back room and dump it into a huge machine. The machine had two spouts. He pumped a wooden handle on the side forcing the milk to come out of the two spouts. Milk came out of one spout and cream came from the other spout. "The machine is called a separator. It separates the cream from the milk," John explained. "But how does the machine know?" I asked. He didn't talk much and he didn't bother to answer. "It's about time you kids went home," he muttered.

Two days later we were ready to leave. Aunt Helen, beaming with satisfaction, stowed our share of pork and sausages under the prow of the boat. Freeman and I sat on the back seat, facing her. A small but determined woman, she planted her feet solid against the bottom of the boat and hefted the oars into the water. "Now hold on and try to sit still." Calm, but doggedly determined, she said, "I don't like the darkening sky over yonder, but if we make good time, I think we can make it home before the storm."

"Yes, I think there's a storm brewing but it's bound to bypass us. Stick to the shallower side of Snye," advised Great Uncle Mitchell as he gave our boat a big push and we shoved off from the dock with a 'swoosh.' Aunt Helen rowed forcefully and steadily. The church steeple on the mainland far in the

MY MOTHER'S SPIRIT

distance served as a beacon. The Snye River seemed placid enough. Eager to get home, she aimed right down center heading for the mainland, instead of heading Great Uncle Mitchell's advice. We thrilled at the sight of our boat piercing thought the choppy water, until the choppy water slapped harder and harder against our boat. As we neared the rougher St. Lawrence it turned from choppy to small waves capped with white foam. The river mist sprayed and soaked our faces. Aunt Helen labored harder, taking longer strokes, forcing the oars to propel us further. The steeple in the distance seemed no closer than when we started. She braced her feet and heaved with all her might trying to keep us inching forward. The waves spilled into the boat. She struggled not only to keep us from capsizing, but also to keep us from drifting over to the St. Lawrence river channel where the currents were much more severe. Still calm, she rowed with determined force.

Trembling with fear, Freeman and I clutched each other, holding on for dear life. I prayed with all my might to my mother's spirit. She must have heard me. All of a sudden Aunt Helen veered away from the mainland and headed across towards Snye. It put us further from our village but it was safer hugging the shoreline of Snye. She rowed along the shallower waters where the currents weren't as strong. Finally, at the narrower part of the St. Regis river, she rowed across right into our cove. Freeman and I jumped out into the sandy bottom to help her. We all heaved the boat up on shore. "There!" she said, unperturbed. "We made it." (Always optimistic, Aunt Helen very seldom frowned or looked perplexed.)

A few months after our harrowing experience, Great Uncle Mitchell passed away. Someone else took over the farm and we received no more free food.

RITUALS, CUSTOMS, GIFTS AND GIVING

We survived and managed to stay healthy from the generosities of others: bits and pieces, now and then, here and there.

From the first day of school in September to the last day in mid June, we lined up first thing every morning to take our tablespoon of cod liver oil. Miss Cassa gave us each a mint-flavored gumdrop she bought herself to help get rid of the god-awful taste of fish oil. When she transferred to another school, no teacher who ever came after her bothered. Most of us resorted to bringing saltshakers from home. Putting a smidgen of salt in the bottom of our spoons helped cut the oily taste and made it easier to swallow. It also kept you from burping up fish oil all day long. After the dose of cod liver oil, we sang our praises of thanks to the government and sang "God Save the King," "The Maple Leaf Forever," and "O' Canada." Then we got on our knees and said one Our Father and one Hail Mary.

A free full-course meal at weddings assuaged my hunger. Good cooks could be counted to turn out bowls of steaming Indian Hash at weddings, and just about the whole village turned out for wedding receptions. Cooks simmered hamburger and onions to form delightful gravy and added mounds of creamy mashed potatoes. Seasonings made the difference and each recipe had its own unique flavor. Some were very tasty—you went back for more; and some were bland or fatty—one serving sufficed. Plenty of sliced turkey, ham, and piles of sliced bread completed the feast. The beautifully decorated wedding cake was cut in small squares, so there'd be plenty for all to enjoy and we could still wrap an extra piece in a napkin to squirrel away for another meal. Often there would be fruitcake, my favorite. At one reception, a drunk standing beside me sneezed all over my fruitcake. His spittle sickened me and I went to get in line for a fresh piece. By the time I reached the table, the cake was all gone. I learned not to let drunks stand near me at future functions.

I could also always count on refreshments served at wakes. The food had been always been the same as long as I could remember: a small white paper plate with a quarter of a bologna sandwich, a quarter of an orange and a store bought cookie (a vanilla cream or the famous maple leaf shaped cookie with the maple cream filling). My hunger intensified when weddings and funerals were few.

MY MOTHER'S SPIRIT

One day in September, Tota and I were blessed with good news. Her grandnephew, Mike Jacobs, from St. Regis Island came to board with us. He'd just gotten a job at the Alcoa plant in Massena. Crossing the river twice a day proved a bit much, so he asked to stay from Sunday afternoon to Friday evening for fifteen dollars a week room and board.

With all that money, we went to Hemlock's store and bought bags of groceries and I ate bologna sandwiches even in the middle of the night when I felt like it.

We had a good Christmas that year. For the last few years, curious about what was so special about midnight Mass, I had teased to go. This time, Tota felt I was old enough and said so. I could go with her. Her arthritis hurt her so, I think she needed me as a crutch more than anything.

I wore my warmest woolens. It gets to twenty below, especially in the dark of winter. Regardless of how cold it got, Tota refused to wear the woolen shawl most elderly women wore in the village. "I look like an old hag in a shawl," she groaned. She put on a black felt hat and her black wool coat with the fox fur collar. The high collar at least covered her ears and she did look fashionable even though her coat and hat were twenty years or more outdated.

In the spirit of giving, it had been a custom at our church for the priest to give out raisin buns to every one in church. The buns were individually placed in big bushel baskets and passed out, one by one, up and down the aisle until everyone got a bun. Tota took two of her biggest white linen napkins, one for her and one for me. I had plans for my bun since this was the first Christmas we weren't dependent on them for our Christmas morning's breakfast.

I had never been inside of the church at night and everything inside looked spooky. The statues, beatific by day, looked more lifelike, grotesque and downright scary. Squeezed shoulder to shoulder with people all taller than me, I had to stand on the kneeling bench in order to see. Tightly packed as we were, it felt steamy enough for warmth but my feet felt very cold. The kerosene lamps gave off a low yellow glow and wafting of fuel oil. We smelled musty, gamy, and I got a whiff of cow manure. Probably, the farmers from the islands hadn't bothered to change their boots. I had never seen so many wedged into the pews. I suspected everyone showed up for the free buns. "The nerve of these 'once a year Catholics' squeezing us regulars, taking up our pews, demanding to share our space," Tota whispered loudly to me. I thought it odd, her saying that. Florence had told me that a few years ago Tota didn't bother to go to church either. I soon got restless and thought the long Mass would never end. I wished I were home in bed. Bored and tired, I wondered why I had ever wanted to see what people did at midnight High Mass anyway. To make matters worse, Tota kept telling me to stop squirming and sit up straight.

This Christmas, thanks to Mike, we were going to feast on ham and eggs and real hot cocoa for breakfast. I planned to wrap my bun and mail it to my father. I had never thought of sending him anything before. We were too poor.

Even so, in the past, Tota had made sure I had an orange, an apple, some nuts, and hard candies in my brown cotton stocking I hung by the wood stove chimney. A package or two would contain a hand-knit pair of socks, mittens or a new scarf. She'd barter one of her prized star quilts, fancy cut glass or silverware for these gifts.

One winter a long time ago, she cut a pine tree bough. She took each individual brush, trimmed the ends off it in a straight line with shears so that each brush stood by its self. She made skirts out of scrap cotton for each brush. Each one looked like a skinny dancer with a ballroom gown. By standing the dancers upright on the seat of the kitchen chair and carefully moving the chair back and forth, and side to side, I could make the pine brush ladies in their fancy ball gowns weave as gracefully as if they were dancing. I spent a good part of the day making the pine brush ladies dance in all directions just by moving the chair ever so carefully.

This Christmas, besides the fruit, nuts and candies bulging in my stocking, there were packages wrapped in pretty Christmas paper piled by the wood bin: a pack of playing cards, a long slim tin of water colors, a box of crayons with their tips all sharpened, and two pads of drawing paper. Mike liked the scarf I knitted for him, too. Tota had given me all her scraps of yarn and had shown me how to do plain and purl stitches to give it a finished look.

The playing cards were from Mike. Tota had a thing about cards. "Tis a devil's diversion," she claimed. But since they were from Mike, she let me keep them so as not to hurt his feelings. But she had to tell me the story of Satan and the midnight gamblers.

"Once there were four men who gambled playing cards with the devil. Delighted in winning, with their piles of chips growing and stacked high in front of them, they went on playing way into the next morning. They didn't even notice that at the stroke of midnight they had grown hooves like the devil. Two short stubs for horns grew out of the sides of their heads. They took on the appearances and personality of the devil and all of them became very cunning and cruel. It's all they ever wanted to do. They had lost their

MY MOTHER'S SPIRIT

souls to the devil. Regular card players were afraid to play cards with them lest they grew horns and hooves too."

I mostly used the cards to do my arithmetic by counting the characters on them, until Mike taught me how to play solitaire. "You know you are playing against the devil when you play solitaire. Don't you?" Tota warned me. "One of these days, when you are playing your game, you'll look up and see the devil urging you on." I didn't take her seriously anymore, especially when I learned there was never any owl up in a tree outside my bedroom window ready to steal my voice. She had made it all up to scare me into doing what she wanted.

"You'd better put the cards up and get your cinnamon bun ready for mailing, if you still want to send it to your father. You should write a note and tell him how you are doing in school. He'd like that," she reminded me.

"Why do that? I've written to him three times and he's never answered. Yet the letters didn't come back. So he must have gotten them. I don't even know what to call him. If he were Mohawk, I'd call him Bubba!" I complained. "Why can't we hire Mose White to drive us to that prison where he's locked up so I can see for myself what he looks like and to find out if he likes me."

"He made me promise I would not ever bring you there to see him."

"Why not? Doesn't he want to see me?"

"Your father is a very proud man. He didn't even want you to know where he was or that he'd been imprisoned. I didn't think that was fair to you…not knowing and always wondering about him. He'll be out soon enough and I do know this for a fact, he'll make it all up to you once the two of you are together again."

"I sure hope so." Feeling better, I carefully wrapped up the bun in butcher paper. Then I wrote the note: "Dear Dad, I miss you," drew a heart around it, and placed it with the bun inside a box. I printed the address carefully like we were taught in school, and asked Tota to check the address. She had Mike mail it for us from the Massena Post Office on his way to work. "The less people know about this the better," she said.

Then winter did its damnedest and even got colder than thirty below. Our activities revolved around the wood stove in the middle of the front room. We ate our meals, read by the kitchen table, and Tota and I slept in the corner of the living room on two cots. Mike took the bedroom right above us, hunkering next to the stovepipe for the warmth. In February, when the slop pail outside his bedroom door froze solid, he found warmer quarters elsewhere. We lost our star boarder.

Not long after Mike left, we were out of food. Then we got lucky again. Mr. Evans, our RCMP, asked Tota if she'd spend the night at our new jail. Since she couldn't leave me home alone with the wood stove burning, I went along too. The new building constructed by the government housed the new jail in the basement. It was a hold-over cell for drunks or troublemakers waiting to be transported to Cornwall for a hearing the next day. Mr. Evans had to lock up a young woman for drunk and disorderly conduct. He explained to Tota that the female prisoner might need another woman as a watchman. Later, Tota explained that he did that so the prisoner couldn't accuse him of rape. We were so broke that for a fee, Tota would do just about anything. We bedded down for the night on two couches in the back room, in view of the jail cell.

For several days I had plenty to tell my school chums. I bragged about spending the night in jail, until Tota told me to shut up about it. Tota had me look up the word "confidentiality" in the ratty old Webster's Dictionary. We were asked to "jail sit" two more times and managed to eke by another winter.

A fresh warm spring day in April lured us kids (me, Annie, Junior, and my cousin Charlotte, from St. Regis Island) towards the cemetery where the grass grew greener with daffodils and yellow crocuses pushing through. I wanted to pick some of the flowers and place them where I was told my mother's grave had been. Tota had told me many times the cemetery was sacred ground holding the remains until bodies turned back into earth. My mother's soul was in heaven with the angels and her spirit watched over me. I think I understood. Yet, we kids whispered among ourselves, sharing tales told by elders mainly to keep us from playing in cemeteries. I had to agree how scary it felt playing here. Eerie looking spooks wafted from the acrid mounds, clouding my imagination. I could envision all the souls trapped in their graves, suffering and withering, not able to go to heaven from evil deeds committed while here on earth. It gave an edge to my excitement—both scary and thrilling. All of a sudden, I spotted the long big shiny black car parked in front of my godmother Julia's house, across from the cemetery. It meant only one thing. Marie had finally come to get me.

"Wan-ta-no-ro!" I yelled, running towards Julia's house. Happily, I pushed the door open with my arms extended ready to hug my friend, Marie. (Wan-ta-no-ro is her Mohawk name.)

I hugged her and took a deep breath of her sweet smelling perfume. Her face next to mine felt smooth as satin. I didn't ever want to let go. A true

MY MOTHER'S SPIRIT

Indian beauty, slender and proud, she looked lithe and graceful in her powder-blue suit. "Have you come after me? My mother gave me to you before she died, remember?"

"Yes, I remember," Marie said, smiling, donning her white gloves. "But not this time." The white felt hat, her trademark, angled smartly over her right eyebrow. The hat confused me. "You're not going already?" I asked sadly, feeling very disappointed.

"Yes, I'm afraid I must." She said, somewhat aloof, "Maybe, someday, you can come for a visit."

I figured she must have had other more important things on her mind. She gave me a dime and told me to go home. I had no choice but to back away towards the door and leave. I sulked all the way home.

"Why the long face?" Tota asked, as soon as I got home.

"I just came from Julia's. Marie's home and she hardly wanted to spend any time with me. I didn't even have a chance to tell her about the scar on my eyebrow from when Lucy hit me with a stick, nor about my spending nights in jail. Someday, she's going to have a hard time explaining to my mother's spirit why she broke her promise."

"I wouldn't hold that against Marie," Tota replied. "It's not easy raising someone else's child. Marie also has to make a living. Besides, you are mine to care for as long as I'm able. Your father will come after you one day."

The next time Julia came to visit, I overheard them talking. Tota must have told Julia how disappointed I had felt after Marie left. I listened close, wanting to hear what Julia had to say.

"I reminded Marie about the promise she made to Mary so long ago," Julia said. "She told me even if she could take her, as Eostenuni got older, if she turned out badly, then Marie would be blamed. If she turned out well, Marie would get no credit for it."

"I guess that's as good a reason as any," Tota replied. "I'm hoping I can hold on until Stan gets a hearing and earns his parole from Danamora. He needs to take her away from here so she can have a chance for a decent life." Then, Tota leaned towards Julia, as if in deepest confidence. "I suspect I might have cancer. My bowels are giving me problems, and I'm losing a lot of blood sometimes."

Hearing Tota worried me even more. I knew about my father imprisoned somewhere near here, but I couldn't even remember what he looked like. I only knew what Tota had told me. I pictured him as ramrod straight, sitting atop his black horse with the military bearing of one who had spent many years in the cavalry, an expert horseman and a state trooper in a gray uniform. Then she had added how women were crazy about him, he was charming, wowing the ladies. I wondered, what would he want with a kid like me? All I could hope was, if he had any intentions of coming for me, he would show up before Tota got worse or died. If he didn't, then I had no idea who'd want me.

As soon as Julia left, I had to know. "Tota, I heard what you told Julia. Why can't you steep some shavings from blackberry stalks like you make for me when I have the runs?" I begged. "You probably have a bad case of diarrhea."

"You shouldn't be listening to our conversation, she scolded, scowling. Then, sitting by her window, she looked far off and it was as if she envisioned a peaceful scene, and her expression softened. "Don't worry. I promise if it gets any worse, I'll ask the health nurse to have Doctor Groman take a look at me the next time he comes to the clinic."

I took comfort in her promise, hoping maybe it was just a little constipation causing the bleeding. I remembered once, when she found blood in my stools, she took me to Miss Barr. Miss Barr explained I probably had a small polyp and that I should be okay, but to keep check on me, and if it happened again to let her know. It didn't. To make sure it didn't happen again, Tota gave me a dose of castor oil every Saturday. And when we could afford it, she'd stir the castor oil in a glass of orange juice. It made it taste worse. Every time I burped I could taste the oil all over again. I couldn't drink orange juice for years and years without tasting the castor oil. It was even worse than taking cod liver oil in school every morning.

CONVERSATIONS WITH TOTA

We welcomed the early spring that year after my ninth birthday. Our pile of wood on the back porch dwindled to a few spindly chunks. Uncle Pete had kept us in supply as long as Tota gave him a few coins now and then when she got a good price for a piece of furniture. I soon forgot about my disappointment over Marie's visit. I worried more over Tota's lack of enthusiasm. She could barely hobble about seeing to my fixing meals and doing my chores, scolding, making sure I did it right. I didn't mind. I'd gotten use to her. Mostly, though, she sat and rested.

We sat at the kitchen table. Tota, with her cup of tea brewed from herbs she called turtle's stocking, I had a glass of water trying to dissolve a cinnamon flavored piece of hard candy left over from my New Year's Day collection. I allowed myself only one piece per day.

"Stop stirring with that spoon and listen to me." She scowled, showing her annoyance. I stopped making the chinking noise. "Mohawk Council wants to rent this house for a meeting place." She sounded tired. "We will be moving back to our other house again as soon as it gets a little warmer."

It should have been good new to both of us. There would be a steady month's rent. I never liked this drafty old house anyway. Instead, my grandmother stared blankly, disinterested, sitting here with her long bony fingers encircling her cup of tonic more for the warmth of the hot brew than for the enjoyment of a refreshing pick-me-up. I wondered why so many people feared her. Thin, frail and bent from arthritis, she could hardly get around. Once a very good basket maker, her knurled fingers were no longer strong enough to scrape, split and prepare her splints for weaving. She still managed to keep up with her knitting as much as possible. "It keeps my fingers from stiffening up like the rest of me," she'd say. Especially when she was hurting. I accepted the news wondering how we were going to manage it. Tota didn't seem up to it.

We moved back to our nice house before Easter Sunday. Tota's sister, Theresa came to help us. Aunt Theresa lived across the St. Regis River (down Snye). I had seen her only twice; once when my mother died and then again when their brother, Great Uncle Mitchell passed over.

Now that Tota was ailing, her relatives felt more kindly towards her. They had disowned her long ago after she took off with my grandfather Tom. "They use to call me 'She Devil' in my youth." She boasted. The only two members of her family who'd bother with her were my Great Uncle Mitchell and her distant cousin, Father Jacobs.

My Aunt Theresa looked worried around Tota. Caring, considerate and reserved, she allowed Tota to do most of the talking, giving orders. They were as different as night and day. Tota was outspoken, sometimes blasphemous even…always spoke her mind. Great Aunt Theresa spoke softly and always in Mohawk. She was as dark complexioned as Tota was fair. I knew why. Aunt Theresa a few years younger than Tota, would not tell me, exactly, but smiled when I said she must not be part Irish like Tota. They were both thin with similar features and Aunt Theresa stood a little straighter. Tota seemed more uppity than usual around her sister. It felt good seeing her acting so chipper.

We were getting ready for church Easter Sunday morning. Tota fashionably dressed, reached for her wide brimmed hat bedecked with fake flowers. As she took the hatpin and placed it between her lips, Aunt Theresa gasped in horror as if she had just witnessed a murder.

"Jesus, Mary and Joseph, you've soiled your mouth," said Aunt Theresa, in mortal fear, pointing at the hatpin between Tota's lips. "Now you can not receive holy communion."

"Oh for heavens sake," scoffed Tota. "After all the sins I've committed in my life time you don't think God's going to mind a little thing like a hat pin between my teeth do you?"

We stepped out into the crisp cold April morning air. Tota held on to me for dear life putting a brave front in her colorful Easter finery. Aunt Theresa led the way wrapped in her traditional dark gray wool shawl covering her head and shoulder showing just her pleasant small brown face. She looked very much like our Blessed Kateri Tekakwitha, *Lily of the Mohawks.*

Aunt Theresa stayed with us for a week and helped us get settled. Tota rallied and was more like her old self. She even had the strength to yank me by the hair a few days later when she found out I sold a bottle of alcohol to the Rubbies.

The day I went to visit Aunt Helen for a game of checkers with Bobby. I passed the shack across the road from her house inhabited by old Boni. Once a nice little house by the river now in such disrepair it could only be called a shack. Every one in the village knew it's where all the alcoholics hung out. There were always three or four of them around and I knew all them by name.

MY MOTHER'S SPIRIT

We called them "Rubbies." When they ran out of the real stuff they drank rubbing alcohol. They mixed it with canned milk and drank it as "white lightning."

I heard, "Hey you! Come here."

I looked over at old Boni in his doorway, motioning to me. "What do you want?" I growled.

Everyone treated them with scorn and no one tried to help them. As long as they kept to themselves and didn't hurt anyone they were left alone. My elders told me to stay away from them. I took my cue from the adults and showed my contempt.

"Here's a quarter for you. Go over to the nurse's office. Tell her you need a bottle of alcohol for your grandmother."

Ready to hurl an insult, such as, "Go get it yourself." I hesitated. A quarter could buy a lot of stuff: five ice cream cones, or bags of candy to last me a month. I couldn't resist. There's no way Tota would ever find out.

Looking over my shoulder making sure no one was watching. "Okay, I'll do it. I'll be right back." I took off running for the nurse's office.

I lied about Tota's arthritis really acting up again. Without too many questions, Miss Barr gave me the rubbing alcohol. "Tell your grandmother I'll be by to check on her the next time I make my rounds," she hollered after me.

I took off running to deliver my booty and to collect my quarter. By the time I got home Tota had already heard about my sneaky errand. She yanked me by my braids, forced me to the chair, and demanded I give up the quarter.

Within the week Miss Barr came for the visit. Tota gave her the ill-gotten quarter. The worst part of it all, I had to apologize for the lie. "Don't worry, I'm sure it won't happen again. As for the quarter, I'll see to it that it gets back to its owner," said Miss Barr. "You can bet on it," she emphasized with a firm nod to my grandmother.

I had to tell Father Jacobs in the confessional. He scolded me almost as bad as Tota. "You've committed a sin breaking one of God's commandments. Unless you're truly sorry and say a good Act of Contrition you'll not enter the gates of heaven." I whispered a sincere Act of Contrition before I left the confessional and immediately said my penance. The next day, Sunday, up in his pulpit he included all us liars and perpetrators in his sermon. Knowing he was talking about me I slid down further into my pew. The consequences of telling a lie for the quarter were very humiliating.

I longed for Tota to be well again. It'd be worth getting a licking, to see her up and about. We were eating supper enjoying our fish. I asked her, "Remember how we once prepared the fish dinner for your rich white friends making some money for all of us?"

"Yes, I remember. What about it?"

"Well, maybe if you showed Aunt Helen and me how to fry fish as good as you do we could serve fish dinners again and make some money."

"Don't be ridiculous. Your aunt has her hands full taking care of Bobby. Why the sudden interest in making money? What do you want now?"

"Annie Hemlock has a bicycle and she's my age."

"I thought so. You want something. Always wanting something I can't afford. Annie's father owns a grocery store. Besides, she's fat and she can very well peddle around town and loose some of that weight. But girls have no business riding bicycles. It's not safe."

"Why not? What's so dangerous about riding a bicycle? Once you learn how, there's nothing to it. Annie showed me how."

"Girls are built different than boys. That's the main reason."

Aha! Now we are gong to talk about sex. I forgot how I worried over Tota's lack of enthusiasm and how defeated she looked.

It's dangerous for girls to ride bicycles. If you lose your balance, you're apt to tear your o-le-ma. (Vulva in Mohawk.)

"Miss Cassa rides her bicycle—a girls bike. It has no cross bar.

"It's too vulgar seeing a girl riding around, having her o-le-ma rubbing together," she said, with contempt, emphasizing her disgust. "A girl should never put anything in her o-le-ma that God didn't intend. She should not ever let any man touch her there, except the man she marries. It's better not to allow yourself to have any impure thoughts about sex, lest you give in to temptation. Take my word for it. I learned the hard way letting that useless young Tom Sawatis sweet talk me into having a go at it."

"Tota!" I cried out, shocked, hearing her mention my grandfather. To think they were young once. And with a grandfather I had seen only twice in my life, I didn't know how to continue. Did her and my grandfather...no I thought. Instead, I went back to discussing about impure thoughts. "Like we learned in Catechism?" I replied meekly.

"That's right," she said emphatically.

It started to make sense. No one ever sat down and told me the facts of life. It came together in bits and pieces, and from hearing this and that from here and there and from this person or that person...like working on a patchwork quilt about sex. Once when I saw Aunt Helen rinsing out small bloody squares torn from bed sheets, I asked what she was doing. She answered, "I'm rinsing out my diapers," and chuckled.

"What do you mean?"

"Someday, when you're older, I'll tell you all about it."

"I'm nine. How old do I have to be?"

Later that day, five-year-old Mary, Aunt Helen's youngest daughter told me what her mother meant. "She wears diaper inside her pants."

Lat year, Bessie, Frankie, Sammy and I, played house in an out-building used for storage. I had a small homemade table and two chairs that my Uncle Jack had built for me. I even had a tiny set of dishes made out of aluminum. We bought food from our houses and ate off the play dishes. Frankie pretended to be my husband. For a bed we used a blanket in the corner of the shed. When Frankie explained what we were suppose to do according to what mothers and fathers did in bed, I revolted and told them all to go home.

Bessie, no older than I, later told me that babies grew inside our belly after a boy did what Frankie was suggesting that we do. She warned me, "You'd better not tell your Tota about playing 'Let's Pretend.' She won't let you play with us no more. Grown ups don't want us to know about all that stuff." I agreed. Tota never knew what we did in the wood shed.

I felt uncomfortable and she seemed agitated. "Tota!" I said, trying to change the subject. "I'm glad to be back in our nice house. Especially, since there's less furniture to dust. I really didn't want a bicycle neither."

"Hmph! Thats good, cause I wouldn't buy you one even if I could afford it. It's shameful for girl to go peddling her ass all over town." She pushed herself away from the table and grabbed for her cane.

It pleased me that she could be her feisty self when she felt up to it.

PREMONITIONS AND SUPERSTITIONS

Tota held on for another summer. She tired easily and preferred to stay in her bed, set up in the living room. I slept on the couch near her bed. Tota had sold most of the furniture to keep us fed and warm in winter. The dining room and the upstairs were totally bare. Uncle Jack no longer came around once Tota's possessions were depleted. There was nothing left he could steal for money.

At age ten, I had the run of the village, and the freedom of knowing Tota no longer had the energy to discipline me. I took care of her.

Still, I missed the good old days. On a hot Sunday afternoon she'd give me a dime for two ice cream cones. The ice cream stand next to the Catholic Church featured two flavors, vanilla and chocolate. We liked vanilla best and I can still taste it to this day. Sitting on our verandah licking our cones, I'd make mine last as long as I could.

"Hard work never hurt anyone," she'd say, in the old days, bustling briskly, doing our chores. And now, that the household chores where all up to me, I had less time for the games other kids played all day long.

One morning Tota asked me to help her get out of bed. "Company's coming. I want to be more presentable."

I was surprised at her sudden enthusiasm, "Who?" I asked, helping her to a chair and reaching for her hairbrush to tidy her up.

"Someone special I haven't seen in a long time. Hand me my light pink shawl so that I don't look so ghostly."

Great Uncle Paul, her brother from down Snye, had sent word he'd be stopping by after church. I had seen him a few times after Mass, when standing outside the church he'd visit for a bit. Wishing he'd accept her invitation to come to our house, I was disappointed that he didn't. He would say that he had animals to feed and then leave. He spoke softly, always in Mohawk, and he looked kindly and unhurried. Like all Tota's relatives, Uncle Paul was small in stature, thin, and unassuming. Tota was the exception. Her strong opinions made her larger than life. Sometimes in the middle of her conversation, frustrated for a better argument, she'd sputter and take off speaking mostly in English.

Uncle Paul's calm manner gentled Tota. She looked relaxed and

MY MOTHER'S SPIRIT

conversed pleasantly. He brought us a hunk of salt pork and half a burlap bag full of new potatoes and onions from his garden. Following Tota's instructions, I made a big pot of "poor man's soup." First I sliced the hunks of salt pork into thin slices and fried it until it was nice and crispy. Setting that aside, I sautéed the onion, which I had chopped up in little bits, in a little of the hot fat. I then added the raw potatoes, cubed in bite size pieces, to the pan of sautéed onions, and stirred until the potato cubes were covered with the fat. Next, I added water to the potato and onion mixture and simmered it all together until the potatoes where done. We all enjoyed the soup. With my belly full, I sat nearby, contented, listening to Uncle Paul's stories.

"Remember the time Mitchell wanted me to saw off his leg because it had turned black and you won't let me? You cured him with poultices of mashed dandelion leaves." Tota nodded. "Theresa had a beau, Abe Jock. You didn't like him. When he went into the outhouse, you locked him in. Hitching up kohsa:tens, you pulled the outhouse backwards. Abe was still sitting on the seat with his feet up in the air."

Tota said, "I did no such thing." They both laughed. Then she said, "But Abe never came back, did he?"

Just as Uncle Paul said he'd better be going if he expected to row across the river before total darkness, a big black bird flew into the window, breaking the glass. It lay dead at our feet. I saw the fearful expression on their faces and a cold shiver ran through me. I remembered an ancient belief about the ill omen of a bird flying into a window. A person in the room would surely die in the very near future. Uncle Paul helped me sweep up the broken glass. He took care of the dead bird. "Mind your grandmother," he whispered, as we hung up the broom and dustpan. "She doesn't have much longer on this earth."

The next day Uncle Pete told us Great Uncle Paul's rowboat was found adrift that morning with no one in it. Expert swimmers dove looking for his body. On the third day, as one of the elders had instructed, a piece of dried bread was cast into the water at about the point where he would have been rowing across. According to ancient beliefs, a drowned body is found where the bread circles; that's how his body was found.

Devastated when told of her brother's tragic drowning, Tota blamed herself for detaining him. The new health nurse, Miss Jacobson, advised us not to leave Tota alone.

Aunt Helen moved in full time, going home only at night. No longer the boss of the house, my freedom flew right out the window.

DOLORES EOSTENUNI STANFIELD

It wasn't all that bad at first. Every Monday, Aunt Helen, had Bobby and Freeman come to our house and we did all our laundry in the great old wooden washing machine in our summer kitchen. The machine looked like a big wooden bucket on strong wide wooden legs, with a heavy wooden lid. A heavy set of wooden gears that attached under the lid provided the churning action. Pulling and pushing a wooden handle inserted on top of the lid turned the gears. The second set of gears on the bottom of the tub turned the same way when a wooden handle thrust into the bunghole on the low end was rotated. Aunt Helen heated pails of water on the kerosene stove. Then she poured the hot water into the washing machine. She added a good dose of lye soap-chips along with all the dirty clothes, and we set to churning the old machine.

To get us involved in good humor, Aunt Helen taught us the words to all the songs she had learned at the convent: "There's an Old, Old, Trail A Winding," "Pack Up Your Trouble In Your Old Kit Bag," "You are My Sunshine," and "If I Had The Wings Of an Angel." She'd harmonize to our singing and we sounded good enough for radio. Bobby liked cranking the handle up and down for hours on end. He had tremendous strength and never seemed to tire. He'd bend up and down, up and down until he got to farting. Then he'd giggle and say, "A fartin' horse never tires and a fartin' man is the man to hire." We'd be useless and weak from laughing. Aunt Helen let us be as silly as we wanted, as long as we straightened up long enough to finish the laundry.

When the laundry was clean she forced the clothes through the wringer. I turned the handle that caused the two rubber wheels to turn, squeezing out most of the water and propelling the flattened pieces of laundry into the rinse tub of clean water. The rinsing began again squeezing out most of the rinse water. When the laundry was finished, she hung the clothes on the line. I helped with the smaller pieces. Bobby and Freeman emptied the tubs. It took us most of the day, every Monday, to do the laundry, rain or shine.

When we were finished we swam until suppertime. The strong swimmers met at the point of the St. Lawrence in back of the church rectory. We'd climb over large boulders to get where the river was deepest and the most challenging. Our favorite game was hide-the-can. Taking the wrapper off of an empty aluminum can, so it shone brightly as the sun under water, we took turns hiding the can so deep behind boulders that anyone finding it had to be a very good diver. Whoever retrieved the can got the honor of hiding it the next time. And the one who could hide it so finding it took the longest was champion for the day. With bloodshot eyes from diving all afternoon with our eyes open, we looked like a bunch of scrawny, shivering water waifs.

After the supper dishes were done, we went outside to join the kids in the village and played hide-and-seek, until it was impossible to discern human shapes from outbuildings. We enjoyed making it almost impossible for the "it" person to find us without someone getting "home free." The empty rain-barrel by the corner of our house served as a good hiding place—except the evening I jumped in after a rainstorm and got soaking wet.

Coming in just before dark had its rewards. Aunt Helen preferred for all of us to be out as much as possible, thus keeping the inside quiet so Tota could sleep—and most often, by staying outside so late, I didn't get a licking.

TAKING CARE OF TOTA
The Whippings Resumed

Tota firmly believed in the saying, "Spare the rod and spoil the child." As long as I could remember, I did what she said or else. No psychology for me. She had no time to play mind games with me. Now in her suffering she no longer cared what I did. But where she dropped the rod, Aunt Helen picked it up with gusto.

Aunt Helen expected me to work as she did. All of us obeyed her. Although kind, she didn't hesitate to lay the stick to my back when she thought I deserved it. It's the way she kept us in order. No matter how quick I darted away from her grasp, she'd nab me. Determined and energetic, she did everything well and with purpose. She also canned, cleaned, and cooked without complaint. She told us she had learned when very young to work hard. That way the sisters at the convent never had to punish her for doing sloppy work. Instead, they commended her for her dedication. She loved to harmonize when she got us all singing. Yet, she refused to sing in the choir or even go to church, and had no time for organized activities. She said, "I do my praying when I'm sewing."

At the time, I didn't hold it against her when I felt the sting and the welt on my back, legs or arms, or where ever she found advantageous to hit. I'd roll up into a ball with my arms covering my head pleading and promising, "Don't hit me, I'm sorry. I won't do it again." She didn't even look angry. "This is for your own good," she'd say, every time she reached for the switch.

Remembering her words brings to mind, one time when Bobby had his spell while playing checkers. We were all concerned, making him comfortable, laying him on the floor, and putting a pillow under his head. Aunt Helen forgot about the tomato and macaroni soup cooking on the kerosene stove. The macaroni scorched on the bottom. Uncle Pete thundered in heavily, expecting dinner. He helped himself to a bowl of soup and cursed, "Damn! This soup's scorched. How in hell do you expect me to eat this?" He thumped his fist hard against the table.

Aunt Helen marched boldly into the kitchen and jutted her face up to him. She came up to his chest. "Yeah? Well I've got other more important things

MY MOTHER'S SPIRIT

to worry about besides feeding your big fat belly."

Uncle Pete got so mad he hauled off and slapped her. I jumped up from the couch and ran all the way to our house. Breathlessly I gave a full accounting of the frightening scene.

"It's probably for her own good," Tota replied.

"How can you say that? It wasn't her fault the soup got scorched."

"It has nothing to do with burnt macaroni. He wants her to put Bobby away in an institution where he thinks Bobby will get better care and your Aunt will not hear of it."

I got punished so many times I should have been better behaved at least. Except with me, punishment didn't do much good. Soon, I'd be getting switched for something else. I doubted if I'd ever hit my kids when I grew up. Switching or the threat of a beating didn't ever keep me from doing what I made up my mind to do anyway. The memory of doing something fun lasted forever. I forgot about the whippings as soon as the pain went away.

Tota, sick in bed, no longer went to church. But she still expected me to keep up with our rigid religious schedule: going to Mass every morning and twice on Sundays, singing in the children's choir and going to choir practice faithfully. Father Jacobs reported my every move to her on his daily visits.

Every time they got together, they argued about the Catholic religion. That Father Jacobs, was the first Mohawk Indian to be ordained a priest, didn't impress her. Both forceful in their arguments, he glibly quoted scripture in Mohawk. She merely dismissed it with the wave of her hand. "Phah!" she'd say with scorn. I've never lived my life according to the Bible."

"How can you be a Catholic, then? Do you believe in the Apostle's Creed?" He'd challenge her.

"Yes! I believe it. I also believe in our Creator and he didn't go writing any big book. The Bible is no more than a history book written about God in God's time by the historians, all men, biased, opinionated and self-serving. Even the monks who deciphered and translated the written words were capable of making mistakes. People in all religions have twisted the meaning around to fit their purposes. Our native peoples were almost eradicated from our own land by Bible quoting Christians, believing they were doing God's work. You spent your life studying, and doing God's work, or so you claim. How much do you want to bet, I'll get to heaven before you?"

"There's no use arguing. I'll continue to pray for you," he said, blessing her with the sign of the cross.

DOLORES EOSTENUNI STANFIELD

"Personally," she insisted, "I think if God ever did appear before us all he'd find us all so far off from his true teachings none of us would muster up." She always got in the last word. The next day he'd be back and they'd start arguing all over again. I think that's what kept her going. She held on into fall.

EARLY AUTUMN

Every fall in mid September, we'd climb aboard Uncle Pete's boat and cross the St. Lawrence to St. Regis Island to harvest wild hazelnuts...Freeman, Donald, and I. (Bobby was now in a home for the infirm in Montreal.)

We picked the big green clusters (shaped like bear paws) off the bushes and stuffed them into our burlap bags. Each cluster held three to four pods with a nut in each pod. In no time we'd have five to six bags full. We'd be home in time for dinner at twelve-noon. We took the bags up to the attic over the summer kitchen and emptied them onto the bare floor, spreading the clusters in a thin layer like a green carpet. Throughout the fall, the green clusters dried up into brittle brown husks. By stomping on the dried husks we loosened the brown nuts from their pods. For a winter evening's entertainment, we'd scoop up handfuls of nuts into our bowls to crack by the warmth of the round wood stove glowing red hot down in the living room. We liked listening to the freezing cold winter winds. That spring, we'd sweep up the brown chaff getting the attic ready for next fall's harvest.

I remembered the many winters Tota and I spent cracking nuts and enjoying the delicious little morsels. Tota would hold the flat iron upside down on her lap, and with a small hammer she cracked nuts for the both of us. She told me stories of days long ago and told me the story of mother earth according to our Mohawk legend in her simple words. It made sense to me when I was five.

Mother Earth rests on the back of a giant turtle. And on Mother Earth grows a special tree called the Tree of Life. Its four roots spread to the four corners, north, south, east and west. Mother Earth nourishes the Tree of Life and the Tree of Life nourishes us and protects us. And above Tree of Life flies the eagle that forever guards Mother Earth.

When thunder and lightning scared me, Tota would reassure me. "Don't be afraid. Thunder is only old grandfather turtle stretching his legs. The lightning is a message from our grandmother sky to Mother Earth that grandmother is about to rain down on us to cleanse and replenish the soil of our Mother Earth. That's why everything smells so fresh and clean after a rain storm." Tota had a believable explanation for all the ills of the world.

DOLORES EOSTENUNI STANFIELD

I resorted to these explanations and memories of pleasurable time whenever I worried about the future. I knew Tota's time to leave us would be soon. I worried some about what would become of me.

I often sat on the back stoop in the sun enjoying the warmth, and daydreamed about all the good that had happened—such as times after Tota had washed my hair and we'd sit outside on a warm summer day as she combed out the tangles. She said my hair was like spun gold drying in the sun.

After a pleasant interlude I'd quietly go back inside to do my daily chores. To please Tota, I carefully dusted old General Pershing. His future looked as bleak as mine. Who'd want this old portrait after Tota died?

The future without Tota would be sad. But I believed that something would turn up. As always in the past, when I worried about something, thoughts of my mother comforted me. My mother's spirit would see to it. And it did.

FLORENCE HAS THE SOLUTION

As much as I loved my Tota, taking care of her during the night and in the early morning tired me out. When she needed to go, she'd awaken me to help her. The chair beside her bed served as her toilet. She could sit on it if she felt strong enough during the day. When she needed to go, I'd flip the seat up and it became her toilet. I'd stand in front of her and help lift her by her armpits. Together we did a quarter turn and she'd land into her chair. When she finished, she'd call me and we'd 'dose-E-doe her back into bed. The maneuver exhausted her. For a scrawny skin and bones grandma, she weighed as much as me. I then emptied her pot, washed it and slid it back under the chair.

Aunt Helen arrived early in the morning with baking powder biscuits for our breakfast. I enjoyed mine with a cup of French coffee. Tota had hers with her medicinal herbal tea. Aunt Helen took care of her by day, bathing, and giving her, her medicine. Most of the time, I'd be tired from being awakened in the night, and I still needed to do my chores. When I heard Florence would be coming home soon to be married, I jumped up in the air and yelled, "Hooray!" Florence could help out with Tota.

There would be wedding receptions at her new husband's parent's house. My mouth watered thinking of all the good stuff to eat and maybe even some fruitcake. Florence and her husband would be living in St. Regis.

Aunt Helen welcomed the news too. She sent me to deliver the message as soon as we heard Florence was home. "Tell Florence I want to see her."

I ran up the hill eagerly looking forward to seeing Florence. I blurted out breathlessly, "Aunt Helen wants you to come over. She needs to ask you something."

"You tell my mother, I have no intentions helping take care of Tota," she curtly replied.

"How'd you know what she wanted?"

"What else would she want to talk to me about? Certainly not about my getting married?"

I let it go. I didn't understand what their problem was all about. Forgetting my disappointment, I stayed and visited most of the morning. She told me about their plans, building a brand new house by the river next to the church.

Florence had a knack of making money like Tota when she was in her prime. She planned to sell nylon stockings door to door. She got the idea while working as a domestic and found out where to buy a quantity of seconds for resale. Nylon stockings were something new and she knew the women in the village would want to buy them.

"Why can't you stay with Tota and me while you are building your house?" I quickly suggested.

"I won't live in Tota's Sears and Roebuck house if she paid me," Florence shot back so fast, my eyes blinked.

"What do you mean Sears and Roebuck house? You can't buy a house from a catalog."

"Yes, you could back then, in 1928. It came by rail to Massena. She had it delivered by truck and hired carpenters to put it together and paid cash with her bootleg money."

"Well I'll be?" Speechless, all this time thinking ours was the grandest house I'd ever seen and only rich people could afford a house like it. Ours even had the gable with it's own two windows sitting majestically above the second floor over looking the street. (The two windows from where people gossiped, someone had seen my mother's spirit the day she died. Tota had 'poo-pooed' when I asked her if it were true. "Rumors, all rumors," Tota had scoffed.) Other people's houses had front porches but ours had a verandah from one end of the front to the other. Disheartened, I sat there looking glum.

Florence changed the subject and described the house her and Angus were going to build.

"I hope it has two bedrooms so I can come and live with you and Angus. Especially, after Tota passes over into the spirit world."

"Is it getting that bad living with Tota?"

"No! I'm getting tired and it's not just taking care of Tota. It's your mother giving me a licking for something or other all the time. It's embarrassing. She doesn't lick the others as much. Just me."

"I've suggested to Angus that you come live with us. He says, he doesn't want the responsibility."

"I'd take care of my self and not be a bother. I don't understand what's supposed to be so bad about me. No one wants me."

"It's not you personally. Most people aren't up to raising someone else's kid...especially a girl. But I know who'd love to take you."

"Really? Who?"

"Martha La France, Rita's mother, they've always been very fond of you.

MY MOTHER'S SPIRIT

Rita wants to go to Syracuse to work but she doesn't want to leave her mother alone."

"If I can't come and live with you then I hope I can go live with them. Rita's been good to me. One Christmas she came and got me and I spent part of the day with them. She even gave me presents."

"Don't worry, I'll talk to Rita. We'll work something out. You'd better get home before you get an other licking."

I walked back down the hill towards home less enthused but lots to think about. I hadn't seen Rita and Mumma in quite some time. The LaFrances were our neighbors when we lived in Tota's hotel. Rita use to take care of me.

"Where have you been all this time?" Aunt Helen asked, knowing all along where I'd been. I didn't answer. After a few minutes she asked. "What did Florence have to say?"

"She thinks I should go and live with Mrs. LaFrance. And you should move over here permanently to take care of Tota. Since you're the ones who's going to inherit this house."

Aunt Helen didn't answer right away. She had a pleased expression on her face. A job well done...not exactly a smile. Or maybe she felt relieved I'd no longer be her responsibility. I puzzled over it. But not for long. I went about my chores wondering how it would be living on the American side with Rita and her mother.

LIFE ON THE AMERICAN SIDE
Wishing the tiredness and cares away

I wished my liniment-smelling, one sick room world, would soon come to an end. My hands, red and chapped, smelled like a Lysol factory from continuously emptying Tota's chamber pot. I sat on the edge of my cot, dead tired, wishing I could sleep some more. Tota needed me to help her. Her stirring and groaning woke me up. She pushed her covers aside, waiting for me to bend over her. "Ohhh!" she cried out in pain as she flung her arms around my neck. I helped her to a sitting position. We swung her legs to one side, ready for our quarter turn-swing into her chair. "Ah! That feels better," she sighed. I waited for her, half asleep. "You're strong for a ten year old." She managed a weak smile. It's the closest she came to complementing me. We swung her back onto the bed, she took a sip of water and I helped her lay back down. Feeling guilty, I couldn't fall back to sleep. I knew I was being selfish, anxiously waiting to hear from Florence whether I'd be leaving here soon, when Tota still needed me.

"Tota, I think I'd like to be leaving to go live with Rita and her mother. What do you think?" I dared to ask, not knowing how she'd reply. She didn't answer right away. I knew she heard me.

"With Aunt Helen here most of the day, and her noisy kids and you, it would be a blessing." She heaved a heavy sigh.

"I wish Donald, Agnes and Mary were old enough to be sent to the Ojibwa School, or to the convent…anywhere but here," I confided, encouraged, that she'd be sharing her feelings with me. "Except Freeman—he helps as much as he can, keeping the water barrel filled," I quickly added.

It's hard work. Freeman would put the wooden yoke on his shoulders and haul two pails of water at a time from the river an eighth of a mile away, until the barrel was full. The village pump from our house with the purest water you'd ever want to drink was only yards away, but we used the well water for drinking and cooking only. There was no water shortage in our village—with two rivers near by. There was an unspoken communal belief that such sweet, life-giving water, should be shared and not wasted. River water was plentiful and good enough for washing.

"Who'd stay with you at night if I weren't here?" I asked, afraid of what

MY MOTHER'S SPIRIT

she might say.

After a long silence, in exasperation, she replied, "Never mind me. Light a candle, and pray I don't have to heave my tired aching bones in this bed much longer."

I'd never do that—light a candle and pray that she leave us soon. "Tota, I'd miss you."

She gestured her hand slightly, as if annoyed.

The following Saturday, Rita came for me. Willowy and slender, she bent down slightly as I flung my arms around her. I hadn't seen her in months. Her broad smile belied her shyness. Her large dark eye glistened, laughing softly at my enthusiasm. "Sit here a minute," I said quickly to Rita. "I'll be right back." I looked eagerly at Aunt Helen, my eyes signaling I needed her help. She read my expression.

"Eostenuni has been edgy all week," Aunt Helen said to Rita as she followed me into the hallway to a dresser for my clothes.

I lowered my voice, concerned, and asked, "Who's going to stay nights with Tota?"

"Aunt Theresa has agreed to come and help," she replied, busily folding my clothes; a set of underwear, three cotton dresses, hand-me-downs expertly altered by her. She had made my slips out of flour sacking and my sun-suits were sewed from cotton remnants. A sudden urge came over me to give her a hug. She hugged me back. I came back into the kitchen, beaming, carrying two brown shopping bags. I tiptoed into the front room and looked as Tota slept peacefully. I turned and followed Rita out. "I'll be back," I whispered to Aunt Helen, who stood holding the door open. She nodded.

When the LaFrance family were our neighbors, living next to Tota's hotel, they knew me as the "Nuisance." Tota couldn't stand me and hired Rita to look after me. From that time on, because Rita and her older sister called their mother, Mumma, I did too. We had gradually lost touch after Tota moved us to the Canadian side. Mr. La France was tall with a white bushy mustache. A stern, fervent Catholic, and fifteen or twenty years older than Mumma, he ordered the women in his household to attend Mass every morning. He didn't approve of Tota's speakeasy, even though he made a good living selling gas to the bootleggers, who gassed up their fancy cars at his one gas pump after visiting the hotel. When he died, Mumma stopped going to church and turned his gas station into her basket-making house. With no one to bother her, she spent most of her time making baskets and smoking her corncob pipe.

DOLORES EOSTENUNI STANFIELD

Phoebe expected me to help care for her three kids; Stanley, five, Linda, four, and Phyllis three. It would only be temporary, Phoebe said, until her husband, Bill, a soldier, came home from the army.

I soon discovered why Phoebe welcomed me as her baby-sitter. Pudgy and breathless, she found it cumbersome and tiring to move around. After having three kids, she failed to lose her baby fat, and became lazy. She was very pretty with hazel green eyes, and crinkled shut when she smiled. She smiled readily and I liked her. I got winded chasing the three kids, and her asking me constantly to hand her this or that, or to go ask Mumma this or go ask Mumma that. I was pooped out at the end of day. It was a good thing we ate well or I would have gotten skinnier. Phoebe liked spending her monthly allowance checks on all kinds of fancy store-bought sweets.

I favored Rita. Dark and plain, she quietly went about her work like a gentle servant, aiming to please. Her easy laughter relaxed me. When I was six, she had given me a standup slate board. I could scroll the alphabet across the top of the board just by tuning the handle on the upper side of it. It came with a soft felt eraser and a box of colored chalk.

She'd be leaving for Syracuse by the end of the week to go to work as a riveter for Remington Rand. I dreaded her going. I'd miss her terribly.

Mumma preferred to stay in her small building next door weaving her baskets and smoking her corncob pipe. Every chance I had, I'd stick my head inside her door asking if I could come in to watch. Mostly I needed to catch my breath from chasing Phoebe's kids…until Phoebe called me. Mumma spoke only Mohawk. A typical Indian woman of forty, reserved, she responded only when she was spoken to. When I came in to watch, she'd keep on weaving. But when she had a visitor, she'd lay her weaving aside, smile and wait for the visitor to speak first. Then there'd be quiet conversation. When I could, I'd sit nearby enraptured. I wished the peacefulness and the restful feeling from the aroma of sweet grass and the splints of the black, brown and white ash trees would engulf me forever. For the time being, I rested feeling contented.

LIFE WITH MUMMA

It felt homey living on the American side in the old LaFrance homestead that stood next to the boundary line. The St. Regis River flowed steadily by a few hundred yards from the back door. I liked padding barefoot down the narrow dirt path to the cove where the cattails thickened. The sights of Indian fishermen casting their nets, the sounds of children swimming and frolicking in the morning sun, and the cacophony of croaking frogs at night were all familiar to me. I could even smell the dank odor of rotting reeds along the river's shallow shoreline. The LaFrance house neighbored Tota's International Hotel where we had lived before Tota sold it in 1933. Rita had brought me back here many times for visits after Tota moved our family to the Canadian side.

Mumma was a tall graying woman who moved with a certain unhurried grace. At fifteen she had married Mr. LaFrance, who was fifteen or twenty years her senior. Half-French, his austere manner relegated her to the corner of the room, where she worked quietly, contented in making her Mohawk baskets of sweet grass and black ash splits. She took pleasure in taking puffs from her corncob pipe. Patient and soft-spoken, we got along great. We shared the double bed in the first of the two bedrooms. Stanley slept on a cot in the corner of our room. Linda and Phyllis slept in the front bedroom with their mother, Phoebe.

Every night I'd lie beside Mumma as she sat up in bed puffing on her corncob pipe. We'd talk quietly about what ever I wanted. The warmth of her body, the subtle fragrance of her pipe, and her gentle voice aroused a feeling of peaceful ease and safety. It soon lulled me to sleep.

The next morning when I woke up, she'd already be at her basket making. Phoebe and the kids would still be sleeping. I'd hurriedly get my coffee (with plenty of milk and sugar) and join her. She'd be sitting by the window with her basket, a mug of coffee beside her. Between sips and a few puffs, she'd weave a bit then stop and rest. I loved watching her rhythmic movements, expertly weaving and rotating the basket on her knee. Her gray hair hung down her back in one long loose braid. Even at forty-five, she had not allowed herself to grow flabby and fat.

Before the month was over, Phoebe talked about joining her sister in the glamorous city of lights, modern conveniences, and movie theaters. She had not wanted to leave Mumma alone. I was the perfect solution to her plan.

Two weeks later, Phoebe and her three kids were gone. Mumma and I settled to a quiet routine. We continued sharing the same bed. Every morning I made our bed, set the table, helped prepare our meals, did the dishes, and swept the floor, so Mumma could do what I knew she enjoyed. I felt useful.

I asked if she'd teach me how to make baskets. "Always start your bottom good and tight with the thicker splints. It's important to have a good strong bottom if you want a firm basket," she'd say as she watched me struggling with the few pieces of splints on my knee.

"Oh damn! Utkum-saluksa!" I'd curse and push it all aside. "To hell with it." I couldn't get the knack of starting. I'd soon get discouraged and want to quit. She'd calmly interlay the pieces down and with the sweet grass she'd firmly weave the bottom to get me started.

"Don't get discouraged, you'll learn soon enough," she'd say pleasantly, taking another puff, sitting peacefully there beside me. Tota would have pushed me aside, done it all herself and called me useless long ago.

Mumma suggested we visit Tota before school started. "To help ease her pain and to say our good-byes before she slips away from us."

I agreed hesitantly. We went the next day. Tota didn't recognize me, and it scared me to see her so ill. Seeing Great Aunt Theresa there helping Aunt Helen pleased me. Mumma motioned for me to sit outside and wait for her. The three of them sat together with my Tota, talking quietly, giving her comfort by their presence as she lay dying. I found Freeman hunched over, sitting on the back steps with his hands between his knees looking down in the dumps.

We sat side by side, both sad and neither one of us felt like talking. I noticed his homemade red wagon next to him. He'd had it ever since I could remember. It was a wooden box painted red, with four wheels recycled from an old pram. It had a handle with a cross bar at the end. Once, when a wheel came off, he had sat by the side of the road crying, "Wahgonne wahgee!" Translated: my wagon is hurt. Remembering how we had teased him about that perked me up.

"Hey Freeman!" I said chuckling. "Remember the time the wheel came off your wagon and you were crying?"

He brightened up and grinned. "Cut it out." He playfully pushed me off the end of the stoop. We stood there laughing at one another. Just then Mumma came out. She nodded somberly. I joined her immediately, giving a small

MY MOTHER'S SPIRIT

wave to Freeman.

We walked quietly side by side. "Mumma, I don't want to come here anymore."

"I know," she murmured. She must have heard me snuffing and wiping my nose on my sleeve; she lovingly put her arm around my shoulder until we got home.

Now that I lived on the American side, I had no choice but to go to the Mohawk School in Hogansburg, two miles away, even though my old school on the Canadian side was but a stone's throw away. Mumma and I rode the Lamondola bus to Hogansburg and bought me a new pair of brown and white saddle shoes at McKenna's General Store. I hadn't worn shoes all summer, except for church, and my old ones were pinching my toes. Apprehensive about going to a new school, excited about riding a school bus for the first time, I had no idea I'd soon be involved in an international dispute.

Our Mohawk Reserve sprawls across the American and Canadian borders. It's of no particular interest to us which side we live on. We are Mohawk first. Evidently it did matter to Mr. Delorme who owned and drove the school bus. A self-important pompous poop, he was a bowlegged dumpy little man with a bulbous nose. He decided to exert his little bit of power.

Mr. Delorme contracted with the board of education on the American side to haul the students. He lived across the road from Mumma's house. The cement obelisk marking the dividing line between the two countries was at the edge of his yard almost across the road from where Tota ran her speakeasy many years ago. He and many of the neighbors resented my grandmother's house of ill repute. He had not forgotten nor forgiven her. He would finally get revenge using me.

On my first day of school, I gleefully looked out the window and saw the little yellow school bus parked outside Mr. Delorme's house. Two girls were getting on. I quickly gathered my new notebook and pencil box and ran out to join them. Climbing aboard, I took a few seconds deciding where to sit from the many empty seats. I took the front seat so I could enjoy the wide front view of the countryside. I felt the rush of excitement and the newness around me right down to my spanking new shoes.

Just then, the short stubby, grumpy faced Mr. Delorme came out of his house and climbed aboard. He saw me grinning at him, eagerly waiting for him to start the bus.

"Hey! You! What are you doing on my bus?"

The angry expression on his face startled me. I stammered an explanation.

DOLORES EOSTENUNI STANFIELD

"I know who you are. You're Agnes Jacobs's granddaughter and you belong on the Canadian side. In the first place, your father's a white man and you have no right to live here."

I felt bewildered and embarrassed to be so singled out by such anger. I glanced at the two other girls. They looked as dumbfounded as I felt.

Mr. Delorme moved to one side to make room for me to pass him. "Get off my bus."

I scooted out of my seat and half stumbled down the step onto the ground. He pulled the lever closing the door, started the motor and pulled away. He left me standing there watching the back of his bus go down the dirt road. It didn't occur to me to walk back to Mumma's house to report what had just happened. Instead, I started walking the two miles to my new school. My new shoes started to hurt, a water blister formed on my heel and I felt thirsty. I passed the customhouse at ten o'clock carrying my shoes.

All cars were required to stop, prepared for a good going over if the customs agent, Mr. Rourke, suspected anybody of attempting to smuggle anything. He saw me and sauntered out and asked why I was not in school.

"Mr. Delorme threw me off his bus," I said and explained why.

Mr. Rourke, an old timer, knew everybody. "You're Stanfield's daughter and I know your grandmother, Agnes Jacobs. You leave everything to me," he said.

By the time I finally got to school and stepped inside, gaping at the spacious halls and the huge auditorium, the acting school principal knew all about me. He had just gotten off the phone talking with Mr. Rourke.

"Welcome to our school," said Mr. Fadden, smiling. I felt comfortable with him right away. He had the waviest reddish-brown hair I had ever seen. I caught a whiff of tobacco and spotted his brown pipe sticking out of the pocket of his brown tweed jacket. His white shirt with a bright green tie showed off his freckled face. Moving swiftly, he gave me a tour of the school: eight classrooms; (indoor) toilets for the girls and one for the boys; and a big room almost like a house with a kitchen, a sitting room and a room with four sewing machines, "The Home Economics room for the girls," he explained. "Across the hall is the Manual Training room for the boys."

Three chubby brown-faced Indian women, wearing hairnets and long white aprons, were cooking big pots of soup in the Home Economics kitchen. Mr. Fadden told me to get in line with the boys and girls waiting to get served. "Plenty of time later to meet your fifth grade teacher, Miss Moran. Enjoy your lunch." He left me. I knew most of the boys and girls from Catechism class.

MY MOTHER'S SPIRIT

We sat together on benches at long tables eating peanut butter sandwiches, hot vegetable soup, and dishes of canned grapefruit sections. I'd never had it so good. I wondered if it was all for real. I even had my own carton of milk. I stuffed the apple in my sweater pocket for later. There'd be plenty to tell Mumma when I got home.

Getting acquainted with my classmates and my new teacher, Miss Moran, took up the rest of the day. I knew I'd like it here. If only Mr. Delorme wouldn't be so mean. First thing I knew the bell rang. The kids got in line and marched to their school busses. There was no use getting on mine. With a Band-Aid for my heel from the health nurse, I started walking.

As I approached customs, I saw the small yellow school bus pulled over to the side. Mr. Rourke motioned to me to hurry. I ran and obediently climbed on past Mr. Delorme and sat on the first empty seat I saw. Everyone looked scared watching me. I didn't dare look at Mr. Delorme. I heard Mr. Rourke say in a very loud voice, "And I expect to see her on this bus every day. Do you understand?" Mr. Delorme didn't answer. I heard later from one of the kids, "Mr. Rourke really gave it to our bus driver."

"Mumma, you'll never guess what happened to me on my way to school," I said breathlessly as I opened the door. "You should have heard what Mr. Rourke told Mr. Delorme. Mr. Delorme almost blew a gasket."

"It's too bad you had to go all through that," she said, slowly laying down her basket. "Many people resented your grandmother for opening the hotel and bringing in all sorts of bad people. He shouldn't have taken it out on you. He needs to remember, she also helped a lot of people who might have gone hungry during the Depression. You mustn't take it to heart. They don't know any different."

The next day I got on the bus as if nothing had ever happened. Mr. Delorme didn't even look at me. As we approached customs, Mr. Rourke stopped the bus. He climbed on and saw me sitting there. "Just checking," he said. Then he climbed back out. There was no love lost between Mr. Rourke and Mr. Delorme. The day I decided not to ride the bus, Mr. Delorme got blamed and got a good chewing out from Mr. Rourke.

THE CONVENT REVISITED

The new brick Mohawk school that I would now be attending was attached to a section of the old brick convent where my grandmother, my aunt, and my mother were educated. Going there, I'd be retracing my mother's footsteps. It would feel like walking on hallowed ground. St. Patrick's Church where my mother prayed with the nuns was next to the school. I could almost see my mother, dressed in her white habit, running and playing with the other young girls, who where also living at the convent.

The Mohawk school, the old convent, and St. Patrick's Church were in the town of Hogansburg. Hogansburg is hard to explain to non-Indians, in that the town is located in the middle of the Mohawk reservation on the American side, yet Hogansburg is not considered as part of the reservation, and all inhabitants are subject to federal and New York State taxes. The Anglos who owned and ran the general stores, post office, and one gas station inhabited the town. I had heard from my elders how the white merchants, Mr. Lantry and Mr. McKenna, owners of the general stores, were known as the merchants who made their living by cheating the Indians.

Shortly after I started school, a pleasant motherly young woman with a familiar face greeted me warmly. All smiles, Norma White told me how she and my mother had lived at the old convent. Now, she taught sewing. "Your mother was like a big sister to me, took me under her wing when I was your age," she said happily. "You'll have to come home with me sometime."

My heart leaped for joy seeing someone who had known my mother as a young girl. There were so many things I wanted to ask Norma. "How about tomorrow?" I hurriedly interrupted.

"Imagine," Norma continued. "Your mother and I lived here and went to Mass next door. I heard what that old mean Mr. Delorme did—throwing you off his bus. Tomorrow it is, then. I have my own car."

I didn't want anything to happen to keep me from going home with Norma. Desperate as I was to learn more about my mother, I said nothing to anyone. Not even Mumma. After school, I waited for Norma and we drove to her home on a state road. She told me stories about my mother, way into the night until I fell asleep.

My disappearance caused Mr. Delorme a lot of grief. Mr. Rourke blamed him for my not being on the bus and called the state police.

The next morning, light hearted, I ran into the school. Mr. Fadden met me at the door, frowning. "Where did you just come from?"

"I came with Norma!" I exclaimed, equally puzzled. "I spent the night with her. Why?"

Everyone's been looking for you, fearing you had been abducted. Stay right here! Don't you move!" He spun on his heals and went to locate Norma. He instructed her to take me home immediately.

"I thought you said it was okay with Mrs. LaFrance?" Norma scolded. "I'm very disappointed in you."

"I didn't lie exactly. I just didn't tell Mumma, cause I was afraid she'd say I couldn't go home with you." I tried making excuses. Norma grew silent and concentrated on her driving. I felt awful.

I saw immediately how upset Mumma looked. She held me to her for a long time not saying anything. I realized then how worried she must have been and I knew she loved me.

A HORRIFYING EXPERIENCE

That morning in October as the bus was pulling out, I looked out and saw Freeman running along side waving. His face had the saddest expression of loss. He looked ready to cry. Mr. Delorme saw him too. He stopped the bus and pulled the door open. I leapt from my seat and ran. I stumbled down the step to the ground. Freeman and I stood there clutching each other. "Tota died this morning," he sobbed. We ran all the way to our old house.

The door to Tota's bedroom was closed. We sat on the stairs and waited for a long time. Finally Aunt Helen came out and saw us sitting there. "I want you two to come home with me," she said dispassionately. "There's nothing you can do here now."

"But what about Tota?" I asked, puzzled.

"She's being taken care off. Aunt Theresa is with her."

We followed her home half running to keep up with her as she cut through and crossed lots. Aunt Helen instructed Freeman to stay home and keep house. Then she took a long look at me. "What?" I asked, puzzled.

"I think I've got a black dress that will fit you. I'll have to shorten it." She went up stairs and in a few minutes, came back down with a black faille dress over her arm. "Here try this on."

Aunt Helen, quickly baste stitched the hem as I sat by silently watching. She finished hemming it. It fit just fine. She and I wore the same size shoes. She told me to put on her black oxfords with the one and half inch heels. "There, now!" she said cheerfully. "Don't you look all grown up?" I walked back to Mumma's carrying the dress over my arm and her shoes in the other hand. Mumma would come back with me later in the afternoon for the wake.

I didn't feel grown up sitting on the stairs watching the sad faces come and go that evening. I could see into the living room where my Tota's coffin was. The undertaker and his helper had taken care of her body here.

For the three days she was laid out, I sat on the stairs most of the time going home only at night with Mumma. We came back early in the day for prayers. Our old house filled with people all day and late into the night. Some were coming in as others were leaving. Tota's body was never left alone. The choir sat at one side of her coffin singing hymns. In between the singing, the rosary was said in unison.

MY MOTHER'S SPIRIT

In mid afternoon and again in the evening, small white paper plates of food were passed. I wasn't hungry but I had to nibble on something. It's an invitation to partake of refreshments, a gesture of sharing a last meal with the deceased. To refuse would be an insult.

I sat on the stairs looking at Tota. Her lifeless faced looked pain free and at peace. Her parched brown knurled hands lying in repose across her abdomen, reminded me of the many evenings we spent sitting by the warmth of the wood stove and she'd crack nuts for us. Just as the empty brown dried up husks on the attic floor to be swept up and discarded, now too, her useless body was going to be put to rest (discarded). I looked over at Great Aunt Theresa sitting by the coffin.

I remembered a time when Great Aunt Theresa gasped in horror as Tota put her hatpin between her lips just before receiving Holy Communion and Tota scoffing at her boasting of her many sins. I closed my eyes and said a quick prayer so that God would overlook such a small offense as the hatpin between Tota's lips. After all she suffered she deserved to go to heaven.

Much as I hated to leave my place on the stairs in mid afternoon, I had to pee. I ran to the outhouse. That's when I saw all the blood in the pit below. It had to be Tota's blood. The undertaker had dumped it in there when he embalmed her body. I cried out in horror. "Oh my God. No!" I could not void. It would be a sacrilege. I ran to the neighbors out-house instead. The sight sickened me so that I could not tell anybody. No one could ever offer an explanation for such an offensive act. Not even Tota if she were alive.

The morning of Tota's funeral, I numbly followed along leaning against Mumma, her arm protectively around my shoulders. The funeral director and his assistant arrived and wheeled her coffin expertly out of our house and into the hearse. Slowly, the hearse carried her casket for her last journey to church. The rest of us walked solemnly behind. After the funeral, there were a few cars lined up outside the church door to take us to the cemetery. Someone directed us into one of them and the line of cars rolled slowly along to the burial place. The choir sang their doleful hymns for the dead meant to evoke the sadness from our hearts. I watched mournfully from under Mumma's arm the entire procedure of laying a body to rest. I could hear the wind rustling scattering the few dead brown leaves between the barren wooden crosses. The river near by muted the sounds of prayers, a hymn, and a distant cough here and there. I heard the silence of my Tota's soul soaring high up towards the sky, free at last.

There would never be a presumptuous stone marking her grave. There would only be the humble generic white wooden cross with the name Agnes Jacobs. She took her most cherished possession with her…her notoriety.

A month after Tota's funeral, Aunt Helen sold the few remaining pieces of furniture in Tota's house (except the portrait of General Pershing…she took it with her). She left Uncle Pete and took her five children to Syracuse, where she started a boarding house for the Mohawk iron workers. In time, she fetched Bobby from the home for the infirm in Canada. I didn't see my cousin and best friend, Freeman again until we were adults.

POKING FUN

Rita came home that weekend to check on us. She and I were sitting on the front stoop talking mostly in English. Now that she worked in Syracuse, she spoke mostly English except in front of Mumma. Trying to cheer me up, she said, teasing me, "I heard you caused an international dispute."

"I like that word—a beaut of a dispute." I kept repeating the word, puckering up my mouth to pronounce dispute. We giggled the way girls do enjoying a private joke. "If I had Tota's big Webster's Dictionary, I could look up dispute. I wonder what became of our old dictionary?"

"International means among other nations. In your case, it involved three nations, American, Canadian, and Mohawk over whether you could or couldn't ride Mr. Delorme's little yellow school bus," Rita said and we giggled.

We tended to inject humor whenever we thought white people did something we considered stupid. We chuckled and snorted with laughter. Poking fun at them helped to ease the simmering in our souls for all the wrongs done to our people. It seemed to me a natural inclination to ridicule our oppressors, while inadvertently striving to become more like them.

Rita, ten years older, was like a big sister. She was a riveter in a defense plant making guns for the US Military. I nicknamed her "Rita the Riveter." Shy and reserved, except with me, she was gentle, always in good humor and naturally graceful. Until she went away to work, she wore her long dark hair straight, falling loosely down her back. Now, her hair was cut to shoulder length and she curled the ends with a curling iron, like pictures of white girls in magazines. She combed out my blond braids and put ringlets in my hair too. Although I did look like the white girls in the pictures, I knew in my heart that I was Mohawk.

"You'll need a winter coat," she said. "Before I leave for Syracuse we'll go to Massena and do a little shopping."

A red furry teddy-bear coat, put on lay-away for me, brightened my day. She promised, "I'll be back again before cold weather and you'll have a warm coat for winter." Then we went to Woolworth's for a banana split.

"Tota and I used to come here, too, for shopping and we'd always have a banana split," I said sadly, toying with the last piece of banana in my glass boat shaped dish.

"You miss your grandmother, don't you?"

"Yep! All the time."

"But you've still got Mumma and me. We'll always look after you."

"Okay!" I said, scooping the rest of the chocolate syrupy banana into my mouth.

MUMMA'S DOWNFALL

I wish I could say Mumma and I lived happily ever after. But it was not to be. A month later, Andy Swamp came a-calling and blew up my peaceful little world into a dozen pieces of very hurtful memories

Andy lived two houses down from us on the Canadian side and we knew him well. He worked at the Alcoa Plant in Massena. Fifteen years younger than Mumma, it didn't seem like he'd be interested in her. A thin quiet little man, and soft spoken, we both liked him. He showed up at our front door one evening with a little brown sack. A gentle rap at the front door and there he stood smiling, waiting to be invited in.

He had a six-pack of beer, a bottle of Coke for me and a pack of cards. Mumma didn't drink nor play cards. But with his gentle coaxing he persuaded her to take a drink. "Come on," he said. "Just one little sip. It will relax you." He taught us how to play gin rummy.

Almost every evening, we'd hear his gentle rap-a-tap and Andy would be standing there with his little brown paper sack. He'd bring wine, whisky, or gin, and always a coke for me. We'd play cards until my bedtime. Then I'd hear them talking quietly downstairs so as not to disturb me. Some evenings, I'd hear the door quietly close behind him and then Mumma would come to bed tipsy, giggling to herself. At times, she'd fall into bed without undressing.

One day just before Christmas, I came home from school, and as soon as I walked in the door they greeted me with, "Surprise! We got married today." In a festive mood, they lifted their glasses of red wine to me as if they were both offering me a toast. Andy wore a gray suit with a white shirt and blue tie. Mumma wore her one Sunday best—a plain black dress with a corsage of white roses pinned to her lapel.

"Andy thought it would be nice to get married before Christmas...sort of a surprise," Mumma explained, blushing like any new bride. Then she giggled, hunching her shoulders like a mischievous kid and said, "By the Justice of Peace."

I thought of Phoebe and Rita right away. If they had known what Andy intended they might have talked her out of it. He seemed so much younger then Mumma.

"Mumma, I've never seen you like this," I said in disbelief. "Do Phoebe and Rita know?"

"They'll find out soon enough," Andy interrupted boldly. For a timid little man, he certainly seemed cocky. Especially with the glass of wine in his hand.

Andy moved in with us that very night. They took the front bedroom; it had a door that locked.

In a jovial mood, to celebrate, Andy took us out to dinner in Massena the next day. He paid for my red teddy-bear coat. He also bought me a pair of white rubber galoshes with white fake fur trim on top. We were happy for a while. Mumma's face took on a cheerful glow.

From then on, every Saturday at one o'clock Mumma and I boarded the Lamondola bus to Massena and met Andy at a tavern. He treated us to a supper of hot roast beef sandwiches with plenty of brown gravy, French fries and a few beers for Mumma and him. Then we shopped for our groceries and rode home on the six o'clock bus.

Soon, Mumma couldn't wait for the once a week shopping trip and got others to buy her bottles of whiskey. She stashed it here and there, pouring it in her tea and sipping it all day long. Often, I'd have to wake her up from her nap when I got home from school, so she'd be okay by the time Andy got home.

One Friday during school vacation, she suggested we surprise Andy by meeting him after work. We rode the bus to the Alcoa Plant. Andy had gotten a ride home with his co-workers. We visited the liquor store instead.

While waiting at the bus stop, she kept taking sips from a bottle wrapped in a paper bag. Embarrassed by the sidelong glances from everyone, I tugged at her sleeve to stop. "Mumma, please." We must have made a pitiful picture; an intoxicated middle-aged Indian woman with an eleven-year-old white girl begging her to stop drinking.

Then it happened. Plop! She dropped the bottle. Three quarters of the bottle sheared off leaving a two-inch bottom intact with shards of glass protruding. Desperate for another drink she stooped and rescued the rest of it tipping the broken bottle to her mouth. I heard a loud gasp, "Oh no!" from the spectators as they watched in horror.

I managed to get the bottle out of her hand and flung it into the trash barrel. She stood, hanging onto my arm, looking over my head with a vacant smile on her sagging face, tottering from side to side. "Please let that bus come soon, before Mumma falls over," I prayed.

Getting her on and off the bus and leading her to our door and up the two steps took all my strength.

MY MOTHER'S SPIRIT

The door opened suddenly and Andy pulled Mumma inside. He took one look at her and slapped her hard. I heard the loud clap of his open hand against her face even before I knew what happened. It sent her reeling backward against the wall. Then he pushed her violently onto the couch. "Sleep it off," he snarled.

I glared at him, wanting to attack him. White faced, with his nostrils flared, breathing hard, he looked menacing enough to attack me. I stood firmly in front of Mumma, lest he try anything. He reacted instantly to my angry stare and backed away apologizing, almost crying in anguish. He collapsed into the overstuffed chair with his hands over his face and stayed there. Mumma was out to the world sound asleep.

Through the rest of that winter, Andy came home with a load of groceries every Friday. Mummy stayed home much of the time weaving baskets. She seemed okay most of the time. I had my suspicions though and hoped Andy wouldn't notice. He left the house often, after the evening meal, to play cards with friends. At bedtime, she began to lie down with me instead of going to her own bed. I could smell liquor on her breath.

Once in a while I would waken to the sounds of the front door closing quietly and I'd hear Andy's movements as he climbed into his bed.

He hardly talked to us at all and stopped bringing alcohol into the house. If Mumma sneaked a drink now and then, where did she get it, I wondered. I became a regular snoop, always suspicious, looking here and there...behind the woodpile, feeling inside of jacket pockets. I even examined the rafters in the out-house. She must have been extremely clever. I couldn't find a bottle of liquor anywhere.

Andy frequented Angus Smoke's pool hall and left Mumma sitting by the kerosene lamp smoking her pipe. She seemed so sad. Some evenings I could talk her into playing cards. "Mumma, let's you and me play a game of gin rummy."

"I don't know? I'm not really any good at cards."

"Yes, you are." I'd convince her by dealing her a hand anyway and she'd have to pick up the cards.

"I really should be making my baskets. I'm at least good at that."

"It's your turn to pick up. Hey! Lemme see. You've got three kings. Lay 'em down. See? If you'd a-done that, you could have gone out. And you'd have beat me."

She sighed, smiled slightly and picked up her pipe. I gave up, picked up the cards and put them away.

Christmas had come and gone. Rita didn't bother coming home. She sent a package through the post office, a matching powder blue cardigan set for me, and a new flannel nightgown for Mumma. Andy gave us a big box of chocolates. I went to church by myself and continued singing in the choir.

Most Sundays after church I'd stop to visit with Florence who lived next to the church. I repeated my embarrassing experience with Mumma and her broken whiskey bottle.

"Andy shouldn't have given her that first drink," Florence said. "Everybody talks about how fast she went down hill after they got married."

"Everybody? I thought we were the only ones who knew about it."

"No! Everybody says about how she never drank until he started visiting her. It's going to get worse. You should write to Rita and ask her if she'll take you with her to Syracuse."

"Maybe I should, but what's going to become of Mumma? She seems awfully lonesome now as it is. Andy doesn't hang around much anymore. Right after supper he's gone to the pool room playing cards or something."

Pangs of doubt, the sadness of leaving Mumma, and not knowing what to do nearly doubled me over. I wished we were talking about something else. I wanted to change the subject. Why couldn't anything ever stay the same? When Andy first came to visit, it was fun. Mumma had brightened up and she had seemed livelier. We were happy. I wished we could be again.

"I'd better be going," I said. "Mumma will start wondering what's happened to me." I made up my mind to ask her if she'd be real lonesome if I were to leave her. I went out in the cold and forgot all about my conversation with Florence.

For a Sunday afternoon entertainment in winter, the farm boys from the surrounding islands crossed over on the ice in their horse-drawn sleighs to pick up their girlfriends. They'd ride around and round the village. Every time a sleigh went by, the kids would take a flying leap from behind a snow bank, and grab onto the high back of the sleigh. With feet planted firmly on the runners, we'd hold on and ride. When we got tired we'd let go. Most of the drivers ignored us, and let us ride. And there were those who'd flip their whip backwards and force us off.

I got home disheveled, my bonnet a-skewed and my face red and sweaty.

"Where have you been all day?" Andy sounded annoyed

I wanted to be cheeky and say, if you'd looked out down the road, you'd have seen me. But after he slapped Mumma, I didn't want to chance it.

"Stayed and visited with Florence, then ran all the way home," I replied,

MY MOTHER'S SPIRIT

at the same time, trying to catch my breath.

He knew what I had been doing. He acted as if it were up to me to keep Mumma company. Since she couldn't drink with him anymore, then he had no more use for her. He continued with his game of solitaire.

Mumma knew where I'd been. She spoke up quietly, "I wish you wouldn't hitch rides like that. You could get hurt or even blinded, the way those boys snap their whips."

I listened to her as I continued hanging my mittens and woolen socks to dry behind the wood stove. "Okay!" I replied, and smiled at her.

"Get yourself a bowl of soup, then you can help me finish dying these splints."

"Mmm! Indian corn soup, my favorite. No one can make soup like you, Mumma." I got myself some soup and sat there slurping it while she worked with her splints.

Andy scraped his chair backward, got up for his coat and he was gone for the evening.

When Andy was home all day helping her dye her splints, she was fine. She worked quietly, scraping, splicing and splitting the black, brown and white ash splints. "You can braid the sweet grass like I taught you. You do such a nice job," she said to me. Today, with Andy's help, she had boiling kettles of water on the kerosene stove and was dying her splints.

"Mumma, your hands are every shade of the rainbow."

Smiling, she said, "And yours will be too. Take these coils of ribbon-thin splints and soak them into those pans of dye." The four dishpans were full of brilliant colors like giant pans of Jell-O...red, yellow, green and purple. "Then hang them on that drying rack See how nice these racks are that Andy designed for me?" She liked his interest in her baskets.

In minutes, I lost myself in a world of peaceful calm as we worked quietly, dying and preparing splints for weaving.

"Mumma, what would you do if I had to leave you one day?" I asked nonchalantly.

"I'd miss you. In a few years you'll probably get married and have a family of your own. For now, I'm grateful you are here with me." She took another puff from her pipe.

"I hope I can live here with you forever," I replied. And I meant it, but I knew in my heart it was not to be. We went on with our work.

ESCAPADES

I did most of the talking. Mumma, weaving with nibble fingers, would stop, take a puff, look over my work and resume with her own. Engulfed in total peace, "Mumma tell me about the time I was three and we lived next door. Mister LaFrance let me sit on his knee and let me pat his mustache when everyone was scared of him. Why did I not fear him too?"

"You weren't afraid of anyone and he liked you. He disapproved of the people your grandmother invited and he wanted to keep you safe."

Mumma kept on weaving and I grew silent. She kept to her self and didn't gossip. Only basket makers came to her for her expertise in basket making. Therefore, she took me by surprise when she asked about Florence.

"She's fine," I replied.

"Did you have a nice visit?"

"I guess so?" I didn't know what else to say. I couldn't very well tell her, Florence and I were talking about Mumma's drinking.

"I heard, she's asked Mose White for his help on getting an early parole for your father."

Mose White, a self-educated Mohawk, made it his business learning about legal matters. He had a car and would transport people for hire, interpreting and speaking in their behalf. Why would Mumma ask me such a thing? I didn't even know if Florence talked with Mose White concerning my father. Mumma must have heard it from one of the basket makers. It was dawning on me that she probably knew pretty much what went on in the village just by listening. Just because she couldn't read nor write, didn't mean she wasn't as intelligent as those who were always insinuating how smart they were.

"Florence hasn't said anything to me about it?" I answered. "Is she really trying to get my father out of prison?"

"That's what I heard," Mumma replied, wetting a tip of sweet grass to her mouth. I grew quiet, wondering why she'd be concerned? Mumma went on with her weaving and no more was said.

I hadn't thought about my father in a long time. I'd never heard from him anyway. It's just like Florence to busy herself with other people's affairs. Not that I wasn't grateful for everything she did for me. I probably was no

MY MOTHER'S SPIRIT

different than these people who thought they knew all the answers and tended to be annoyed with Florence, because she DID know more than they. She usually gave good advise. Yet she annoyed others to the point where they wouldn't listen to her just for spite. Much like throwing away a perfect jewel because of it's ugly box. She even annoyed me at times.

She started telling me how to behave as soon as I turned eleven. I didn't like her tone of voice...always insinuating. She reminded me of Tota; opinionated and sarcastic. When Florence told me to stop hitching rides on back of sleighs I paid no mind, but when Mumma's asked me, I stopped.

My twelfth birthday on March 2nd had come and gone. No fanfare. We didn't make a big deal about birthdays and I didn't get any presents. Mumma reminded me the morning of my birthday how nice she thought I was becoming. My teacher and classmates sang Happy Birthday that day and that was it.

That spring, the older kids started hanging out with Francis Johnson, fifteen. He knew a lot more about our Indian traditions. He accused us of behaving like white people. We admired the way he looked with his one long braid hanging down his back. He had his own Indian regalia and wore moccasins. He invited us to his house on the Canadian side and taught us drumming, dancing and singing traditional Indian songs. "As soon as we get good enough," he said, "people will ask us to perform at weddings and special events."

We heard there would be a wedding reception at the Kateri Tekakwitha Center April 1st. "This is it," he said. "Our big chance." So ten of us rehearsed at his house every day.

On the day of the wedding, six of us showed up, a scraggly bunch, each wearing some part of Francis's regalia. I wore a beaded headband. Sam and Frankie each stuck a turkey feather in their leather headbands. Bessie and Bella Mae wore shawls and leather moccasins. Cloistered in the back entrance hallway, no one paid any attention to us. The adults were too busy putting food out on the long tables.

Peaking into the hall bedecked with crepe paper streamers, pink and white paper foldout wedding bells, I drooled at the sight of all the food. Then I spotted the wedding party coming in.

The plump bride in her long white satin dress clutched her veil trying to keep it from billowing in the wind. Her six bridesmaids in long puffy maroon satin dresses traipsed in with six ushers in black tuxedoes. The tuxedo-suited groom and best man held the doors open. The wedding party looked like they had just posed for the society section of the Sunday *Massena Herald Tribune*. Except for brown faces and dark Mohawk features they looked more like a white wedding party.

The hall quickly filled up, hungry guests scrambled into the folding chairs set up to the long tables laden with steaming bowls of Indian hash.

Francis hissed, "This is it." TUM, tumm tumm tumm. TUM, tumm, tumm, tumm! He came out beating his drum, wearing his mid-plains long feathered bonnet. TUM tumm tumm tumm! The scraggily six of us followed close behind toe stepping to the drum beat like we'd seen in the movies.

Everyone seemed amused, except the two mothers of the wedding couple. They expressed their annoyance over our pesky performance with scowls. That's when the best man walked over. "What do you kids think you're doing? Who put you up to this?" he scowled.

Francis stepped up to him upping his chin proudly, "We are honoring this occasion with a traditional dance." Father Jacobs hurried over and stepped between them. "Here, you kids, take off your costumes and get something to eat." Francis turned about, highly insulted, and padded off with his long feathered bonnet swaying behind him. The rest of us, hungry and thirsty, stayed and partook of the wedding feast. We did not regroup for any further celebrations. No one ever asked us to.

GOING TO THE MOVIES

Every Sunday after noon, I managed to get out of the house in time for the one o'clock bus to Massena. I'd join the kids going to the matinee. It was easier when Andy wasn't home. He preferred that I stay home with Mumma. If he got away first, then, I knew Mumma would give me the money to go.

My girl friends on the American side were Christine and Dorothy and I always insisted we sit up front. "Better to gaze at our idle, Dana Andrews," I'd say. The truth being, I couldn't see, and they'd go along with me. Chewing our popcorn, we'd moon over the love scenes between Dana and Irene Dunne. We saw a lot of war movies and we idolized the handsome actors in military uniforms. We agreed in unison. "Oh! They're so handsome...Oh my God!" Christine swooned over Van Johnson.

Whether we wanted to or not, we learned a lot about the war going on some where in Europe we called "overseas." THE EAR AND EYES OF THE WORLD loomed up on the screen right after the cartoon, and before the main feature.

The movies of World War II were the most disturbing. Showing the cruelty of German soldiers by actors in German uniforms made a lasting impression. Especially the one showing soldiers ushering small Jewish children into a big tent. There would be cots inside and doctors and nurses would draw blood from the children's thin puny little arms. Most of the children couldn't get off the cots from losing so much blood. I grew fearful of needles ever after and could never bring myself to donate blood. After seeing this one movie, we filed out into the sunny afternoon. Dorothy and Christine looked as pale as I felt. We rode home in silence. I couldn't get my mind off these poor little children.

As soon as I walked in the door I knew Mumma had been drinking. She slept soundly on the couch and didn't hear me come in. "Mumma wake up. Please! Before Andy gets home." I needed to get her perked up. Although disheveled, she woke up in time and I aired out the room. I hustled around quickly and fried some onions and potatoes for supper.

When either Andy or I were around, Mumma kept her self busy with her baskets. The one time Andy came home before I did, he blamed me for her being tipsy. He acted very brusque with the both of us. "If you'd been home, she wouldn't have started drinking."

Luckily, I got off the school bus before he got home from work. Most often Mumma would have that familiar glassy stare, vacant smile, and pretending to be sober, so much so, she'd make no sense. I'd start getting supper urging her to lie down and rest. Sometimes, Andy wouldn't come home for supper. When he did, I'd get a whiff of bar room smell. At least he drank in moderation and I didn't see him intoxicated. He provided for us. But I no longer knew what to expect. Most of the time he came home in a sour mood and nothing I said or did made any difference. Worst of all, Mumma's drinking became almost constant. I didn't know what to do about it.

A SECRET SMOKE

Early one spring morning, my girl friends, Mabel and Cezzie, both from the Canadian side, walked over to visit me. We sat for a while on the steps to our front stoop and gazed out to the road, and beyond to the old lacrosse field. We were nine, and we didn't have much to talk about. For something better to do, I suggested it was high time we sneak off somewhere and had a smoke. Enthused, Cezzie volunteered to get the quarter for the pack of cigarettes from her grandfather, grouchy old, Mr. Delorme. The same grouch who threw me off his school bus on my first day of school to the American side. She could sweet talk her grandfather and get anything she wanted from him.

"Tell Mr. Hemlock the Camels are for your uncle," Mabel suggested, acting so much the wiser than Cezzie and me. Mr. Hemlock threw the pack of Camels on the counter, without giving Cezzie a second look. She merrily skipped down the steps with the pack in her hand. We chose the abandoned outhouse in back of the old lacrosse field. I had the box of matches I had secretly taken from Mumma's supply. We lit up.

"I always smoke mine right down to here," Cezzie said, indicating the bottom inch of her lit cigarette.

"I thought you said you never smoked before?" I asked, piercing my lips together and closing my eyes to take a puff, holding the cigarette between my thumb and first finger.

"Look at you," Cezzie sneered. "You don't even know how to hold it."

"I do so. I just don't like getting smoke in my eyes."

Mabel flipped her hand about with the lit cigarette, imitating Bette Davis. We puffed some more without much conversation. After a few more puffs, I spat out, "Mmwah! Ahh!" After the second cigarette, when I ran my tongue around the lining inside my mouth, it felt as if it was lined with brown felt. I wished we had bought something to drink.

"My mouth tastes like all that shit below," I said.

"I know," Mabel agreed. "Mine does too."

Cezzie spit in the pit and said, "Pee yew!" We soon found it boring, not much fun, and we all looked pukey.

"What are we going to do with the rest of the pack?" Mabel asked. "I sure don't want to be caught with it. My mother'd kill me."

"Let's get rid of the evidence," I suggested. "We'll rip up the cigarettes, burn the matches and throw everything in the hole. No one will ever know we were in here."

"Good idea," we agreed. We hurriedly lit up everything, and threw it all in the two holes of the seat and closed the door behind us. We crept through the tall grass to our houses, none of us feeling too chipper.

"Thank God!" I thought. It was Mumma who came to the door.

"Where did you disappear to this morning?" she asked, concerned.

I didn't have to say a word. I reeked of all the malodorous smells of an outhouse. She knew as soon as she saw me what I had been up to.

"You look green as a turtle," she said.

"I feel like it," I muttered and climbed the stairs on all fours and went to bed.

She came up behind me with a glass of water. "Drink this, all of it."

Feeling miserable, I prayed that if I lived, I'd never smoke again. She placed the empty slop pail by the bed, reached over and smoothed the hair off my face.

In our haste to get away, we hadn't noticed the smoke seeping out from the bottom of the outhouse. The accumulation of years of paper work, the pages of the Sears and Roebuck catalog, had ignited. The old dried up wooden building couldn't contain the blaze leaping from the pit below. By the time neighbors came out with buckets of water the outhouse had exploded into a roaring fire.

"It must have been those damned hoodlums hanging around with nothing better to do," old Mr. Delorme grumbled.

Spring blossomed into a brilliant summer. Two more weeks and school would be over until September. We eagerly scrambled into our seats on the school bus for the ride home. Mr. Delorme stopped at the garage across from Mr. Lantry's general store. "I'll just be a minute," he growled.

We dared one another to run in and steal something and get away with it before we got chased out. A bunch of us tumbled out of the bus and dashed into the store.

"Hey! You kids. Get outta here," one of the old biddy sales clerk yelled at us. We angled for the door but not until I'd swiped an orange.

On the way home I held the orange in the air and the kids cheered.

"You kids keep that up, I'm stopping this bus," Mr. Delorme threatened. We grew quiet. My guilt got the better of me. I didn't want the orange anyway. Mumma would be disappointed if she heard what I had done, so I left it on the bus.

I HEARD MUMMA CALL MY NAME

That Sunday morning right after early Mass, I kept my head down and walked faster as I passed Florence's house. Lately, she'd been watching for me, calling out and detaining me to wash her dishes accumulated from the day before, and giving me only fifty cents. It would take almost two hours and I couldn't stay that long, although the fifty cents would have covered my expenses for the show and a bag of popcorn.

Andy, on the sly, had told me, as I was leaving for church, "Stay around and keep an eye on Mumma today until I get back. I have to see a friend about a dog." That's the excuse he always used when he didn't want to say where he was going. I heard him, kept my head down and didn't respond. Shortly after I returned, before I could rustle up something to eat, a car stopped out front. With out a word he got in back and it sped away.

Mumma had gone into her little house next door to work on her baskets and must have seen him leave from her window. An hour later Mumma came in tipsy, needing a nap. I suggested she lie down. The bus would be coming soon and I needed to get away. I was thinking Mumma would sleep it off and she'd be okay. I quietly took fifty cents from her dish of change in the cupboard and went out to join the kids out front waiting for the bus.

The movie, *It Happened One Night*, with Claudette Colburn and Clark Gable, wasn't all that interesting. I kept wondering about Mumma. After the movies, cavorting with friends while waiting for the bus, I felt fine. As soon as we settled down into our seats, I began to get the jitters thinking about Mumma and not knowing how she'd be. And I didn't want to face Andy. He'd surely be home by now.

I sucked my breath and entered the house cautiously. Mumma, although disheveled, was braiding sweet grass, and appeared to look busy, probably for Andy's sake. Andy hardly looked up from the letter he was writing. I suspected Mumma had covered up for my being gone.

"We've already eaten." Mumma got up from her chair. "Here, let me get you something to eat."

"No," Andy said. "Let her be. If she's old enough to go tramping all over Massena and be gone all day, she's old enough to get her own supper."

I reheated leftover fried potatoes and Indian fried steak (thick slices of bologna fried in bacon fat). I cleaned up my mess. Both seemed to be ignoring me anyway. There was a lot of daylight left. I bounded out the door to play hide-and-seek with the gang.

Rita came home on a Friday, that last weekend in June. It was like old times. I joked, acting silly, and Rita caught my mood. We giggled over nothing. Mumma brightened up, watching us while quietly puffing on her pipe. We both enjoyed having Rita home. Andy acted the timid little man and stayed out in the shed puttering looking busy. That night over pillow talk, almost whispering so as not to disturb Mumma and Andy in the next room, Rita told me I'd be returning to Syracuse with her for the summer.

"Why?" I asked. "What about Mumma?"

"She's going to be okay." Rita told me about Andy's letter. "He thinks you're getting out of hand–even stole money from Mumma to go to the movies. Besides Phoebe wants to go to work and needs you to baby sit."

All day Saturday, while I was getting ready to leave, Mumma sat idly by, puffing on her pipe. She watched me gather my stuff, fold my clothes and put it all in my two shopping bags. Rita cleaned house. Mumma liked making a basket, not doing housework, although our house always had that clean pleasant aroma of sweet grass and splints. I thought maybe Rita would find Mumma's liquor stash. No one discussed Mumma's drinking. I wondered if Andy had told Phoebe and Rita about it. If, as Florence said, everybody was talking about it, then Phoebe and Rita must have heard by now. I certainly wasn't going to bring it up.

Everyone quietly went about their business. Andy made himself scarce down by the river. So I kept busy too, until it was time to go.

I hugged Mumma long and hard. "I'll be back before school starts," I promised. She smiled and cradled my face with the palm of her hand for just an instant. The feeling of her touch upon my face lingered for a long time afterwards.

Rita and I rode to Syracuse with her friend Susan Hemlock. Susan dropped us off in front of Rita and Phoebe's apartment over an antique store on Geneses Street. The front entrance had stairs leading up to a long dark hallway lined with old junky, dusty, musty-smelling furniture. The hall door opened into a small living room. Six of us were expected to fit in the three rooms. Rita and I were to share the studio couch in the living room. Phoebe and her three kids slept in the one bedroom. The apartment at least had a bathroom with hot and cold water and a flush toilet. We couldn't all fit in the tiny kitchen at one time. The range, refrigerator, sink, and a kitchen table with

MY MOTHER'S SPIRIT

four chairs took up all the space. The back entrance, off the kitchen, led downstairs into a small fenced in yard.

"It's dangerous going down the front stairs and out into the heavy traffic. One of you might get hit. Always use the back stairs. Okay?" Rita cautioned.

I had no choice but to entertain Stanley, six, Linda, five, and Phyllis, four, in the small yard all day.

I heard about the Burnett Park Zoo, and found a way to walk there with my three kids. We could spend the whole day looking at the caged bears, lions, and a few monkeys. We preferred playing in the park rather than being cooped up in the back yard. Sometimes I took them to the matinee to see a good kids' movie if Phoebe gave me the money.

When Rita and I wanted to see a good movie, we went to a much bigger theater. There, a huge pipe organ rose up from the bottom of the stage. During intermission, a spot light shone on a small slim beautiful blond woman in a gold sequined dress seated in front of it. I watched in wonder as she played the many layers of keys simultaneously, and her feet tapped-danced on the pedals at the bottom. The thin curtains on the stage opened and the words of the songs she played appeared on the screen. You could sing along by watching the bouncing ball landing on the words to the rhythm of the song. I sang to my heart's content. Rita couldn't carry a tune and didn't even try. She enjoyed just watching and listening.

I convinced Rita I knew the layout of the streets and went about without fear. Then one time, I went to a matinee at the small dinky neighborhood movie by myself and sat up front. As soon as the lights dimmed and the movie started, a man sidled into the seat next to mine. His hand went right up inside of my leg. I yelled out, "Hey!"

"Shush!" he whispered. "It's all right. I thought you were someone else."

I jumped up from my seat and ran up the aisle and out unto the sunlit street. I walked home fast, looking back every so often, afraid he'd followed me. After that, I no longer felt free to roam the streets. The big city had lost it's magic. I didn't even bother telling Rita about the nasty man.

I longed to be home with Mumma and playing hide-and-seek all over the village with my friends. I wished I were near a Catholic Church, so that I could go light a candle. Then, maybe my prayers to go back to the reserve would be answered. I wanted out of this city. Rita and Phoebe didn't go to church, so I didn't either. My Tota had told me a long time ago why it helped to light a blessed candle. You lit a candle just as you would light a bonfire if you were lost, hoping to attract someone's attention to come and rescue you, or to hail a ship far off if you were stranded on a deserted island. The candle flame alerted the saints that you were in need of their intercession with God. I believed in lighting candles. It made perfect sense to me.

We were in the middle of World War II. Materials were so scarce that even shoes were rationed. And I needed shoes. Rita had no way of getting coupons for me. I knew I was Mohawk living on the American side, but I had no papers of identification to show whether I was Canadian or American. I didn't seem to be either. Since I didn't have coupons I had to wear felt slippers.

To make matters worse, during the hottest days in August our refrigerator went on the blink. The landlord blamed the war for the fact that he couldn't fix the fridge. The miserable heat and not a breath of fresh air continued day after day. I had to wait for either Rita or Phoebe to come home and go to the store to buy whatever it took to fix our meals. I had placed a ham bone in the warm fridge the day before. I thought I could gnaw some meat off of it, enough to hold me over until someone got home. When I turned it over, I saw two white maggots crawling on the plate. I quickly threw the bone into the garbage pail.

To keep Stanley, Linda, and Phyllis comfortable enough, we pretended the tub was a swimming pool. They splashed one another and had a good time. I'd take them down into the backyard to dry off. Then I gave them a drink of Kool Aid.

That's when I heard Mumma's voice calling me, "Eostenonni," plain as day.

"Mumma," I cried out. Thinking she must have come for a visit, I ran back up the back stairs, ran down the hall, and down the front stairs out onto the street calling, "Mumma!" I looked around eagerly. Recognizing no one, I went back up the stairs and back down again to the backyard. The queasiness in my gut me made me ill. I sat on the bottom step and cried.

At four-thirty that afternoon, Rita came home looking very troubled. I knew something bad had happened. She usually came home in a happy mood. Then Phoebe came in. She'd been crying. They told me that Mumma had died that afternoon.

Rita made arrangements with Susan to drive us home. We shoved our belongings into paper sacks and left. "We'll stop along the way for a bite to eat at some nice restaurant," Rita said, trying to be cheerful. The three little ones brightened up, but the rest of us looked grim. I didn't feel like eating. Fitfully, I tried to nap with the three kids in the back seat until we got home.

Andy moved out without a word almost immediately. Rita and Phoebe

MY MOTHER'S SPIRIT

reclaimed their house. The good women of the village came in and helped get the house in order. My three charges and I were relegated to Mumma's basket-making house. Cots were set up for us and that's where we stayed.

I had no desire to view Mumma's body when she was bought back from the funeral home. I knew they had her wearing that black dress, the same dress she wore for her wedding, less than two years ago. The sweet smell of flowers sickened me. I wanted nothing more to do with death. I busied myself with the care of Stanley, Linda and Phyllis. I loved them and took good care of them. They comforted me in their gentle, childish ways—leaning on me or just laying their hands in my lap, sitting very close. Most of the time we huddled together, sitting on the door stoop.

A neighbor explained how Mumma had been taken to the hospital in Massena. She had died of cirrhosis of the liver a few days later. It took the alcohol only two years to kill her. Except for the funeral Mass, the ride to the cemetery, and the sight of her coffin being lowered into the ground, I preferred to remember Mumma the way she was…lying side by side…taking puffs from her corncob pipe…knowing she loved me.

NEW DEVELOPMENTS – NEW STRUGGLES

After Mumma's funeral, we went around in a daze. Rita, restless, wanted to return to her job as Rita the Riveter. I believed she just wanted to be out of here. Phoebe hated her job in a meat packing plant and had no intention of going back. "Might as well stay home and wait for Bill," she sighed heavily. Bill had been gone for over two years and she hoped he'd be discharged soon. Me? I would rather have had it the other way around—for Phoebe to go and Rita and me to stay. But I had no say in the matter. It would have been fun here with Rita. She did a good share of the household chores. Phoebe sat and smiled a lot, but I did all the work. With her constant, "Hand me this or hand me that," or "go see what they're up to," I didn't have a minute's rest. At least Phoebe wanted me because I was useful.

I had my hands full when school started that fall. Phoebe couldn't wake up early enough to help with Stanley. He hated getting up for school. I had to pull him out of bed, dress him and get him to eat breakfast. Struggling with him on the bus took all my strength. Mr. Delorme looked meaner than ever, having to sit there and wait while Stanley and I created a scene every morning. One morning, Mr. Delorme got so mad at us, he got out of his bus and threw a pail of water at us. To make matters worse, several times, Stanley's first grade teacher took me aside and suggested that Stanley needed a bath.

Two weeks later, after school on a Friday afternoon, I joined in for a game of tag with the older kids. One of them accidentally tagged me too hard. I went down on my knees on a broken beer bottle and got a deep two-inch gash on my right kneecap. I grabbed an old sheet from the pile of rags in the corner of the shed, tore off a strip and wound it around my knee to stop the bleeding. I wanted to go see Miss Barr, the health nurse, whose office was a few houses down on the Canadian side. But remembering the ruckus I had caused over the school bus incident, I decided I'd better not. I didn't care to be humiliated again. When the throbbing eased up, I tended not to think about my knee.

Sunday, I woke up in the middle of the night with a terrible thirst. My knee throbbed worse than ever. I prayed, "Please let there be a glass of water by my bed." I knew I couldn't hobble down the stairs. Miraculously, I reached over and there it stood, a glass half full. I gulped it down thinking I had never tasted anything so satisfying. My knee had swollen to the size of a red cabbage and

MY MOTHER'S SPIRIT

was just as purple.

Luckily for me, Rita came home that Sunday. She took one look at my knee and yelled at Phoebe, "How could you let her knee get so infected?"

Phoebe played ignorant to my hobbling around with the rag tied around my knee. "She told me she hurt it playing tag. How did I know she cut it on a broken beer bottle?"

Rita took me to Miss Barr's office. Miss Barr didn't care which side I lived on. She bandaged my knee and told me to come every morning until it healed properly.

If Tota had been alive, she probably would have washed out the cut with lye soap and warm water, then applied the broad green leaves of the dandelion plant for the chlorophyll to draw out the infection. Florence would have slapped a hunk of salt pork on it. It seemed so long ago, when Tota and Florence had doctored me with home remedies and Indian medicines. When that didn't work, as a last resort, Tota would visit the health nurse.

Rita and Phoebe both claimed the homestead, causing a rift between them. They argued all week long. It didn't feel right. Mumma hadn't been dead all that long. Rita got so mad, she hit Phoebe with the wooden spoon she had in her hand. "This is my house," Rita cried. "You've let it get dirty as a pig sty."

"Easy for you to criticize," Phoebe retorted. "You don't have three kids to chase all day. Besides, it's as much my house as it is yours."

"What do you man, chasing kids all day? Eostenuni is doing all the chasing, taking care of these kids, and doing what little that gets done around here. I've a good mind to take her back with me."

It reminded me of that time long ago when I was three and we lived next door. Phoebe had said something hurtful. Rita had picked up the teakettle of boiling water and chased her threatening to scald her. I must have sensed danger because I scooted out the back door to fetch Mumma. She had come running in time to take the kettle away from Rita, scolding them. Phoebe was always at a disadvantage. Always chubby, she couldn't run as fast. Rita moved easily and swiftly.

The bickering continued all that week. I felt almost relieved when Rita left with her friend Susan that Sunday afternoon. I couldn't understand it at the time. Ordinarily, Rita and Phoebe both tended to be easygoing with pleasant dispositions. Why, all of a sudden, did they argue all the time? They couldn't seem to get along.

Right after Phoebe received her allotment check, we ate very well. Toward the end of the month, we fell back on peanut butter and bologna sandwiches, and Kool-aid. I became the chief sandwich maker. One school morning at the end of the month, our food supply had completely dried up. I had fifteen cents in my bank. I hurried to Hemlock's store for a can of Campbell's vegetable soup. I no sooner had it opened and was heating it on the stove when the school bus honked for us. I turned the burner off and I ran, dragging Stanley, and left the soup for someone else to enjoy. It's a good thing we got hot lunches at school, or we would have gotten awful hungry. When I got off the bus, I found the pan empty, left on the sideboard for me to wash.

I had it pretty good, though. I didn't mind. My three charges followed me around like baby ducklings...except on school mornings. Stanley resented my waking him up so early. Linda was pudgy, with big dark brown eyes and straight dark brown hair. She was the most docile and lovable. She followed me everywhere. Phyllis, the youngest, was leaner but tended to be feisty for one so tiny. I called her "Little Bullet."

It became a joke. Every Saturday morning Phoebe would give a big sigh and tell me to set up the washtubs. Then I'd have to wear the yolk across my shoulders, and carry water, two pails at a time, from the river until the tubs were full. We didn't have a washing machine. Phoebe scrubbed the clothes on her washboard. She'd be red, sweaty and tired in no time, way before the clothes were all washed. She left the colored clothes for next time. And they'd stay in the corner on the floor of the back porch until they were moldy and beyond saving. The soapy clothes that did get washed got one rinsing and were hung out to dry. Our supposedly white pile became dingy gray forever. I hand-washed my own clothes and hung them up to dry. Wash and wear, back then, meant I looked rumpled but fairly clean.

Phoebe preferred to buy new clothes for herself and the children. It wrecked her budget but we managed to squeeze by each month. We were happy. Then Bill wrote to say he had been discharged and would be home soon. She went into a tailspin; clean the house, mop the floors, Eostenuni do this and Eostenuni do that. Everyone went around smiling from ear to ear except me. I barely had enough energy to climb the stairs to bed. I wasn't sure what would become of me, but I felt so tired I no longer cared.

Bill came home and everyone fawned over him. For an Indian, he had very light brown, wavy, almost curly hair. His faced looked chiseled, masculine, and so perfect, with a broad forehead and a strong square jaw. His muscles bulged and his sinewy arms rippled with steely strength. He had broad-shoulders and the narrow hips of a dancer, and was just as light on his feet. He teased Phoebe over the forty pounds she had gained since he last saw her. He'd cuddle her anyway and said he didn't care. He told everyone she was the prettiest girl on the reserve. And she was, I had to agree.

He didn't like to work around the house any more than she did. But, he at least hauled our water from the river, relieving me of one heavy chore. They partied every night and did a lot of bar hopping. That's all they talked about to the many friends who dropped in constantly. I stayed home and looked after the little ones. Phoebe didn't drink. I suspected she kept up with him to keep other women away.

One afternoon, Bill shadow-boxed in the kitchen while I swept the floor. He swung around flexing his biceps. He showed me an iron set of four rings welded together in one piece. "What are those?" I asked. He demonstrated, slipping the set of rings over his fingers and flexing his fingers into a fist. Then he smacked his fist into the palm of his other hand.

"These are brass knuckles."

I winced, imagining what would happen to the face that got in the way of Bill's punch. "You're not going to fight someone, are you?"

He laughed. "You never know. I like to be prepared."

Sometimes he'd come to breakfast sporting a cut above an eyebrow or a bruise on his cheekbone. He drank coffee by the pots full.

When I heard him telling Phoebe he'd have to look for work soon, my ears picked up and I listened hard. He mentioned looking for work in Syracuse. She replied that if he went, she and the kids would go too. Wherever they went, I prayed I wouldn't have to go with them.

Rita came to my rescue. She came home unexpectedly one day. I couldn't believe my good fortune. A few harsh words were spoken between her and Bill. Before the week was over, Bill, Phoebe and their three kids had moved out. Rita and I were left to ourselves. I wondered how we would manage with Rita out of a job.

"Rita, how are we going to live?"

"I'm going to take in sewing. Don't worry. Something'll turn up."

I don't believe Rita planned it this way—it just happened. She had bought a case of beer and kept it cool in the root cellar. A few days later a friend dropped in. "Say! Would you happen to have a cold one?"

"Yes! It just so happens, I do. Eostennoni, go down and bring up a couple of bottles."

I ran in to the kitchen, removed the throw rug covering the trap door, shinnied down the ladder into the root cellar and fetched the cold beer. The friend threw a quarter on the table. Soon, others came and the quarters multiplied. Before we knew it, Rita and I were in the beer business.

Running our illegal beer parlor.

From then on, friends came in for a social drink throughout the day. They'd throw quarters onto the table and down into the root cellar I'd go. Rita replaced the empty case with two full ones…then four, and so on. She wore an apron with big pockets and soon they were stuffed with bills. I rolled up the quarters in wrappers. We made a good team.

I developed more confidence, I was better dressed, and I made a new circle of friends at school. I was eager to pal around with Christi Cornstock, blondish, tall and sexy, she reminded me of Ginger Rogers. Dorothy Philips was our comforter, short and pudgy. Priscilla Laughlin, tiny, mischievous and pixie-like kept us giggling. They were all a year or two years older than I. That fall, the teachers announced we'd soon start rehearsals for the Christmas play. The four of us rolled our eyes. "Honestly! How childish!" we complained. Priscilla, a very good singer—better than I, was to dress as a turkey, and sing and gobble. I was to wear a crepe paper Christmas tree costume and sang "Merry Christmas To You." Rita volunteered to help sew our costumes. But Christi, Dorothy, Pris and I had more grownup stuff to talk about.

The three of them huddled together and commiserated over their monthly miseries. I'd sympathize, not wanting to admit that I had not started yet. Thinking about the whole bloody mess made me uncomfortable. Tota and Aunt Helen had implied by their actions and sarcastic remarks that it wasn't anything to talk about. When I did start a few months after my thirteenth birthday, I felt too embarrassed to tell anyone. One day, while sorting out the laundry, Rita asked me, "What in the world is happening to all our washcloths?" I broke down and confessed. She looked at me and laughed. "Why you poor kid. Why didn't you tell me?" She gave me a box of Kotex. I felt better after we had a brief discussion. I knew I could tell Rita everything.

We had visitors every evening, sometimes as many as eight. They kept me busy shinning up and down the ladder and casing up the empties, but I didn't mind. I enjoyed the camaraderie…that, and all the ohwi'sta' (money) in our pockets. If a guest became rowdy, Rita maneuvered him out the door. Most of the time they sang Indian songs. I sang right along, including the risqué ones—Hahaha, yo wey suh ya ga na' onon:ta:ke, to the tune of "Little Brown Jug." (Hahaha, It's so nice to touch your breasts). Or they'd sing a little ditty in Mohawk meaning: "Come on my friends, let all go to Caugnewage to see

MY MOTHER'S SPIRIT

our girlfriends we like so much."

Two men would be conversing quietly and, all of a sudden, they'd be crying over something or other. Then the women would be sobbing, crying over how great it felt to be in good company and that Rita...she's the "salt of the earth." Soon they'd all be crying. That's when Rita would announce. "Sorry! We've run out. It's time to go home." Then they'd all stagger out.

But one very cold night in December, Rita let harmless old Mr. Jackson sleep on the couch. He lived alone and she didn't have the heart to turn him out. In the middle of the night I woke up and heard movement downstairs. I crept down three steps and looked down into the sitting room. In the low gray glow of the kerosene lamp, I watched the old man getting up. He must have mistaken the wood stove for a tree and aimed at it, relieving himself. The instant his urine hit the hot stove, it sizzled a yellow steam wafting the most acrid smelly stench. It stung my nostrils. The strong ammonia spray could have aroused the dead. Rita jumped out of bed and flew down the stairs. She hurried the old man out the door, opened both doors wide open and threw nutmeg all over the stove. We allowed no more inebriated guests to spend the night.

That following spring late in the night, a horrible fight broke out in our kitchen—a terrible tragedy really. It's a wonder someone didn't close us down and send Rita to jail. Dundee, barely eighteen, from two doors down the road, came to join the four guests sitting around the kitchen table. He was a likable scrawny kid with a bashful smile, and his nose wrinkled when he grinned. He'd already been drinking when he came in. Smiling, he pulled up a chair and squeezed in between two women.

I felt tired and decided to go to bed. The loud boisterous talk late into the night never bothered me. I could sleep though an earthquake. No sooner had I gotten into bed than I heard a thunderous pounding at the back door. I ran into the storage room over the kitchen and looked down through the register. Dundee's brother-in-law, Bunion Burlyhead, over six feet tall, pushed his way into the room, mad as a bull and hollering for Dundee. Dundee kept on grinning, wrinkling his nose, sitting between the two women as if they were going to be his protection. Rita jumped up and placed herself between Bunion and Dundee. Bunion pushed her out of his way with one arm, knocking her against the wall. Everyone cleared out giving Bunion wide room to do his damnedest.

I watched in terror as Bunion hit Dundee in the face with his fist again and again, mashing it to a pulp. Dundee, offering no resistance, crumbled to the floor. Bunion tossed him up on his shoulder as if Dundee were a rag doll with his arms and legs dangling. He took him outside. I saw the clots of blood on the floor where Dundee's head had lain. They looked like clumps of liver. Once outside, Bunion swung Dundee by his legs and whacked Dundee's head against a tree, and left him for dead. A car pulled up alongside, two men stuffed Dundee into the front seat and sped away to the hospital. Dundee survived but was never right in the head afterwards and he never regained his speech. The story we heard was that Dundee had volunteered to bring a case of beer to a party. But he stole the case from his brother-in-law. And that's the reason Bunion almost killed his kid brother-in-law.

Rita and I laid low and stopped selling beer. I continued going to church and singing in the choir. If Florence knew we were selling beer on the sly, she never mentioned it. She and Rita were good friends. Maybe Florence took into account that at least I had a place to live. Rita finally got to her sewing. She got some material and made me a summer outfit, a pink princess dress with a vest to match for church. She did alterations and kept busy—at least for a while.

INVADING RITA'S PRIVACY

I enjoyed having Rita to myself again. Measuring me for a new dress, she joked, "You're developing a little 'bozoom' there." She teased me about the small mounds on my chest.

We giggled. I didn't mind. I snorted, "As long as they don't get bigger than Christy's. Her's looks more like two small cantaloupes."

Rita giggled, " Young men say anything bigger 'n mouthful is a waste."

"Why Rita! What a thing to say!" I acted shocked, then mock-disgusted. We were enjoying ourselves. It was the first time she had given any inkling that she, too, must have liked boys. If she were lonely, she didn't say. She seemed contented. I didn't think she had a boyfriend.

Then one night I heard voices from outside our bedroom window.

It was a hot stifling night in July. Our unscreened bedroom window was raised to the maximum. I tiptoed quietly and stuck my head out the window to see where the voices were coming from. Whaaay! I couldn't believe it.

I saw two couples sitting down below on the front stoop. Rita sat on one side with a man who had his arms around her. On the opposite side, sat Susan with her boyfriend. Each couple was back to back. Susan and her boy friend were kissing too. What shocked me more was knowing who these men were—fathers of the kids I hung around with. Susan's boyfriend was rubbing her breast as they were kissing. Rita and her boyfriend were chewing on each other's mouths. The two couples were so busy feeling each other up. I watched quietly, thinking if I were to spit on their heads, they'd probably never feel it. Just as, when walking across a bridge, I liked to spit into the fast flowing river below, then run like mad to the other side and watch my spit in a frothy foam flowing down the river. Tempted to spit, I could have easily generated a big wad of it from watching the salacious scene. After a while, I decided not to. I didn't want Rita to know I had a balcony seat to her love life.

I thought of the scandalous talk my discovery would cause—I'd be the entertainer of the month. I relished the tales I'd tell only to my closest friends. I continued watching them until I grew tired. I crept back to bed knowing I could never reveal my secret to anyone. I didn't want Rita to be hurt by it nor to cause embarrassment to my friends. Remembering Mumma's words that gossip caused more harm than good, I vowed I'd never tell. And I never did.

DOLORES EOSTENUNI STANFIELD

For the longest time, I kept wondering if Rita and her lover were seeing one another. Playing detective, thinking of when they might have gotten together, all of a sudden I remembered Rita saying she had to get right back to Syracuse after Mumma died. Her boyfriend was an ironworker and away at the time. Then, when she came home, I remembered seeing him in church with his family. His daughter sang with me in the choir. I felt so sorry for Rita.

SUMMER'S TEMPTATIONS
Field of Sin

I swear, Florence could read my mind. I dropped in for a visit after church, sitting opposite her, I glanced out the open door and saw a teenage boy working on his bike. I hadn't seen him before. I took sidelong glances at his dark lean sinewy body, naked from his waist up. Careful not to let on what I was thinking, I kept up with my idle chatter. Lately, she'd been lecturing me about boys. It annoyed me. She sat sorting and folding laundry, not paying any attention.

"His name is Mickey Taylor," she said.

"Who?" I replied, feigning disinterest.

"That boy you keep looking at. He's from Caugnawaga visiting his grandfather, Tsitso." (Tsitso is Mohawk for fox. Everyone called him Tsitso because he looked like a fox.) Tsito lived across the road.

"I'm just curious. I've never seen him before. He's kinda cute."

"He's only here for the summer. He's sixteen and too old for you. I suppose all the older girls will probably be after him. I want you to stay away from them. The way these girls act nowadays—asking rides from these boys on their bicycles!"

"Why are you telling me all this?" I frowned.

"For your own good. You're not a little girl anymore. You need to be careful, and not take chances."

"What do you mean, take chances? What chances?" I played innocent. Rita must have told Florence about my periods. "I'm going home," I said in a huff, and left before she had a chance to say anything else.

The older kids favored the village pump as their hangout. I considered myself older, and no longer wanted to be out at the point swimming and competing, hiding the same old tin can. That was kid stuff. I liked it much better with the older kids, hanging out, flirting or just talking.

That day at the pump, I gasped when he appeared. He hesitated, acting shy. Quickly, I whispered to Betty Dey, as if I didn't know, "Is that Mickey Taylor?"

"Yes," she answered, neither one of us taking our eyes off of him. He laid his bicycle on the ground and walked over to the pump. He filled the blue-enameled community dipper and drank from it. Then he carefully hung it back in its place. I didn't miss a single movement of his bare brown back glistening like bronze in the hot sun. He wore only his tight black denim jeans and moccasins. His hair was cut short like the rest of the boys except his had a slight wave to it. His eyes were emerald green. His tan made his perfect teeth gleam a brilliant white.

I stared as if mesmerized. So did the other girls... none of us saying a word. After a lull, Sammy, who knew him, asked, "What gives?"

Mickey grinned, without answering. He blended in and became one of us.

At the point behind the Catholic Church not far from our favorite swimming place, a clearing, surrounded by tall weeds, provided the perfect hideaway for serious petting. We called it the "Field of Sin." If a couple were to raise their heads above the tall grasses, they'd see Brother Andrew hoeing in his garden. And if Father Jacobs had dared to venture out a few yards from the sanctity of the rectory, he'd have walked into a muddle of entangled limbs, and have heard enough grunts and groans of rapture to provide material for his homilies to last him for many months to come.

This is where I wanted Mickey to bring me. But, I had to get his attention first. For harmless sport, boys gave their favorite girls a ride on their bicycles. Girls rode sidesaddle on the cross bars and the couple would circle around town and eventually end up for some necking in the privacy of tall weeds. There were many older girls to choose from. Mickey tended to ignore me.

It became an obsession. I'd hurry with my chores helping Rita clean our beer parlor so I could be out at the village pump as the gang began to gather. If having impure thoughts could be considered a venial sin, then I had many and was ready to commit a really big one. It would surely plunge me into hell forever. I didn't care. If I couldn't get him to notice me I thought I would surely die.

Then one day, I had my chance. He came peddling up close and jumped off, sauntered over to the pump and took a drink. Watching his bronzed body sent a shiver through me. As usual, he turned his back and talked to the guys. I walked to the pump as if to get a drink. Instead, I threw the dipper-full of icy water at his back. He jumped, flailed his arms in fright and turned to look as I took flight. He gave chase, caught me in short order and grabbed both my wrists. He stared at me, and then grinned. I didn't resist, letting him hold onto my wrists, grinning back at him. He looked as if he didn't know what to do with me. Then he let go but stood near by. The others laughed and went on with their horsing around. Mine was a childish prank and the excitement died

MY MOTHER'S SPIRIT

down quickly. Mickey and I exchanged eye contact. He went for his bike and I followed him. He held his bike upright and I hopped on ready to ride sidesaddle. He pushed off and away we went.

He peddled leisurely up the road. I leaned back as much as I could against his chest and felt his perspiration against my shirt. I listened to him breathing easily. Closing my eyes I hung on to his wrists desperately, hoping we'd head toward the point. I held my breath as he followed the path leading to the back of the church rectory. By the time we reached the field, I was wet with desire. Eager to hop off, I couldn't. He kept his bike upright with his arms outstretched firmly holding onto the handlebars. His feet were planted firmly on the ground. In the long silence of seconds, I could hear him breathing. Now what?

Then he spoke to me in Mohawk with that slow drawl of his. "You should never let anyone talk you into coming here. At least not until you're a lot older." I felt more embarrassed than disappointed. I couldn't think of anything to say. After a few moments, he pushed off and took me straight home, going right by Florence's house. He let me off in front of our house. "See yah around!" he said over his shoulder as he peddled on his way.

The next day, hoping to see Mickey, I went to visit Florence. She lit in to me as soon as I appeared in the doorway. "What were you thinking of, riding around with that boy from across the road. Are you crazy?"

"What's wrong with that? Nothing happened," I protested.

"Maybe not this time. But sooner or later, you'll be rolling around in the grass like those boy-crazy girls. First thing you know you'll get yourself pregnant."

"Well! You should know. Is that how you got pregnant so Angus would have to marry you?" I shouted, preparing for a good argument.

"I'm telling you for your own good. Rita had better keep a tighter rein on you. I'll be so glad when your father comes after you before you come to some bad end."

"Just because you got pregnant, doesn't mean it's going to happen to me," I sneered.

"Go on home. It's impossible to talk to you. You're too thick-headed to listen."

"All right, I'm going and I'm never coming back. You can scrub your own dirty dishes from now on. I grabbed the open door and slammed it shut as hard as I could to let her know how angry I felt. I went straight home, hopping mad. I forgot about Mickey.

Rita glanced at me. "Who'd you get into an argument with—you look meaner an bear."

I slammed my body into the nearest chair. "That Florence makes me so mad sometimes."

"She has that effect on many people, but she means well," Rita replied calmly. "She's concerned about you. What did she scold you for this time?"

I sat at the kitchen table toying with a spoon and tracing the flowered pattern on the oil tablecloth, almost digging at it. I told her about Mickey and blurted out the whole story about how I wanted him to take me to the "Field of Sin"' and how unfair I thought Florence's accusations were when nothing happened. As I talked my tracing became lighter until I had nothing left to say. I put the spoon down.

She listened quietly. After a pause, she said, "I'm glad you told me about it. Promise me that you'll always come and talk to me when something like that happens again. Mickey must be a nice boy. But you need to be careful. Not all boys are that considerate or conscientious."

I sat at the table thinking, then said, "Okay! I promise." I went about my business feeling much better.

A few days later, I went to visit Florence as if we had never hurled an angry word at each other. As in the past, we argued a lot, but soon forgot what it was all about. And neither one of us ever said, "I'm sorry." She told me that Mickey had gone back to Caugnawage. I kept the pain of disappointment to myself. At fourteen, I think I understood the reasoning behind Florence's concern. I knew many young single girls who got pregnant. Just about every family had their oldest daughter bear a child out of wedlock. Often she didn't marry right away and her parents ended up taking care of the child.

The elders groused or gossiped about the parenting practices of the younger generations. Yet they accepted it as a matter of course that boys will be boys, testing their virility, and sowing their wild oats. Girls took all the responsibilities for their own fertility. As they provide fertile ground for the sowing, so shall they reap. Young men were not chastised, as if it were their birthright to experiment before marriage.

Honestly, why should Florence be so worried about me anyways, I thought. I couldn't possibly get pregnant. Not me! I was too young.

FLORENCE'S BIG SURPRISE

Rita and I started selling beer again. This time, we were very selective who we sold it to—more like a private club. I had saved enough money to buy my own case of beer for resale. Adding up the profits in my mind gave me a boost of self-confidence, at fourteen, earning my own money. I looked forward, sometimes treating my friends to a banana split before the movie matinees on Sunday afternoons.

The first Sunday in July, anxious to get home from church, I hurried past Florence's house. She'd probably heard about us selling beer again. I didn't have time for any more lectures. I suffered through Father Jacobs's, homily and that was enough. I had to help Rita some before the bus came. "Damn! To late," I muttered. I heard Florence calling me. I pretended I didn't hear her.

"Eostenuni! Get over here!" She ordered. Florence never said please, nor asked in a friendly manner. She yelled louder. "There's someone here to see you."

I saw the shining maroon sedan parked by her house. Curiosity got the better of me. "Who?" I asked, crossing the road. "I can't stay long. I'm expected home to do chores. I don't want to miss the bus for the matinee."

As soon as I stepped in the doorway I saw the lean middle-aged white man spring up from his chair with his hand extended as if to shake hands. I stood there scowling. Instinctively, I knew who he was. His nervous chuckle told me he felt as awkward as I did.

"Go ahead," Florence said, giving me a slight push towards him. "Give your father a hug." I managed a weak "Hello," and stood there feeling stupid.

She gave me that, "What in hell is the matter with you," look, signaling me to be more spontaneous. I sat on the edge of the chair opposite him.

He introduced a neatly coifed, dark haired women sitting on the couch as Clare. She remained seated and smiled, nodding slightly. Almost immediately a much younger gangly, curly-headed blond jumped up and gave me a hug. "Hi!" she said. "I'm Ginny." Her zestful behavior put me a little more at ease.

All during the conversation, my head turned left to right like watching a tennis match. They talked at me. My father remained standing quietly by his chair watching me and smiling. Ginny, it seemed, talked non-stop. Not really listening, I couldn't grasp half what she was saying. I took quick glances at him instead.

I tried to remember what all others had told me about him. They were right. He did look handsome. Slender, neat and trim, with out that middle-aged paunch, I could see why women liked him—especially this woman named Clare.

We listened to Clare, Ginny, and Florence for about twenty minute. I looked nervously at Florence wanting her to come to my rescue. I needed to get away if I were to catch the bus. Florence ignored my anxious stares. I mumbled that I needed to get home.

The ebullient, big as life, Ginny, jumped up immediately and gave me another hug. I liked her. Clare said they had to get going too. "We have a long drive ahead of us yet," she said and sidled over to my father—as if to inform me that she had first dibs on him. She stood up to her full height in her black patent leather high heels. Her shoes seemed to push her ample bosom higher. She reminded me of a baby buffalo.

My father made another attempt at a friendly chuckle and failed miserably. He reached into his trouser pocket and drew out a fistful of bills. Before he had a chance to hand me any of it, I pounced at him, put my arms around his middle and hugged him. I laid my head on his chest, breathing in deeply the acidly odor of cigarettes, perspiration, and laundry soap. The strength I sensed in him felt comforting. I hugged him for a long minute. I thought, let this be a signal to any woman who thinks she can sidle up to my father and claim him for her own.

He held me to him, and patted the back of my head. We shared a moment between us. "I'll be back next Sunday," he said quietly. "I hope you'll come with us for a visit next time."

I nodded and turned to leave. Clare had already dismissed me with her vacant smile. I ignored Florence, as I sprang for the door. I'd deal with her later.

Ginny loped out the door with me. "Isn't your father just the greatest! hubba hubba!" she gushed. I frowned at her, and kept on walking.

WITH MIXED EMOTIONS

"How come you're so moody?" Christy wanted to know. "Chezze, you're just no fun today."

"Oh! Leave me alone," I growled. Dorothy didn't say anything. Quiet herself, I found her more comfortable to be with. She let me be. How could I tell them about my father? They wouldn't understand and would want to know more. I couldn't tell them he'd been in prison all these years. I'd have to make up something. They didn't say good-bye when I got off the bus and I didn't either.

I ran up the back steps and flopped into a kitchen chair. Rita had no time to talk. She was entertaining visitors, a woman and two men. I knew them all well. One of them was the married man I saw her that night petting to high-heaven. I gave him my most menacing scowl. Overwhelmed with doubts about the future and there sat the man who was apt to ruin Rita's life. Yet, I couldn't say anything. I soon grew weary of all of them and I slipped away to my room.

Early the next morning, I left a note for Rita. "Gone to see Florence."

I went around to the kitchen door. Florence stood by the kerosene stove stirring a pot of what looked like bubbling syrup. I ambled over and took a look. "What are you making?

"What does it look like?" She sounded irritable.

She made mock maple syrup by boiling sugar and water and flavoring it with Mapleline whenever she needed money. Then she peddled it door to door as pancake syrup with that real maple flavor.

"Florence! How come you didn't warn me my about father's visit? You let me stand there in front of him like a complete idiot. I had no idea."

"You ARE an idiot. You don't know how to appreciate a good thing when you see it. I knew sooner or later, he'd be coming. If I told you, you probably wouldn't have bothered coming over. Since you and Rita started selling beer again. You've gotten conceited, a 'Miss Know It All.' Rita knew it would only be a matter of time before he showed up."

"Rita knew about this?"

"Of course she knew. I didn't say too much about it. I didn't want to get your hopes up. I wrote telling your father to come here instead of going to

Rita's. With you and her selling beer, what would he have thought? Selling beer is illegal on the reserve. Rita's lucky she hasn't been arrested by now.

"Illegal? What do you call making fake maple syrup? Isn't that illegal? What's the difference?"

"A lot of difference. You're a minor. She could go to jail and you'd be put in a foster home. If you ask me your father couldn't have gotten out at a better time, before you got into some real trouble."

"Damn you! Florence? You make me so mad. What sort of trouble? Why are you always insinuating how bad I am?"

"Well, I know how boy-crazy you're getting." She kept stirring her damn syrup.

"It takes one to know one," I hollered. "Tota told me how bad you were. You chased after Angus until you got pregnant. Then you got kicked out of high school because you smuggled American cigarettes in your book bag and sold them to the Canadians."

"Don't talk to me about Tota. God, how I hated that woman." Florence laid the spoon down and glared daggers at me.

Good! I knew I had her really mad now. I had the sudden urge to laugh at her.

"If it hadn't been for your grandmother, you're father never would have been sent to prison. You're just like her, mouthy, never grateful for what anyone does for you."

"What are you talking about? Everyone says it's you who's just like her—acid tongue, pretending to know more than anybody and good at insulting people. So! Tota sold bootleg whiskey. You sell fake maple syrup."

"You little snot, I've had enough of you. Go on home! No wonder Angus says you're as sassy as a fart and twice as nasty."

"You tell Angus he's nothing but a cocky lacrosse player, walking around like a Jim Dandy. Who cares what he says? I'm going home and this time I'm really never coming back." Fuming I stomped off and slammed the screen door—hard

"Eostenuni! Come back here." She called after me, calm as could be.

Her sudden change of tone caused me to stop. "What do you want?" I asked, still angry but I obeyed and went back inside.

"The reason I've worked so hard getting your father released is because I've known him since before you were born. He's a good man; he's always been good to me. Believe me, you'll have a lot better life with him."

"I know," I said. "But what about Rita? What am I going to tell her? She's

MY MOTHER'S SPIRIT

been good to me too."

"Don't worry about Rita. She'll get along. It's not as if you're going that far away. You'll be able to come and visit her often."

"Do you think so?"

"Sure, why not?"

Feeling a lot calmer, I determined to have a good talk with Rita as soon as I got home.

We sat at the kitchen table talking. I had a glass of milk and Rita had a cup of coffee. We sold beer but she never drank any. She drank a lot of coffee instead. "Rita, how can you drink so much coffee?"

"Maybe it's because it keeps me brown." We giggled.

I told her all about my father's visit. She smiled and seemed real pleased. She patted my arm. "Don't worry. Everything will work out." All that week we prepared for his visit. You'd never know we sold beer by the time we got done airing out the place. She lengthened some of my dresses and sewed a red cotton dirndl skirt for me to wear with my white peasant blouse. With my black patent leather Mary Jane's and my blond hair cut in a pageboy, I could pass for a white girl.

My father showed up the following Sunday around noon, with Clare. I asked about Ginny. Clare answered briskly, "She had to work." I hid my disappointed by not saying anything. They didn't stay long. My clothes were packed in one shopping bag. I fully expected to be gone only for a short visit. I hugged Rita real hard and told her I'd be back soon.

Just the way Clare opened the rear door of the maroon sedan let me know who owned the car. Dad only did the driving. She held the door open as if she expected me to get in as soon as possible. I obeyed and she shut the door firmly. She got in the front seat, I sat in back staring at her broad fat neck. Dad stayed behind for a few minutes talking to Rita. I saw him offering her money. She shook her head no and kept her arms wrapped about her. As soon as my father got behind the wheel, Clare skootched right up to him and sat real close.

I waved to Rita as we pulled away, craning my neck and looking back as long as she stood there. She kept her arms wrapped around her, hugging herself for dear life. She never waved. I looked back until I couldn't see her anymore.

Dad didn't keep his promise. I didn't see Rita again for three years.

EXPLORING ON MY OWN AND FINDING A GEM

Clare announced we'd take the leisurely, scenic route though the Adirondacks. Scenic to her maybe—she enjoyed Dad's company in the front seat. I sulked riding in back. All I saw were miles and more miles of desolate woods. It took two hours to get to Star Lake.

Finally, Clare sighed. "Here we are."

Dad drove to a big old white wooden building in the center of town with the sign: Star Lake Hotel. Before we were half out of the car, Clare said to Dad, "Stan, let me show her to her room. You must be tired. Relax and I'll join you in the lounge shortly." I grabbed my shopping bag ready to follow her.

"See you later, babe," Dad said to me. Surprised, I stopped and looked up at him. He hadn't said much during the trip and nobody ever called me babe. I liked it. And I liked his tanned good looks. The silent type, he reminded me of Gary Cooper.

I followed Clare, climbing two flights of stairs to the third floor. She opened a door to a dinky little room with a sloped ceiling. If I were any taller, I would have had to crane my neck sideways to avoid hitting the ceiling. It had a single bed with a white chenille bedspread, a dresser, and a stuffed faded green chair by the one small window with white lace curtains. The small room smelled of the old dry narrow varnished boards lining the walls and ceiling. She walked over to the window and pulled down the green shade. "You should lie down and rest for a while."

I gave her a quizzical look. I hadn't lain down in the middle of the day since I was a kid. Why in hell would I want to do that? I couldn't wait to go exploring.

"The bathroom is the door next to you. Here's a gift to help you feel at home." She handed me the small package wrapped in white tissue paper with a pink ribbon, that I saw on the dresser as I entered. "Thank you," I mumbled.

"Dinner is at six. I hope you'll like it here." She closed the door quietly behind her.

I sat on the bed and opened the package. It contained a toothbrush wrapped in cellophane. (What did she think, I wouldn't know enough to bring my own toothbrush?) I handled the small white comb, and smelled the perfumed bar of soap. Included was a box of sanitary napkins. It would surely come in handy in a few days. Maybe she wasn't all that bad.

I had to visit the bathroom. The small, all white, room had a bathtub with clawed feet just like the one Tota and I had in our Sears and Roebuck house. It would be nice soaking in a tub with bubbles up to my chin. No more having to sponge bathe in a little basin on Saturday nights. I ventured out into the short hall. The door to the room opposite me stood slightly ajar. I poked in and detected my father's scent. I recognized his shirt. I picked up and examined the bottle of nail polish on his dresser. Who'd be using nail polish in here? Clare said she had her suite on the second floor... interesting. I took the back stairway and ended up in the kitchen.

"Well, well," said a smiling, short plump middle-aged woman wearing a red bandanna and a white food-stained apron, her arms extended ready to give me a hug. "You're Stan's daughter. Let me be the first to welcome you." I disappeared into her ample soft bosom. "I'm the cook, the name's Olive." Just then, Clare came around the corner. She looked surprised to see me.

"I thought you'd be resting after that long trip." She took me by the arm and led me into the dining room.

It was a big sunny room with lots of tables covered with white tablecloths and four chairs at each table. Its many windows faced the street and it had its own entrance. Clare explained to always use that entrance when I came in off the front porch. The other front door opened into the lounge and she didn't want me going in there. I almost gave out with a La-de-dah! Big deal! But I didn't say anything.

Dad came in from the lounge, grinning. "Hi, babe!" He pulled out a chair and joined me. He sipped his beer while I looked around and stared at everyone. Clare, acting as hostess, led a couple to their table and then showed the six or seven others who drifted in where to sit. She walked towards us and Dad jumped up and pulled out a chair for her. As soon as he sat down, her plump fingers closed over my father's hand. I noticed she wasn't wearing nail polish.

Olive lumbered in juggling three plates loaded with food. She placed them in front of us unceremoniously, not at all careful how she placed them. Clare frowned but didn't say anything. Olive said, "There." And winked at me. She waddled back into the kitchen. When she came back in again serving others, my eyes followed her movements. She treated everyone the same way...a silent, here's your food now don't bother me again. The voices of the diners made the room hum. Clare did most of the talking at our table. My father listened and I concentrated on my pork chop not paying attention to the conversation. He saw me put my fork down after eating my apple pie. Touching my hand, he said, "You're excused." I hurriedly pushed away from the table.

"Mind you," Clare called after me. "Stay around." I didn't bother to answer.

I sat on one of the many white Adirondack chairs on the long front porch watching traffic. Shortly after, my father came out and sat next to me. "Well, babe—"

"I think it's going to be fun getting to know the place." I chimed in, not waiting for him to finish. We sat there in silence enjoying the evening breeze, until he said, "Ready to go inside?" He offered to walk me to my room.

"Might was well," I said. "There isn't all that much to do around here." Instead of going into my room, I walked ahead to his room. "Whose nail polish is this?"

"It must be Ginny's." he replied. "She came in here from time to time and did her nails while cleaning and making beds."

"Will she be here tomorrow? I can't wait to see her again."

"Clare didn't like her goofing off so she fired her."

"Does Clare own this hotel?"

"Yes."

"Oh my God! I'm in for it now! I'd better be getting to my room then. I'm kind of tired anyway."

"Good night, babe. Don't forget to lock your door. If you need anything let me know."

I dutifully tiptoed and gave him a peck on the cheek and went to my own room. I must have been tired. It was the earliest I'd gone to bed since Rita and I started selling beer. I didn't wake up until daylight the next morning.

I dressed hurriedly and went down the back stairs into the kitchen again. "Well, well, an early bird." Olive gave me a hug. She easily looked about Mumma's age. It would not have been right to call her Olive. I decided to call her Mrs. Mills. Still wearing the large white apron and the red bandanna around her short gray curly hair, she was stirring a big pot of stew—tomato with big chunks of green peppers. "What'll you have for breakfast?" she asked.

"What's that you're cooking?"

"Homemade spaghetti sauce."

"I'll have some of that. It smells awfully good."

"For breakfast? Don't be silly, it's for dinner tonight! Here, take a look at

MY MOTHER'S SPIRIT

this." She handed me a menu.

To make it easier on her, I chose a bowl of corn flakes. I knew cornflakes, my favorite from way back when the Jona kids shared theirs with me, when we had nothing to eat at our house. Instead of the watered down canned milk we poured on it then, there was this lovely pitcher of fresh creamy whole milk.

"Here's a glass of fresh orange juice and some toast and jelly. The boss says I gotta feed you good." She plunked a banana beside my bowl. "The boss don't want nobody hangin' around here. It distracts me, she says. So eat enough to last you till lunchtime. Lunch is between 11:30 and 2. Don't be late or she'll make you wait till five."

I looked at the orange juice and gagged. I could almost taste the caster oil from when Tota use to lace my juice with it. "I don't care for orange juice," I said apologetically. I worried over how I'd know when to come in for lunch. I'd never owned a watch. No one at home wore one; we went by Indian time.

"Here's a glass of grape juice. No big deal. Arlene is coming in at ten. You'll like her."

"Who's Arlene?"

"My daughter. Works as waitress, tends bar in the afternoon."

Before I had a chance to take my dishes to the sink, she'd swooped them up and had wiped the table clean.

"Is it all right to look around?"

"Lordy! Yes. The boss sleeps till almost noon. She don't bother me none though." Mrs. Mills chuckled. "How that woman likes to lay down rules. Use to be a prison matron. What she says goes in one ear and out the other. No one else will work for her and she knows it. She can lay down the carpet all she wants. I just dance all over it. She did a little jig singing, "Sweet Georgia Brown!" She chuckled again and went on humming.

Her funny talk eased my mind. I peeked into the darkened, dank, stale cigarette smelly barroom. It reminded me of our outhouse. I eyed the big metal contraption larger than a breadbox on a table in the small room between the bar and the dining room. "It's a slot machine or a one armed bandit," yelled Mrs. Mills from the kitchen. Later, Arlene showed me how it worked. When you put nickels in the slot and pulled the handle, if the pictures of the crazy acting red cherries behaved and ended on the straight black line, a bunch of nickels came flowing out of its spout. After the first time I tried it and a few nickels came tumbling out, I played it every chance I got.

I liked Arlene right away. Especially after she showed me how to punch a key on the cash register so that the drawer sprung open and I could help myself to a handful of nickels. She cautioned me, "Just don't do it when someone else is tending bar." Later, though, I learned that Arlene added the shortage at the end of the day to my father's bar bill.

Arlene, short and chunky, had so many freckles splattered across her face she looked brown. Her carrot red tight curly hair contrasted with her colorless eyebrows and eyelids. It looked like she didn't have any. With her right eyebrow perpetually raised, she had that "I don't give a damn what you think, like it or lump it" expression. She stood solid and took no guff from anyone.

She opened the bar at ten in the morning, plugged in the juke box, and let me sit on the bar stool watching the colorful lights bubbling along inside the tubular casing of the juke box. "Listen kid, you scat outta here if someone comes in, okay?" I nodded.

The cheery glow from the music box got me to singing.

"Put another nickel in, in the nickelodeon, all you ever get is music, music, music."

"Hey! Not bad," she said. I sat at the end of the bar singing all the songs I knew. Two men came in. No one said anything and I kept on singing. Arlene grinned. A couple came in. I kept on singing. All of a sudden she must have spied Clare. "Scram, kid." she warned, lowering her voice. She hurriedly handed me two bills from a brandy snifter sitting on the bar. Gee! Those two guys must have each put in a dollar. Feeling great I made a fast getaway out the front door.

For something to do, I followed the dirt path back of the hotel to the lake. I stood there in awe. My eyes followed the bend of the shoreline around to an opening and beyond that to another lake. I remembered the explanation for the Star Lake. It consisted of five smaller lakes meeting at the center to form one large one. The spring fed, deep, emerald green lake, surrounded by towering evergreen trees, lay hidden at the foothills of the Adirondack Mountains. I gazed at the shimmering beauty of a million sparkling jewels scattered over the sun kissed waters. The nicely landscaped garden estates of the wealthier summer residents were on the opposite shore. I breathed deep the fresh clean fragrance of pine and balsam. I treasured my discovery like a gem in my hand to admire. I thought of my mother. I felt the pleasure of her spirit smiling down on me to see me so blissfully at peace in such a beautiful place.

THE IRONY OF IT ALL

Clare stopped me at the front entrance. "Dolores, would you please come in here for a moment? I'd like to talk to you." I wanted to wash up before Dad returned from work, but I followed her up to her sitting room. She seemed relaxed. Maybe she hadn't heard about my singing and hanging out in the bar. Her stupid rules were getting on my nerves, such as not hanging out in the kitchen and talking to the cook, or not going swimming alone. I'd been swimming by myself since I was seven. She didn't want me playing the slot machine, either. Her, acting so nice made me suspicious. I chose a soft comfortable chair to sink down in and waited for her to speak.

"How would you like to go shopping with me tomorrow? You could use some decent clothes."

"Why? What's wrong with my clothes?"

"Well, nothing really. I just thought you'd like some new ones. I would like to buy you something nice. I've often wished I had a daughter to buy nice things for."

I became more suspicious. Now she wanted to buy me something.

"Wouldn't you like someone to help you shop for clothes? Like a mother, sort of, someone to talk to?"

"I have a mother."

"What an odd thing to say. I thought you mother died when you were very young."

"She did, but she still watches over me. Wherever I am or whenever I need her, something always turns up and I end up okay. Right now, I have Rita and Florence acting on her behalf."

"Hmm! Well! Never mind then. We'll talk about it some other time. It's time to wash up for dinner." A smile tucked at one corner of her mouth.

She followed me downstairs. As soon as I saw my father sitting at the bar, I walked up and leaned against him. I defied anyone to tell me I shouldn't be in here. His eyes lit up—he was glad to see me—but he kept on talking with the man on the other side of him.

Even in his scrungy gray work clothes, he still looked good. He had nice wide shoulders and sat with his back straight. He let me lean against him as I listened to the men talking. He finished his beer, and pushed his glass away.

He refused another, put his hand on my forearm and we both stood up. He led me into the hallway. I liked him being mine. No wonder Clare made out as if he belonged to her. And trying to butter me up all of a sudden—I made up my mind it wasn't going to work. I followed him up to his room. The bottle of nail polish still remained right where I saw it last.

"Have you seen Ginny since she got fired?"

"Yes! A couple of times—she's around. Why?"

"Just wondered. Clare wants to take me shopping. I told her no."

"Why not? We've had a talk. She really likes you. But she thinks you don't like her. She's trying. I think you should go."

"You do? You're not in love with her are you?"

He laughed. "Is that what's bothering you? Are you worried some woman is going to drag me away from you?" He grabbed me by my shoulders and smacked a kiss on my forehead. "Your mother's the only woman I ever loved. There! Does that make you feel better? Go get washed up and I'll see you at dinner." I hugged him in the middle, then let go.

Clare was standing by the front entrance greeting her guests when I came in from the kitchen. She looked at me as I walked to our table. I gave her a great big triumphant smile.

As soon as Dad came in, she sidled up to him. He pulled her chair out for her. Right away, she placed both of her big fat ugly hands over his. "Mr. Hymes called today. He'll be here Friday afternoon," she said in a soft voice. Dad didn't answer.

"Who's Mr. Hymes?" I asked.

"Your dad's parole officer."

MISTER HYMES

I heard all the particulars from Mrs. Mills early the next morning at breakfast. I asked her if she knew Mr. Hymes.

"Yes, indeedy. Mr. Hymes, Clare, and her husband worked together for the county jail many years ago. Mr. Hymes was the correctional officer. After Clare's husband died, she bought this here hotel. Mr. Hymes, as your dad's parole officer, got him a job at Jones and Laughlin's Steel in Benson Mines and made arrangements for your dad to board here. That's how Clare got her hooks into your dad."

"You think so?" I sensed a conspiracy.

"And here's something she shouldn't be doing, and that's setting up drinks for him, knowing full well he's not supposed to be drinking. But when he come home from work thirsty, what's the poor man to do?"

"What's wrong with my dad having a drink now and then?"

"He's not supposed to touch alcohol while he's on parole. If you ask me, she's got your father right by the 'you know what.' One wrong move and she's going to turn him in. You mark my word."

I stared at Mrs. Mills, trying to understand it all.

For as long as I could remember, Tota had said Dad was in prison. Now he was out but still not free. It didn't seem right to me. To make matters worse, Clare acted like she had some kind of control over him.

"He's got to toe the line. And one of these days, Clare's going to jerk that line. Know what I mean?" Mrs. Mills, shaking her head, went back to her work.

I wanted to meet the mysterious Mr. Hymes, the overseer of my father for the next seven years.

Clare didn't need to remind me to wear something nice for dinner. "Don't you have something else besides your red skirt and that white blouse?" But, she had to say it. She annoyed me more than ever.

Mr. Hymes must have arrived early. As I came down through the kitchen, I spied Mrs. Mills working near the area Clare claimed as her office, a small space cordoned off at one end of the kitchen by cabinets. I saw Clare sitting at her desk talking to a dignified, well-dressed, older man. Mrs. Mills busied herself working near them. I saw her cocking her head to one side, as if trying to hear what they were saying. No wonder she knew so much. More power to her, I chuckled to myself. I grinned and waved, loping through on my way to the dining room.

Dad came in the front entrance as Mr. Hymes emerged from Clare's office to join us. They shook hands as if they were old friends. Just then, Clare looked in. "Dolores come here for a second."

"Now what?" Reluctantly, I got up from my chair. The two men started to stand up as if they were going to come too, but sat back down as I sauntered out into the kitchen.

I glared, anxious to know what the hell was so important that she had to call me in here.

She ushered me into her office and pointed to a chair. "Perhaps you should give the men a chance to talk. Have you thought any more about us going shopping?"

"Yes! Dad said I should go." I thought it would please her and so she'd let me go back into the dining room.

"Fine, let's go one day this week when it's not so busy and make a day of it, shall we?" Her usually dull face turned a shade brighter. She sounded more upbeat. "Try to be more enthused at dinner. It's important to let Mr. Hymes know you've adjusted."

"Whatever you say, Mrs. Hutton." I deliberately emphasized her last name to let her know I knew the score. I bounced out of her office and went to join my dad and Mr. Hymes.

Both men got up as I approached our table. Dad pulled my chair out for me. Then he introduced me to Mr. Hymes. Mr. Hymes shook my hand and held it as he stood there smiling at me. I smiled back, not sure what I should say. I liked him. If I had been given a choice for a grandfather, I would have chosen Mr. Hymes. He was soft spoken, unhurried and kindly; I felt comfortable listening to him conversing with Dad. Then, Arlene arrived with our dinner. I struggled trying to cut my steak. With a twinkle and a smile, Mr. Hymes suggested, "Maybe we should let your dad cut your steak."

Dad took over, looking pleased. And I beamed over the special attention. I showed my best lady-like manners, keeping one hand on my lap, taking small bites and chewing with my mouth closed.

I answered all Mr. Hymes's questions. I learned then and there that white folks liked to ask a lot of questions.

"Yes, I like it here just fine, and Mrs. Hutton's real swell." Dad looked on approvingly and I felt proud of myself too. After enjoying a dish of vanilla ice

MY MOTHER'S SPIRIT

cream (my favorite) for dessert, Dad said I could be excused.

Hmm...what to do now? Guess I'll play the slot machine. After just three nickels, hot diggety! I hit the jackpot. The nickels came tumbling out so fast I had to lift up the hem of my skirt to catch them all. The diners, including Dad and Mr. Hymes, came to see all the excitement. Everyone including Mr. Hymes cheered. "Way to go, babe," my dad grinned. Clare came out and glared at me. She didn't look too happy.

I sensed her displeasure and backed out of the room, holding on to hem of my skirt. I hurriedly dumped the nickels in a shoe box and went back down to join Dad and Mr. Hymes. They looked jovial, sitting at the table waiting for me. Even Clare broke out with her half smile, while dad enjoyed his cigarette. Shortly after, Mr. Hymes said he had to get going and we all got up with him.

Smiling, Mr. Hymes shook my hand. "Pleasure meeting you, young lady! Next time, you'll have to show me how to play that machine."

I thought, what a nice man. I knew my dad had a good friend in Mr. Hymes.

GOINGS ON ABOUT TOWN

The next morning, I went down to the kitchen to show Mrs. Mills my winnings. Arlene gave me a handful of coin wrappers. "Here, kid. You'll need these." Chuckling, she went back behind the bar. It took me awhile to roll my nickels. I kept counting and putting the nickels in neat little piles. "You'd better get that done and get out of here before the boss comes down. Out of sight, out of mind. If you know what I mean?" I heeded Mrs. Mills's warnings. I hurried and gave my booty for Arlene to cash in for me—thirty-five dollars worth.

I spent the next few days close to the hotel, mostly sitting on the porch. I got a kick out of watching Star Lake's summer residents. They walked in groups and took up the main road, holding up traffic, and refusing to get out of the way. Most of the shop owners resented them for taking over their town. Mike the butcher, at Tears General Store said, "Too damn uppity and nervy." One day, I watched wide-eyed in disbelief when Mike came around the counter waving his meat clever at a fussy big-bosomed lady. He held her package of meat in the other hand. She sputtered and accepted the packaged meat without further ado, and hurried out of the store.

Tears Store sold everything from nails, barbwire, groceries, and meats, to jewelry, clothing, shoes, and lingerie. It's where Dad bought me my first wristwatch, a Hamilton gold watch for a hundred dollars. I took pleasure in looking at it hundreds of times a day. Three weeks later I broke it to smithereens turning cartwheels.

Charming and quaint best described the picturesque hotels, the swankiest being, Star Lake Inn with it's own golf course. I frequented Sparrow's Sugar Bowl wedged between two hotels and across from Gerald Marshal's gift shop. But usually, when I wasn't sitting on the porch enjoying the parade of tourists, I'd be with a group of kids at the beach behind the Star Lake Hotel.

One bright Saturday afternoon, while I was sitting on the front porch, Gary Young, eighteen, an acquaintance of Dad's whom I had seen many times in the bar, approached me. "Hey kid! Care to walk with me to Sparrow's for a sundae?"

"Wait, let me ask." Sticking my head inside, I called, "Hey Clare! Is it all right if I go for a sundae with Gary?"

MY MOTHER'S SPIRIT

"I guess so," she replied absentmindedly. Gary and I took off walking to the Sugar Bowl. Gary was a scrawny kid, but I liked his bright laughing blue eyes and his funny sense of humor.

He made a big thing over my choice of ice cream. "Vanilla! With all the many flavors, you chose plain vanilla?" Gary drawled. "Make mine cherry with lots of chocolate syrup— I like cherries," he said to old man Sparrow. Sparrow leaned way down into the ice cream tub balling out the scoops and putting into a glass sundae dish. He looked mad all the while he was heaping goops of chocolate sauce all over the ice cream. Then he plopped some whipped cream on top and topped it with a bright red cherry and placed the concoction in front of Gary. I took mine in a plain sugar wafer cone. Gary joked, "Did you ever see such a sour-faced old man running a sweet shop?" I had to agree, Mr. Sparrow did have an ugly, grumpy puss. I'd never seen him smile. I let out a giggle. We enjoyed our treat, laughing at Gary's making fun at just about everything.

We left and meandered along towards the hotel, fully expecting to sit and continue guffawing on the front porch. As we reached the front step, Dad came charging out and grabbed Gary by the front of his shirt, almost lifting him from the floor. "You stay away from my daughter. If I catch you anywhere near her again, I'll kill you," Dad snarled at Gary. Dad's distorted angry face frightened me.

Gary's eyes were as big as saucers and he looked scared out of his wits. I had never seen my father so mad. I ran inside and stood at strict attention next to Clare behind the bar.

Dad came back in white with rage. He glared at Clare, as he roared, "You go up to my room." I knew he meant me. I ran up the stairs quickly, then stopped halfway and listened.

"Really, Stan. I don't know why you're so angry and making such a big fuss. Gary isn't a bad kid. He's just being friendly." Clare attempted to gloss over the hateful scene.

Dad's voice low and controlled, menacing, he spat out his words "You don't know anything about him. I work with the guy. From now on, she's not to go anywhere without my permission. She's my responsibility. Not yours."

I slowly continued up to my room and waited until dinnertime. I had no idea Dad had such a ferocious temper. He didn't say anymore about it and I certainly wasn't going to either. The frightful episode lingered, putting me on notice. For a mild-mannered gentle man, Dad could be explosive.

THE NEED FOR INFLUENTIAL FRIENDS

Dad acquired a secondhand black Ford pickup truck. Dad reassured me "A little the worse for wear but it runs good." We went bouncing around neighboring towns. It felt like riding on the wings of freedom in that little old rattletrap. Much to Clare's distress, she no longer had her hand on Dad's pulse. We came and went as we pleased.

We visited the dairy farm three miles over in the next town, Oswegatchie. The panoramic view of sloping green hills in a rural pastoral setting, with the two church steeples far off in the distance, reminded me of picture on a calendar. Dad's long silences no longer bothered me; I enjoyed letting my mind wonder. I felt safe and happy just to be with him.

The farm belonged to Rod Langevin, an old colleague and friend of Dad's from when they were both state troopers and members of the elite Black Horse Chapter assigned to the Malone barracks during Prohibition. Rod Langevin and dad were both tall, straight, and no nonsense types, but Rod liked to talk. He knew about my mother and he's the one who told me a lot about Dad: how Dad, in his younger days, had liked to box and had sparred with Gene Tunney.

Dad and I enjoyed visiting with Rod's wife Thelma and their four kids. I liked horsing around with the two older boys, Max and Frank, my age; the two daughters were much younger. Rod told me, years later, how he'd hoped Max and I would hit it off. At the time, I found Max too much of a clown and farm life didn't interest me.

I remember the day when Rod, along with others of considerable influence, had to go to bat for my father—the day Clare decided to make trouble.

Clarence Backus, the honorary mayor of Star Lake, also testified in my dad's behalf that day. Mr. Backus liked Dad from the first time they met. Dad and I took his canoe many times.

I loved paddling around the lake with Dad. He paddled smoothly through the placid waters while I enjoyed the scenery. One time, Dad needed to get something as we neared the shoreline of our hotel. "Now stay here and I'll be right back," he said as he dragged the canoe out of the water. Five-year-old Bobby, playing at the water's edge, near by asked for a ride in the canoe.

MY MOTHER'S SPIRIT

"Sure." I said, "But just a short one." He climbed in, I gave the canoe a big push and the canoe slid through the water, slick and quick. Before I realized, we were almost in the middle of the lake. I heard dad hollering at me from shore. "Get that kid back here!"

"He can't swim!" Cried out, Bobby's mother, as she came running to the water's edge.

I succeeded in turning the canoe around and paddled back. Dad grabbed the prow and heaved the canoe up on the bank. "Jeezz!" he cursed. "What in hell were you thinking? The kid didn't even have a life jacket on."

"I don't know why you're so upset. Nothing happened. Even if it did, I'm a good swimmer, I'd have saved him."

"No, you couldn't. I don't care how good a swimmer you think you are. He'd have dragged you both under. You scared the hell out of me. Wait for me at the hotel. I'll take the canoe back." I did as he said and didn't argue.

There were no more canoe rides after that. I had to amuse myself in other ways. Occasionally, when I knew Clare wasn't tending bar, I'd come in for a snack and look into the middle entryway, and if there weren't many in the bar, I'd feed a few nickels to the slot machine. No one noticed except Arlene and she didn't care. This one time, I came bounding around the corner and caught Mrs. So-and-so and Mr. Whatsis engaged in a clinch, kissing with his hand up her dress. At my "oops," they quickly disentangled, and I backed out just as fast.

Arlene wanted to know all about it. She gave out with a hoot and a cackle, chuckling off and on. I sat at the bar, sucking on a straw, slurping my coke, enjoying myself and retelling my tale just to get her chuckling again. A customer walked in and I high-tailed it out of there. If Dad found out, he'd have been furious.

Clare, Dad and I continued dining together. But I sensed a cooling off between them. Clare no longer touched him when she sat down to join us. She did most of the talking, most of it small talk about the hotel. I continued to ignore most of it until she asked Dad if the trip to New York City was still on. I perked up. "A trip? When? Who's all going?" Neither one of them answered, as if they didn't hear me, Clare got up to tend bar. Dad got up too and said he needed lighter fluid from Tears store.

I automatically followed him. "May I go with you? I need a new pair of sandals."

He hesitated for a second. Then replied, "Sure, babe." We ambled out of the hotel.

"What did Clare mean?" I asked again. "Are we going on a trip?"

Dad had a habit of not answering right away. It's as if he had to think how he'd reply. Finally, "I'm thinking about it. Not sure yet. We'll discuss it later." He broke off and I didn't push it.

To change the subject, I told him about Arlene and I snickering over Clare propositioning the liquor salesman. That got his attention. "Did Arlene tell you that? Do you know what the word means?"

"Sure! Clare wants to hire him as her bartender, so Arlene can do the bedrooms besides waitressing. She's not too happy about that. Says she might quit."

"What about this new bartender? Have you seen him?"

"Yep! His name is Bob Barnes. She had him in her office and Mrs. Mills said Clare practically seduced him right there, before she lured him up to her parlor."

Dad looked amused and forgot to say anything about my hanging out in the bar with Arlene. He grinned. So I added the clincher.

"Afterwards, I heard Arlene telling a customer that Clare acted like she wanted Mr. Barnes to put the blocks right to her right there."

"Jeezz! How much time do you spend in that barroom with Arlene? You're not allowed in there." He frowned and I knew I must have said too much. I shut up after that. We walked into the store, both appearing glum. He paid for his lighter fluid and followed me into the clothing and shoe department. Jenny, one of the store's two clerks followed us listening intently as I described exactly what I wanted.

Jenny always paid attention. I imagined she probably would make a good mom to some kid like me. Engrossed in trying on the sandals, I forgot all about Dad. I straightened up to look at him for his approval. Uh oh! I caught that unmistakable look between them—a meaningful eye contact—a signal maybe. She complimented me on my excellent choice. But I suspected something else pleased her more than my buying a pair of shoes.

I doubted if Clare knew about Jenny, the way she pounced in on me a few days later while I waited for Dad in his room. The door stood slightly ajar. I decided to polish my nails with Ginny's nail polish. All of a sudden, Clare came bursting in, pushing the door wide open. "It's not good for you to be in his room all the time," she said breathlessly, obviously accusing me of something sinister.

"Why not?" I replied, expressing my annoyance.

"Because he's a man and men have temptations."

MY MOTHER'S SPIRIT

"What do you mean? I don't know what you are talking about?"

"I think you know exactly what I mean. You're not as innocent as you pretend."

Anger welled up inside me and I had a sudden urge to lash out. "I'm going to tell him what you said," I said angrily.

Her sullen face lifted and her tone softened, as if she regretted what she had just said, "I don't doubt that you will."

I felt powerless, not knowing how to hurt her back. I ran out past her and locked myself in my room. I thought about it for a long time, lying on my bed. Tears stung my eyelids. I doubted if I could ever mention this to Dad. He'd be so angry, no telling what he'd do. Considering how mad he got at Gary Young.

We continued dining together. Again, Clare bought up the subject about going shopping. I found it strange that all of a sudden Dad looked amused. So I said, "All right."

"Fine!" she said. "How about tomorrow, right after lunch. We'll make a day of it. How's that?"

"Okay," I replied and went on eating.

Clare and I went to Ogdensburg the next day. I enjoyed being the center of her attention. On the way home, she asked if Dad had said anymore about going to New York. I told her no. She replied, "I think it would be nice if we took my car. Wouldn't you agree?"

"I don't know." I stared blankly at nothing, listening to the drone of the tires, it seemed forever. In the silence of my mind's eye, I soared to the empty sky above. Then, Splat!! A bird flew into the windshield—an ill omen—I knew.

A TRIP TO THE BIG APPLE

A day shopping with Clare in Ogdensburg, wasn't all that bad. She had her hair done by a woman named Gladys, while I leafed through a *Modern Romance* magazines. Intrigued, the titles lured me wanting to read on, until Gladys handed me a comic book. Shortly after, Clare looked at the mirror pleased, patting her dark hair curled high on her head adding to her height. She did look nice. I tended not to notice her top-heavy bosom forced up by a girdle nor her narrow hips and bandy legs.

After visiting three department stores, patiently waiting while I tried on many dresses, we agreed on one we both liked. She was buying. I let her have the last say.

She suggested we have a sandwich in a hoity toity tea shoppe. We were served a pot of tea to pour into our fine bone china cups. My Tota had much finer china, fancier, and we'd lift our cup to the lip with a palm around it for the warmth of the brew. Clare lifted her teacup daintily with her pinkie up. I made no pretense of copying her. I gulped my tea holding my cup Tota's way while enjoying my cucumber and watercress sandwich.

"I'm eager to see your dad's face when he see's how nice you look in your new out fit."

I replied, "Me too."

We left to come home, I enjoying the scenery while she drove. "Are you always this quiet when you're riding around with your dad? Just where do you go anyway?"

"Yep! Dad's not much of a talker. I like it that way. We usually ride around going nowhere in particular." I went on with my sight seeing.

Sunday, I put on my new pink dress. It had white puffed sleeves; a tight bodice laced in front to the waist with a full gathered skirt. With my white hat curled up on each side like a Dutch girl's cap, I thought looked down right spiffy. After church, eager to show Arlene my new outfit I went into the bar and spun around. She laughed loudly and snorted, "You look just like the girl on a can of Bon Ami."

Dismayed, I let it pass. "I don't care," I retorted and went into the kitchen for a snack.

Dad seemed preoccupied and didn't notice my new outfit. Later that afternoon, he informed me that we'd be going to New York City in his truck. He didn't take Clare up on her offer to take the Buick, even though it was newer, bigger and more comfortable. Instead, his friend, Dick Hitchman went with us.

I had fantasized about the trip all week long. Dad said he'd show me his stomping grounds and the gymnasiums where he trained as a boxer. Most of his relatives lived in the small towns near the city. "We'll be meeting them too," he said. "The whole bloody lot of them."

Clare seemed okay the day we were getting ready to leave. She gave me a red leather shoulder bag with a twenty-dollar bill tucked inside the matching wallet. She put her arm around my shoulder and gave me a squeeze. I smelled her lemony perfume and I thought how nice. Mrs. Mills gave me a hug and Arlene gave me a smack in the behind. Climbing in between the two men, I felt snug as a bug and we took off.

Dad drove through the Adirondacks to Albany, our old black truck chugged along chewing up the winding and hilly roads, until finally, just before nightfall, the big city of skyscrapers—The Big Apple loomed in front of us. I had heard about it plenty of times. Mohawk iron workers, most of them, relatives and friends, helped build the giant steel structures. I felt real proud of my Indian heritage.

The old truck wheezed into the parking lot of the Holland Hotel, shimmied and belched. We let it rest for three days. Dick disappeared into the big metropolis. Dad and I walked to everywhere—Times Square, mostly, and eating plenty of chop suey in Chinese restaurants, sandwiches in automat and cafeterias, and sweets in bistros. The streets teemed with throngs of people in so much of a hurry. I would have bumped into most of them if dad hadn't held a firm grip of my elbow steering me ahead. The city reeked of rancid body odor, burnt onions, gas fumes and not a breath of fresh air anywhere. My head pivoted in all directions, to the tops of high rises and from left to right trying to take in all the sights at once. We ducked in to see the Rockettes at the Radio City Music Hall to catch our breath.

That first night alone in my hotel room, I could still hear honking of cars, sirens and the hum of elevators. The noises didn't bother me. I'd slept through much worse when Rita and I ran our beer parlor. In spite of the noises, a pang of loneliness came over me. Thoughts of my mother, fourteen years earlier, pregnant, lonely and scared while dad looked for work during depression, saddened me. I finally fell asleep through sheer exhaustion.

The next day, August 14th, 1945, the day World War II came to an end was the biggest thrill of my life. We were caught in the excitement of it all. Everyone went wild celebrating in the streets. Men in uniform were hugging and kissing young girls. I saw that young sailor winding his ways towards me for a smooch. Dad must have seen him too. Dad grabbed me by the arm and pulled me out of the sailor's way. The sailor whizzed right by and grabbed someone else. I knew he was aiming right for me, missed and grabbed that nurse in her white uniform for that most reprinted image in LIFE Magazine. By pushing me into a movie hall, I felt robbed of my moment of glory. I'll never forget that day in history. Dad and I were a part of the crowd when the whole city went wild with jubilation. I'll also, never forget the movie we saw that afternoon, *For Whom The Bells Toll* with Gary Cooper and Ingrid Bergman and I felt the earth move.

On the third day, as we check out of our hotel, I saw a black man on the sidewalk with a sign. I walked up to him to see what the sign read. Instantly, I heard my father's angry voice, "Get away from that nigger." I stopped abruptly.

Stunned, I said. "DAD! You called that man, nigger. Why?"

"Get over here," he snapped. "You're blocking traffic." He gave me a slight push towards the parking lot.

I'd seen a few black people in Cornwall before and Tota had explained their plight. She had told me to call them negroes with respect.

We walked to our truck in silence. Confused by the change in his attitude, I found it hard to believe he disliked people of color. He threw our suitcases in back and left me to fend for myself. Before, he'd opened the car door for me and made me feel so grown up.

The more I thought about it, the more agitated I became. I broke the silence with a spiel about what I had learned in the movies about the Holocaust. The persecution of Jews by the Nazi and how horrible, I thought, most white people were to Negroes and Indians. He interrupted. "You don't know what you're talking about."

"I do so," I shot back. "Didn't you just call that old black man a terrible name?"

With his mouth a rigid line, through clenched teeth. "SHUT UP!"

I sunk down into my seat and pouted all the way to High Land Mills. Then, as we were entering the city limits, he had the nerve to suggest that maybe it would be wiser if I didn't tell his people about me being an Indian or that I lived on a reservation. "Give them a chance to get to know you first," he said.

"And what? Deny that my mother's people are Mohawk Indians?" I cried out angrily. Not a chance. I steeled myself. Never.

MEETING MY FATHER'S PEOPLE

Oh Boy! Did I have news for him! I remembered Tota telling me how, right after he had been sent to prison, two well-dressed women, who claimed to be his sisters had come to visit us. They'd asked to take me back with them but Tota had refused. She told me that Indians didn't give away their Indian children to white people—no matter what—and I was Indian. So his relatives knew all about me. I don't know why I didn't think to tell him this before. Now I'm glad I didn't.

All of a sudden I perked up, eager to meet the bloody bunch of Englishmen. Dad was so nervous, he smoked one cigarette after another, and his hands were shaking.

He didn't need to be nervous. As we pulled into the driveway, they all rushed out to greet us; his brother Jerome pumping his hand, his two sisters, Muriel, and Margie, hugging him and patting him on the back. A brother-in-law, Walter, offered a firm handshake and smiled at me. A sister-in-law, Margaret, tiptoeing, kissed him on the cheek. The two older ladies with snow-white hair, Great Aunt Phil and Great Aunt Sally, stood back waiting for Dad to hug them. I stood with my best smile, waiting. The women hugged me last.

"This is a special occasion, and it calls for a celebration," said Aunt Phil, the tallest and older of the two elderly ladies. "Jerome, go down cellar and get a bottle of my root beer."

Uncle Jerome, an agile little man, darted for the cellar door. His wife Margaret patted a place beside her on the couch, inviting me to sit next to her. Right off, I said to her, "I'm half Mohawk and I live on an Indian Reservation."

Aunt Margaret hugged me close and said, "I'm Bri'ish, born in Carlisie, England, came to this country as a little girl." From then on she called me "My Indian Princess." Ample bosomed, plump, and the most talkative of the women, she monopolized my attention asking me a string of questions. Her prominent two front teeth emphasized her pert little nose that constantly wrinkled as she talked. Her words bubbled with laughter.

Aunt Margie, the oldest of Dad's siblings, reserved, slender and tall like him, stood to one side talking with Dad. I found it hard listening to three conversations all at once. I thought it strange they all carried on conversations at the same time. The Mohawks, even, when drinking in our beer parlor, never talked all at once. They took turns, with plenty of lapses in between. But not these sophisticated white folks; they sat up straight on the edges of their chairs eager to jump in to do their share of talking.

Aunt Margaret, chuckling, talked about her four children. I'd be meeting some of them tomorrow, she said. Then, Uncle Jerome handed me a glass of the most delicious root beer I ever drank. The rest were drinking sherry in small glasses. He sat next to me, smiling, and whispered, "Your Aunt Margaret does all the talking in our family. She's much better at it than I am."

Aunt Muriel, my dad's youngest sister, a pretty little woman, sat quietly listening to her husband, Uncle Walter. He was entertaining the two Great Aunts with tales of his own.

My father coughed nervously and asked if anyone minded if he had a cigarette. Immediately, Uncle Jerome stood up and invited the men to tour the factory, a huge building behind the house. Aunt Margaret's non-stop talking was getting to me, so I jumped up to join them, too. We sauntered across the road to the very long low building—the A. G. Hall Fishing Line Factory. Great Aunt Phil and her husband, Uncle Capp, had owned the factory and Uncle Jerome ran it for them. When Uncle Capp died, she sold it to a German company and Uncle Jerome stayed on as manger. I followed behind listening to him explaining about all the bobbins, knobs and gismos. I soon found it boring, left them and went back into the house.

Great Aunt Phil hauled out the old family albums and we poured over them. Squinting, she explained who the ones in the photos were and where the photos were taken. She was the matriarch of the family and she had seen to the welfare of my father and his siblings. She pointed to the photo of an ornate old Victorian house, their summer cottage in the Catskills before Uncle Capp died. They were neighbors of George M. Cohen, the great American composer of patriotic songs.

I asked about the older portrait of a pretty, fair young girl with her hair in a pompadour. "It's my youngest sister Sophie, your grandmother," Aunt Phil answered. "She died at fifty. Uncle Capp and I, not having any children, took her three youngest, your dad, fifteen; Uncle Romie, eleven; and Aunt Muriel, eight. Your Uncle Joe and Aunt Margie were older and already on their own."

I pointed at the picture of a kindly old grandmother, noting the resemblance to Dad. "That's your Great Grandmother Stell, your father's beloved granny. He went to live with her when he couldn't stand the rest of us anymore," Aunt Phil continued. I noticed she rolled her eyes and wore that

MY MOTHER'S SPIRIT

"sweet suffering" patient smile, when she was amused.

As soon as the men returned from their tour, the women got up, saying they had to be leaving. They hugged one another amid a flurry of good-byes. "Now don't forget," Aunt Margaret caroled, "We'll be expecting you for breakfast, tomorrow." The flurry of voices subsided and they were gone.

"Time for supper," Aunt Phil said as she hobbled into the kitchen. Once tall and solidly built, now bent, she walked with a limp, from a broken hip. I followed, offering to help. For something to say, I asked what we were having. She answered, "Pig's ass and garlic," straight out, upping her face proudly. I liked her style...don't ask asinine questions and I'll give you no spoof. She didn't waste her time with idle chitchat.

Aunt Sally, the more genteel of the two, looked diminutive beside Aunt Phil. She was equally witty. When I passed her the plate of little fancy cakes, she replied, as if slightly amused, "No thank you. I've had elegant sufficiency. Any more would be vulgar superfluity."

I practiced that phrase over and over till I mastered it. Then I repeated it every time I wanted to show off.

The next morning, Dad and I walked over to Uncle Jerome's house for breakfast.

While Aunt Margaret and I were doing the dishes, she gave me the low-down on the Stanfields.

"They called your father the black sheep of the family. Restless, always running off to join something or other, he enlisted in the cavalry and went chasing after Poncho Villa into Mexico. Did you know your dad was wounded in France during the First World War? Then he became a state trooper and got mixed up with bootleggers, lived with Indians, and landed in prison. We didn't hear anymore after that. Our letters came back unopened. Don't tell the great ladies I told you all this. They're a secretive bunch. They like keeping things to themselves."

I didn't have a chance to say, "Cross my heart and hope to die." She kept on going. "Aunt Phil married Uncle Capp, a state assembly man with money. They tried raising your father, Romie and Muriel after their mother died. Shortly after, your father ran away to live with Granny Stell. Instead of sending my Romie to college, they had him working in their factory. They doted on Muriel, sending her to Syracuse University with a fur coat—the works, and gave her a good education. After all those years, of my Romie dedicating his life to running their factory, they sold it out from under him. He's about out on his ear with hardly a pension to speak of."

DOLORES EOSTENUNI STANFIELD

"What about Great Aunt Sally?"

"She never married—traveled all over the world as secretary and companion to a famous opera singer. Can't remember her name. Anyway, while they were in this country, Aunt Sally arranged to have your father take singing lessons. He had a good tenor voice. But, your father, never sticking with anything, took off again. Many years later, the opera singer retired. By that time, Aunt Sally found that life had passed her by. She was almost penniless. Aunt Phil took her in. They've been together ever since."

"My grandmother once told me about two women claiming to be Dad's sisters who came to visit us. Would that have been Aunt Muriel and Aunt Margie?"

"Yes! Aunt Margie is great for keeping tabs on everyone and is just as secretive. They never told me what they found out. I had to pry it out of Romie. Your Aunt Margie is tight-lipped with me. Her and her big nose. They all have that prominent nose. She calls it the classic Roman profile. I call it the famous Stanfield beak. Except for your Aunt Muriel. She's the nicest in the family. Now my pet, I want to hear all about you!"

Before I had a chance to tell my story, and to protest about the noses of the Stanfields—I didn't think they had big noses at all—Dad called to me to accompany him on yet another visit.

We walked to Aunt Ada's house, Uncle Joe's widow. She briefed us on how Joe had died in a hunting accident. "A little over a year ago while out hunting with our two sons, Joey and Jimmy, his gun went off as he climbed over a barb wire fence, killing him instantly. We tried to let you know, but we didn't know where to reach you."

Dad and Aunt Ada embraced, consoling one another. I stood by, not knowing what to say. She turned and hugged me. "My! You look so much like my Jimmy." She brightened up and pointed to photos on the fireplace mantle. The two sailors in their navy blue uniforms looked handsome. The one she pointed out as Jimmy looked a lot like me.

I kept meeting cousins all day. Aunt Margaret's youngest, Norma, ten, was chubby, fair, and affectionate. She kept following me around. Aunt Margaret, all of sudden, suggested to Dad that he let me enroll at the same school as Norma. "I think you should let our princess stay. She'd be such good company for our Norma." Even though they weren't Catholic, they were planning to send her to a parochial school.

I looked at Dad with my most serious scowl. No! Dad declined her offer. After two days with strange relatives, I could hardly wait to get started on our

MY MOTHER'S SPIRIT

trip home. After lots of hugs and many goodbyes, we finally drove away. Dad looked relaxed and happier than I'd ever seen him.

Dad remarked, "It went better than I expected. What did you think of them?"

"Not bad. Especially Aunt Margaret, she's the most friendly. Though she's plenty burnt up about the way Uncle Romie's been treated after years of devoted service."

"Better him than me. Jerome's always been the quiet one, contented to be in one place all his life. I would have gone crazy if I had stayed. Too bad about Joe, though, surviving World War I, then dying in a hunting accident. I didn't even know about it until now." Dad grew silent, staring ahead, and concentrated on his driving. I felt sad too, even though I never knew poor Uncle Joe. I moved closer to my Dad.

Visiting New York City was exciting, but I liked Star Lake better. The picturesque little village suited me. I enjoyed swimming in my clean green crystal lake. And I looked forward to our Sunday afternoon walks again. Dad always walked easy, as if marching in a parade. He'd carry his newspaper under his arm. When I tended to slouch, he'd tap me on the shoulder with the rolled newspaper to straighten up. He'd say, "Head high, shoulders back, let your legs carry you and walk as if you're stepping on broken egg shells." I stepped up boldly, squared my shoulders and walked like he did.

To while away the many miles on the road as we drove home, I went on with my daydreaming and pictured all the fun things I'd be enjoying again soon.

But no amount of daydreaming could have prepared me for what awaited us when we got home.

ANYTHING BUT A HAPPY HOME COMING

We pulled into our hotel parking lot around seven. "Here we are, babe!" Dad sounded as relieved as I felt.

"I'm glad to be back," I said, giving him a peck and jumped out of the truck, excited over the many stories I'd be telling Arlene and her mother. I even looked forward to seeing Clare again.

Clare, half smiling and acting very solicitous, held open the front door for us. She invited us to come in for a chat. "After you unpack and unwind from the long trip." I took it to mean, in her sitting room.

I took a peek in the lounge hoping Arlene would be working. My face fell, when I saw Bob Barnes the new bartender behind the bar. No matter, I thought, time for visiting with Arlene and Mrs. Mills tomorrow morning. I prepared for a good soak in the tub with bubbles up to my chin.

After my bath, I came skipping down in my robe to her sitting room. I heard them arguing. Already? We just got home. Puzzled, I stopped and listened. "You need to think of her schooling. Growing up with Indians, she lacks social skills. She doesn't even know how to hold a teacup," I heard Clare say. She mentioned a private school. "The best in the country. I can afford it." Just then, Dad came storming out. "Think about it." She hollered after him.

"Over my dead body!" he answered angrily. I stood there staring with my mouth open. "Pack your bags. We're checking out," he ordered.

I was in the truck with my shopping bag full of clothes in five minutes. Dad jammed his stuff in back and got in. He stepped on the gas spinning his tires; he headed for the home of his friends, Roy Myers and his wife Dorothy. I ended up sleeping on their couch. Dad got a room at a boarding house almost next door to Clare's hotel. Myra Smith and Roy Place, the local sheriff, ran the boarding house.

Dad wouldn't tell me what Clare had said that got him so hopping mad. "You don't want to know," he said firmly, and I left it at that.

Fortunately for us Clare didn't get her revenge. Mr. Langevin later told me that Clare had resorted to blackmailing Dad and had threatened to report him for violating his parole. Several of Dad's influential friends, including Mr. Hymes, testified at the hearing in Dad's behalf. Dad could have been sent back to the Dannemora State Prison to serve out the rest of his time. I asked if I could go to the hearing too. "I'm not a kid anymore. I need to know what's so bad you can't tell me."

"I don't want you involved in any of this." Dad forbade me to go to the hearing. "Now drop it!" Whatever his reason, he refused to talk about it and I never found why he could have been sent up for seven more years.

I think the folks around me told funny stories about the Prohibition era to make me feel good again. Roy, greatly amused, told stories of the local priest, Father Burbough.

"Father Burbough sat on his pomposity playing cards with friends while the feds, acting on a tip, searched the house for illegal whiskey. They searched the place and found nothing." Roy snickered, enjoying himself. "Father Burbough and his card playing friends had stashed the hootch beneath the table where they were playing cards, with some of it hidden under his skirt. Why, the best people in Star Lake bought whiskey from the bootleggers." The list of former Star Lake bootleggers went on and on.

I liked staying with the Myers' in their small three-room cottage not much bigger than a dollhouse. Roy played his guitar and taught me words to an old folk song.

I got a girl named Crossed Eyed Sue
As pretty as she can be
With a great big wart on the front of her nose
And a face like a sour apple tree.
Crossed Eyed Sue and a kangaroo
Were very much alike.
For the kangaroo, it hopped all night
And Sue, she hopped all day.
Oh! I've got a girl named Cross Eyed Sue,
Her eyes are red, and lips are blue,
Dimpled hair and curly cheeks,
Her false teeth rattles and her glasses creak...

"You should buy this girl a guitar," Roy winked at me, and I agreed. But, I guess, Dad had other things on his mind. I rarely saw him. Dorothy sorted out my wardrobe and made a list of clothes I'd need for school.

That September, I showed up at Gerald Marshal's one room schoolhouse in Star Lake. A kindly and dedicated teacher, he told Dad I'd need some tutoring. I had failed all the standardized tests, and Mr. Marshall couldn't determine what grade I belonged in. His expression conveyed the seriousness of my being so far behind for a girl my age. I stayed after school everyday trying to catch up.

Then Dorothy took sick. I had to find a new home. I pleaded for more stability to my life. "Please, Dad, let's get an apartment. I'll keep it clean and everything. Then we can come and go as we please."

"That's what I'm afraid of. You need supervision, babe. With me working overtime, you'd be home alone too much and I'd be reported to Child Welfare Services."

Rod Langevin persuaded the Durham family in Oswegatchie to take me in as a boarder. Mrs. Durham and Thelma Langevin were sisters.

The Durham's and their two daughters, Marian, my age, and Sarah, twelve, were Baptist and urged me to go to their church. I didn't mind. They sang good strong hymns and I enjoyed belting out the "Old Rugged Cross."

One day, Ora Griffen righteously declared, "What's this? A Catholic girl going to a Baptist Church. Well! We can't have that." Her and Mrs. Ritz were two staunch Catholics in the County Farm and Home Bureau in Oswegatchie. Most of the matrons in town were members. Mrs. Griffen and Mrs. Ritz attended the Catholic Church in Fine, seven miles away. The following Sunday, Mrs. Ritz dutifully took me to her church. I sang in my best angelic pious soprano voice… "Ave Maria" and "Come Holy Ghost."

When I couldn't recite prayers in unison with the congregation, Ora said I'd have to attend Catechism classes and learn them.

"I do so know my prayers," I protested. "Our Mohawk priest, Father Jacobs, taught us our catechism. And he's my grandmother's cousin," I added with emphasis.

"Well. We don't know that," she persisted gruffly. "It sounds like gibberish. We can't understand it."

"But I'm not saying my prayers to you. I'm saying them to God!"

Mrs. Ritz, matronly and more diplomatic, chimed in with her beguiling voice, batting her eyelids. "Why don't you attend classes with my Barbara? Just to keep her company. Before you know it, you'll be saying your prayers in English."

I gave in. Every Sunday, she and her daughter, Barbara, sixteen, gave me a ride to church.

Then I got a big crush on Earl Fletcher the star basketball player in high school. I went berserk over him. Earl, the best looking boy I'd ever seen, went to the Baptist Church. He lived next door to the Durhams. The following Sunday I went back to the Baptist Church with the Durhams and sat right in

MY MOTHER'S SPIRIT

front row, belting out "The Old Rugged Cross."

I enrolled in the Oswegatchie Union Free School, a small school with all twelve grades and an enrollment of a little over a hundred students. Thanks to Gerald Marshal's tutoring and on his recommendation, I was placed in the seventh grade. He reassured me. "Not too embarrassing for a fourteen year old student."

Earl, two years older and a senior, didn't notice me at first. He had more girlfriends than he knew what to do with. When I learned that he played snare drum in band, I begged Miss Hain, our music teacher, to let me play the bass drum. "Please let me learn how to play the bass drum. All my life, I've wanted to learn how to march to its beat." (I didn't let on, that I hadn't ever thought of playing in a band.) Before long, I stood proudly by his side beating on my drum. He coached the junior girls' varsity basketball team. I learned how to play basketball and got on the team. During a game with a competing team I coaxed him to let me play. Crazy with enthusiasm, and eager to show off, as I ran out to the center, I caught the ball and dribbled it across to the other side. Our team booed me off the floor. He didn't put up an argument when I quit. "Just as well," he agreed. "But, you've got a mean beat. Keep it up." It cheered me up a bit when he said that, and I knew he was getting to like me.

Knowing Earl and the players practiced after school and sometimes after supper, I'd go out and sit on the guardrails in front of our house, waiting for him to walk by coming home from ball practice. One evening he failed to show. I finally went inside and got ready for bed. Just then I heard the school bus returning from a game. I ran out in my robe and sat waiting for him. We were sitting on the guardrails laughing, enjoying our talk, when Mr. Durham looked out and saw me.

"Get in this house!" he roared. "You've no business talking to a boy outside in the dark in your night clothes. I've never seen such scandalous behavior!"

Another time I managed to see Earl alone was going after the mail at night. Our tiny post office, located an eighth of a mile up the hill from our houses had two mail runs a day. The second mail run came in at six and Mrs. Humble, the post master would sort it. Earl always picked up their mail. So I started going after our evening mail. I'd rush through the supper dishes, timing it right so I could walk back down the hill with him. If I were really speedy, I'd get to walk up the hill with him to double the thrill.

We enjoyed skating on the pond between our houses. In winter, Earl shoveled it and we skated every chance we got. My skates kept getting loose, or so I said, and Earl would tighten them for me each time. On weekends we skated way after it got dark by the light of the streetlight. He and I would be the last to leave, or unless Mr. Durham called out ordering me to come inside.

In spring, knowing how sound travels on water, Earl and I arranged a time to talk across the pond from our upstairs windows. I'd rush through the supper dishes. When I heard him whistle, I'd fly up the stairs for our tête-à-tête.

"What were you doing just now?" he asked this one time.

"Doing dishes," I replied, annoyed that I had almost missed his signal. "Most of the time I have to do both, wash and dry. Marian is so slow. No wonder she's fat. It's quicker for me to do it all so I can get up here in time. I almost didn't make it this time."

"I wish I were there with you. We'd do them together. We'd never get them done 'cause I'd be hugging you instead."

"Do you really like me that much?"

"You know I do."

"Then, how come you're going steady with Lillian? Every time I think you like me, you're going steady with someone else."

Just then a thunderous roar: "Get away from that window." Mister Durham had been standing on the back porch listening.

Mr. and Mrs. Durham were so upset with me they informed my father I'd have to leave at the end of the school term. "She's too much of a responsibility and a bad influence on our girls," added Mrs. Durham.

That spring, after my fifteenth birthday, Miss Lease, our eight-grade teacher and our Senior Girl Scout leader, got us enthused about putting on a formal dance. We'd sew our own gowns to earn merit badges, invite boys, dance to records, and have refreshments. We gleefully set the date for May, and chose our theme song: Hoagie Carmichaels' "Star Dust."

Miss Lease and our home economics teacher kept us scouts busy sewing on our gowns. My gown of white dotted Swiss looked pretty decent and fit nicely. In between sewing, we chirped about whom we were going to ask to be our dates. My friends teased me saying they knew whom I'd be asking. Just to show them, I deliberately asked a boy from another school who went to our Catholic Church, Bernard Welch. Marian ended up asking Earl.

Finally, our big evening arrived. We had decorated the hallway of our school as an intimate area to dance in. The records were chosen and stacked; the junior girl scouts were in their places ready to serve the refreshments.

Bernard came to the door with a corsage, his mother had made from the

MY MOTHER'S SPIRIT

flowers in her garden. He and I walked the few yards to the school. Wanting to impress the Durhams, I used my best manners and told Marian how pretty she looked. She did look pretty in spite of her being quite pudgy. She was really a sweet girl and, ordinarily, we got along quite well.

As soon as the dance started, Earl and I fixed my dance card and he claimed every dance. He held me close, and we swayed to dreamy rhythms of slow tunes as we drifted farther and further away from the lighted area. We swayed out to the outer edges far from the chaperones. We ignored everyone else. Before the dance ended, Bernard took off with one of the helpers. Marian went home with her mother. Earl walked me home and I landed in the doghouse for the rest of the school term. After that Earl and I kept our meetings a secret.

Dad told the Durhams I'd be leaving at the end of June to spend the summer with his relatives. Thoroughly disgusted with my boy-crazy behavior, they couldn't have cared less.

Our school had such a small enrollment, there were only three seniors graduating. The school board decided to hold both the grade school and the high school graduation ceremonies on the same night. Because I had skipped a grade and was now an eight grader, Earl and I ended up on stage together. He, as valedictorian of his class, and I, as valedictorian of the eight grade, both gave a speech. He planned to attend Cortland College in the fall. Evenings, we'd walk over to the school and sit on the steps and talk. One time as we stood on the front steps, I stood one step higher. We kissed. He gave me his identification bracelet and I gave him my gold ring with my Initials: DJS

Miss Lease lived in Newburg, seventeen miles from Highland Mills, the hometown of my relatives. She had it all arranged. We'd travel by bus and Uncle Romie would pick us up at the Newburg bus depot. At the end of August, we'd return together and I, then would board with the Fletcher family. I couldn't believe my good fortune. Earl and I would be living in the same house. The two months we'd be apart seemed like forever. We agreed we'd write to each other every day.

A BROWN WREN IN A GILDED CAGE
The summer of 1946 in Highland Mills

Our bus rumbled into the Newburg terminal that last day in June. Miss Lease and I shuffled along behind the slow line of passengers disembarking. Eager to begin a new adventure, I mumbled, "I wish these slowpokes would get out of my way."

Uncle Romie leaned on his black ford coupe, waiting. Resembling my father in looks but much shorter, and with out that military bearing, he stepped forward and helped us with our luggage. He offered to drive Miss Lease to her house.

"No, no! Thanks, my brother Matty will be showing up soon." Miss Lease, twenty-four, was nine years older than me, we were the same height—petite at five feet two. She talked non-stop, especially on the bus. Mostly, she talked about her Italian family. I felt as if I knew them all personally. I recognized her kid brother swaggering towards us. With an air of confidence, he called out, "Hi, sis!" and grabbed her suitcase. After pleasant introductions and saying goodbye, they went one way and I followed Uncle Romie to his car.

He maneuvered the little coupe expertly out of the terminal. I stiffened, holding my breath and wide eyed at all the traffic coming at us from all directions. His quiet manner and the amused expression on his face reassured me that he knew the city and I had nothing to fear.

Riding with Uncle Romie felt much like riding with dad. Uncle Romie wasn't very talkative either. He did ask about Miss Lease. "Bright eyed, pert and perky, your friend. What's her name again?"

"Elana, Miss Lease, I mean. She's Italian, born in Italy, came to this country as a little girl. Her father, an American citizen, during the first World War went back to his homeland and married his Italian sweetheart. Miss Lease, the oldest of his four children, three girls and a brother, went to a Southern university cause it's cheaper. They live in the Italian section and she's invited me to come to dinner sometime. She says her mother cooks a seven course Italian dinner when company comes. Maybe I can ride in with you the next time you come here."

He smiled, looking straight ahead, not answering. I took that for a yes. It felt good riding with my very own uncle, a white man even if I didn't know him very well.

I thought about my Uncle Jack, a Mohawk, who tended to be indecisive and tolerated Tota's insults. I hadn't seen him in five years. Last I heard, he worked in a logging camp somewhere in Northern Canada. I missed him a lot.

I moved a tad closer to Uncle Romie and stopped talking, enjoying the silence between us. In no time at all we pulled up in front of Aunt Phil's house.

The two Great Aunts came out on the front porch, their faces lit up, happy to see us. Aunt Sally, more agile and two years younger than Aunt Phil, led the way upstairs to show me to my room. Uncle Romie followed with my suitcase.

Dazzled by the airiness of the large bedroom I twirled around admiring the four large windows with white organdy curtains. I likened the flowery wallpapered walls to a country garden. It had been Aunt Sally's room. She had moved into the room across from me, no larger than a closet.

My first evening meal with them, we sat down to a simple supper of rolls, soup and a salad. The two genteel old ladies were non-practicing Episcopalians and not accustomed to saying grace. I bowed slightly, and made a quick sign of the cross. Aunt Sally, with her failing eyesight, must have thought I was brushing something away from my face. She asked, "Is there a fly in here?"

Aunt Phil, I soon learned, cooked gourmet meals. I thought her homemade rolls where the best I'd ever eaten—but as I buttered the other half, I saw a bug in it. I threw the roll across the table, jumped out of my chair, ran down the hall to the bathroom and coughed up my mouth-full of food into the toilet. Dismayed, Aunt Phil looked over the basket of rolls. The bug turned out to be a caraway seed.

Eager to get to know my cousins that first week and for them to learn about me, I answered their many questions. Never shy about my Indian heritage, I explained, "No, we don't live in teepees. I sleep between two sheets like everyone else. And please don't make that stupid noise hollering with your hand cupped to your mouth, 'wahooing.' We don't do war cries."

These cousins, related to me through my father, were just that—only cousins. I didn't sense the closeness I felt with my Indian cousins who were more like my brothers and sisters. On the reserve, we snickered at or stuck our tongues out at the white folks, who rode through our village gawking to get a better look at us. As if they were on a safari—viewing natives in their own habitat. All of a sudden I felt strange with these white folks—my relatives.

I already knew about Uncle Joe's two sons, Jimmy and Joey, in the Navy. I heard several times how I looked enough like Jimmy to be his sister. It rankled me. I believed I resembled my mother instead.

Uncle Romie's two older sons, Walt and Rod, had just returned home from the service. Aunt Margaret kept running after us with her Brownie camera putting me in between, snapping pictures. Not that I minded. Acting coy, I flirted with them, thinking they were so good looking. Cousin Noel, twelve, wasn't interested in girls, and had better things to do. Norma tagged along everywhere I went. I met Aunt Muriel's five children later when she invited me to spend a few days at their summer farmhouse in Chester.

One day I came in from hanging out with the kids in the neighborhood. I mentioned the names of the kids I had just met. Some of them were Italian. Aunt Phil lowering her voice and told me not get too chummy with some of them. "It's better to hang out with your own kind." Puzzled, I wondered just how many around here were Indians? Maybe, because I resembled my father a little, she forgot about my being half Indian.

My Aunt Margaret never forgot and made a big fuss over me. She called me, "My Indian Princess," right from the start. She seemed delighted when she learned that I had taken piano lesson. She decided that I should keep up with it. Every afternoon, I went to her house to practice—except that she enjoyed playing the piano more than I did. She'd pop into the living room to give me pointers and end up taking over the keyboard. Then we'd sing all the old favorites: "Sweet Rosie O'Grady; Peg O' My Heart;" "There's a Tavern In The Town;" and "Ole Sol O Mio," and many more.

After all that exertion at the piano, we rewarded ourselves with a treat. Every day she'd send me to Belding's Drug Store for a pint of Neapolitan ice cream and we'd split the pint between us. "You need fattening up," she'd say. "And I'm already plump. Best to be plump and healthy than to be scrawny and sickly." A few years later, I learned she had been diagnosed with sugar diabetes.

I suspected that Aunt Phil and Aunt Sally weren't all that fond of Aunt Margaret when Aunt Sally confided in me one day. "Did you know that your Aunt Margaret took our Jerome away from her own sister. Priscilla seemed quieter and much better suited for him." Then dolefully, Aunt Sally sighed, "I guess, he preferred Margaret."

My two great aunts weren't all that fond of Aunt Margie either. Aunt Phil enjoyed telling me about the time Aunt Margie, who professed to be a

MY MOTHER'S SPIRIT

Christian scientist, came and left her son Robbie, with them for the week she needed to be away on a trip. Little Robbie, six, at the time, had a badly swollen knee. The two aunts were very concerned and skeptical when Aunt Margie reassured them that through her prayers, he'd soon be healed. Robbie sobbed and sobbed over his aching knee. Aunt Phil whisked him away to the family doctor and Robbie's knee got better. When Aunt Margie returned, she triumphantly declared that Robbie's recovery was due to the wonderful healing power of prayer. Aunt Phil rolled her eyes, smiling mischievously. "We never told her what we had done."

"Oh!" added Aunt Sally, "remember the time Margie was ill and complained about all those mysterious symptoms? She had all kinds of diagnostic tests done to get to the bottom of what ever it was that ailed her."

True! Aunt Margie, did study her bible, but she was quiet about it—not at all boastful or righteous. I liked my Aunt Margie, who went to great lengths to make our summer interesting. My cousins, Mally, fifteen, and Joan, fourteen, where my Aunt Muriel's daughters. Not having daughters of her own, Aunt Margie doted on her three nieces. She took us on excursions up the Hudson River by day-liner to Albany or down to New York City. She took us to plays, good restaurants, and museums.

Sadly, though, I soon discovered, that she, like my father, showed her dislike for colored people. One day, on the sunny streets of New York, she suddenly glared at the large young black man standing near by. "Look at that big black buck," she sneered. I looked at her not knowing what to say. I thought it odd; she'd talk like that when she took the Bible seriously, studying it like a biblical scholar. Other times, gracious, tall and dignified, she sounded like Miss Manners herself.

Getting to know my two great aunts tickled me the most. They liked entertaining, graciously, sipping sherry and sitting straight, with perfect decorum. I contrasted this scene to our beer parlor on our reserve. There, everyone liked drinking beer right out of the bottle. Anyone who asked for a glass was given a jelly glass. Our beer parlor friends joked, and made gentle fun of one another. But, not these two cultured ladies. They talked about more important matters very intelligently, discussing their opinions about politics or cultural events such as plays, books, and society in general.

Except when Aunt Sally and Aunt Phil were by themselves. Every after noon, they had their sherry, smoked one cigarette each and played bridge. Then they'd argue about points and accuse each other of misplaying their hand. Aunt Sally would always indignantly gave in first, throwing her hand down. "I'm not playing with you again, ever," she'd say, squaring her shoulders, and thrusting her head upward, sitting as if she were queen Victoria. The next day they'd light up, sip their sherry and play as usual.

On the days when I expected a letter from Earl, I'd come to the dinning room table with a happy heart. Sure enough, there'd be his letter propped up by my place setting. Aunt Sally would be eyeing me with an amused expression. They'd excuse me while I bounded up the stairs to read it in the privacy of my bedroom. I'd tuck it under my pillow intending to answer it later. One time, Aunt Sally asked. "Is he your beau?"

"I guess so," I replied. To change the subject, I asked if she ever had a boyfriend. "Were you ever in love?" I asked Aunt Sally. "How come you never married?"

"Don't worry, my child," she answered coyly." I've had my moments." Aunt Phil just rolled her eyes. We enjoyed our supper in silence contented to be in each other's company.

Aunt Margaret had told me that a long time ago Aunt Sally had been engaged to a handsome young soldier the family didn't approve of. He went off to war and never returned. She never loved another.

THE AFFABLE MR. MALLET

Mr. Mallet, the spry, seventy year old affable salesman for the A.G. Hall Fishing Line, Inc., and I boarded the Greyhound bus in front of the barber shop on Main Street in Highland Mills, early on a rosy Monday morning of 1946. Mr. Mallet, in his tan linen suit, complete with pale green tie, straw fedora, brown and white spectator shoes, followed me down the long narrow aisle. I spied two empty seats, side by side and squeezed my skinny frame quickly inward and sidled into the one by the window. Mr. Mallet sat down beside me. The bus rolled onto Route 17 and we headed for New York City. This was supposed to be the first of many such trips, intended to broaden my education by spending the summer with my father's people.

"There's many a time I've squired the ladies on such trips, but none as fair as you, my dear." Mr. Mallet told me about his 'heydays' in the 1920s and how he wowed the ladies by taking them on excursions to the city just as he was doing with me today. Even with flabby jowls, thinning white hair, bushy eyebrows and sagging facial muscles, he was still gallant, and the swagger to his steps made women of all ages passing by to turn and take a second look. I took some comfort in knowing I was dressed in my best—my Dutch girl outfit, white socks, and saddle shoes.

We settled nicely in our seats, and for the sake of conversation, after a few miles of silence, he opened with, "Tell me young lady, what do you think of euthanasia?"

"Well, to be honest, I've never been there, but it sounds to me like it would be a nice place to visit. Is it in Asia?"

The telltale signs of a smile around his eyes, gave away his moment of amusement, but with a straight face, he replied, "No, my lady, euthanasia is a word. It means mercy killing."

"Jesus, Mary and Joseph," I blurted out. "The meaning of the word sounds so much more sinister. What's merciful about killing someone? Euthanasia. It sounds like a type of dance. Swing and sway with Sammy Kay. Like when you help end someone's life, you should feel happy about it."

"I take it you don't believe in helping to end the suffering of one who's afflicted with a painful terminal disease?"

"No way. I sure wouldn't want to make it legal for someone to decide it was my time to go. To be gone from this world—departo! Like rubbing his or her hands together for a job well done. There! I've just done my good deed for the day helping the poor bugger die. Sending the poor suffering soul on the road to purgatory. Besides, my grandmother always told me, the reason we all have to suffer on this earth before we die is because it's our Creator's way to help us in doing penance for sins we've committed here on earth. Then when it's time for us to let go, our souls will soar on the wings of angels to the heavenly domain of the Great Spirit where our souls will happily dwell forever."

"Interesting way of putting it. Your grandmother, I understand, was Indian. She must have had a great influence in your understanding of life. Your philosophy, so to speak, to be so sure of life after death."

"Yes! Tota and her cousin, Father Jacobs, explained it all, in our Catechism classes. Don't you believe in your soul living ever after?" Mr. Mallet didn't answer. I took that as a no. Poor man! We rode in silence for a while. I enjoyed the lull, giving me a chance to take in the scenery whizzing by.

"Tell me young lady, what books have you read recently? Who's your favorite author?"

"I can't actually remember, except our seventh grade prose and poetry in English class. I read comic books mostly, Archie, with Veronica, and Jughead, and the Sunday funnies. Just the other day, Aunt Sally gave me this ancient old book with a faded green leather-bound cover, titled *Scaramouche*, while I was relaxing on the front porch. I can't understand most of the words and it's boring. But I promised I'd try my best. I've been dragging it around. One thing I've learned about all of you though, I mean, white people in general, you all can't bear to see me sitting by myself, enjoying just being quiet and thinking. Right away, you all got to be saying something or trying to get me doing something, thinking I must be bored."

Mr. Mallet smiled and closed his eyes until the bus came to a stop and we got off. Time Square all over again, cars and taxicabs honking, people pushing you along, the same garlicky smells, hot smelly odors of burnt onion, human sweat and not a breath of fresh air anywhere. Just like last year when Dad and I stopped here on our way to visit our relatives. Mr. Mallet led me by the arm into a magnificent restaurant called Childs or something like that. A man in a black tuxedo showed us to our table and seated me. The dining room was elegant, cool and spacious. I felt as if I were stepping into a smooth rhythm of sophistication. This is where I could very well say, "No, thank you.

MY MOTHER'S SPIRIT

I've had elegant sufficiency. Anymore would be vulgar superfluity," and not be laughed at for being so pompous. But, of course, I wouldn't say it. I wouldn't want to embarrass my elderly escort who was being so gallant. Another waiter came to take our order. Mr. Mallet said, "May I take the liberty of ordering?"

"Yes, please," since I hardly could figure what all was on the menu. I looked sideways at the other diners hoping they didn't notice how awkward I felt. It was the first time I ate Lobster a la Newburg, the tastiest seafood I ever tasted. I took the toast points and mopped up every bit of the creamy sherry sauce. Mr. Mallet looked please watching me enjoying my lobster stew. He must have appreciated my being enthused and impressed about the many sights we took, because he kept saying, "This is only the beginning, my dear." He kept patting my hand, even as we settled back in our tight but cozy high-backed seats for the ride home.

Long after that memorable trip, Aunt Sally told me what Mr. Mallet said about me. "Very opinionated for a young girl her age who doesn't fully understand what she's talking about. And she reads only comic books." Despite his unfavorable opinion of my literary tastes, he continued sending me big fat rolls of Sunday funnies by Parcel Post every month until his death three years later.

LEARNING ABOUT LIFE ON BACK COUNTRY ROADS

Aunt Muriel invited me to spend the last three weeks of my vacation at their summer farm in Chester, a rural community thirty miles from New York City. They maintained the gracious large old white Victorian farmhouse on acres of rolling green hills and fields. The red barn stabled two riding horses: Ginger, a sleek mare, and the stocky quarter horse, Mickey. Aunt Margie and Uncle Ernest lived in the studio apartment over the barn. I slept in their spare bedroom.

My cousins, Mally and Joan, expert riders, taught me to saddle the horses and how to post so my ribs no longer came down with a thud against my navel while riding. I rode Mickey, and most often it was Mally who accompanied me riding Ginger.

One morning while riding along a back country road, we met Marcy, twelve, who lived in a small dilapidated house by a fork on that road. Curious, we dismounted to let the horses rest in front of the house. The yard, bare of grass, was littered with broken toys. A ragged old couch under a tree graced the outdoors. Three small children, a boy, five, and two girls, four and three, were climbing and jumping all over it. Marcy looked after them while their mother worked at a tavern in town. Mally and I got a kick out of listening to Marcy tell us bawdy jokes. Titillated, we went back again the next day. This time, she taught us a dirty song we wouldn't dare sing in front of anyone. We delighted in singing the song over and over.

> Walking down Canal Street, knocking on every door.
> Goddamn son of a bitch, I couldn't find a whore.
> When I finally found one I wiggled it around.
> Goddamn son of a bitch I couldn't get it out…

It got worse as the words continued. We learned all four verses in one visit. I also heard the term "white trash."

Marcy reminded me of myself when at ten I had to take care of Stanley, Linda and Phyllis. Our reserve had no such phrases for poor people. Indian trash? Hardly! We were all poor and didn't know it. Marcy had a generous

MY MOTHER'S SPIRIT

heart and offered to share peanut butter sandwiches with us. She reminded me of the Jona kids who shared their lard and sugar sandwiches.

After a few visits, Mally and I tired of singing the song and took other roads looking for new adventure. I forgot about Marcy.

For a special treat one afternoon, Uncle Walter, an advertising executive, drove Mally, Joan and me to New York City in his big town car to show us how a radio program was broadcast and how advertising was done. Sitting inside a glassed-in compartment reserved for radio personnel and their families, we watched the actors hovering over mikes reading their lines from the radio program, The *Romance of Helen Trent*. With sound effects, three people at another mike sang a jingle, a commercial about E - Z squeaks, squeaking oil.

The next morning, I looked forward to sharing the highlights of our trip with Aunt Muriel. My few moments alone with her, usually in the kitchen while enjoying my oatmeal, were most memorable. She listened quietly, amused, and her hazel green eyes twinkled. She prepared a delicious dish to surprise us for lunch. I never heard her raise her voice despite six of us running in and out all day long. She was gentle, sweet and petite, with a waist so tiny it was hard to believe she had five children. She lovingly put up with all of us while taking care of her youngest, Tommy, five. David and Barry were typical boys nine and eleven, who preferred to play at the next farm down the road.

Later in the morning, Aunt Margie would come over from the studio and help Aunt Muriel for the day. While Aunt Muriel was easygoing, Aunt Margie tended to be more rigid, insisting on a timely schedule for meals and such: a midmorning snack at ten; lunch at noon; a snack at three and a formal dinner at six when Uncle Walter arrived home and presided at the head of the table.

One afternoon at harvest time, the Rowe family at the next farm invited us all to help prepare corn for freezing. We picked, shucked, and scraped, until each ear was bared to a cob. Then we were treated to homemade ice cream and fresh strawberries. With all this good eating, I no longer looked like a broomstick.

From the start, Aunt Margie called me Lorry. I didn't care for the nickname. It reminded me of a carriage with a fringe on top. I let it pass. I had it too good to complain about a name. I became more upset when she insisted on cutting my hair short. "It brings out the waves. You'd look more like your Dad," she said. I had finally gotten it long enough so I could braid it again. I wore it in an easy ponytail. It became a challenge keeping busy so she didn't find me sitting still long enough for her to fetch the shears.

A week before I'd be leaving, Aunt Muriel and Aunt Margie busied themselves mending and hemming dresses that my cousins had outgrown or were tired of. I thought myself fortunate that I was properly clothed. From Aunt Helen sewing slips for me from flour sacking, and making shirts, skirts and shorts from remnants, to Rita sewing me complete outfits, I had always had at least two or three changes of clothing. But never did I have so many dresses to choose from as I did now. Feeling like a princess, I twirled around in the mirror admiring each new dress.

Shortly after I returned to Aunt Phil and Aunt Sally's house, Uncle Romie called to say we'd be riding into Newburg the next day. Miss Lease and her family were expecting me for dinner.

He took four of us kids: Norma, Noel, myself and a neighbor, Billy McClennon, a year or two older than me. Billy and I ended up in the rumble seat. Right off, he put a choke-hold around my neck, supposedly for safety from the blast of wind that hit us. The wind whipped me across the face and took my breath away. To make it worse, Billy started kissing me. I clenched my teeth, banged our mouths together and I bruised my lip in the process of Billy's passionate kiss. By the time we got to Miss Lease's house, my hair was tied into knots and I looked like Methuselah.

Disentangling myself and getting my wind back, I patted my hair down and rang the doorbell. Uncle Romie and the rest of them went on their way to do their shopping. Miss Lease and her family engulfed me in their kitchen talking all at once, half of it in Italian. "Mama mia!" What a family!

I remembered the trick we used to pull when we wanted to break the monotony from class work. We'd get Miss Lease talking about her family…non-stop. I knew about her mother, her sister Jeannie and all her boyfriends. We even knew their names. Jeannie was the good-looking sister and Billie, her kid sister, wearing glasses, was the plain one. Matty, according to Miss lease, was the brother who supported them all. A real charmer, he didn't want to get married because he had it too good at home. I enjoyed dinner of spaghetti, chicken, ravioli - seven courses, including spumoni ice cream for dessert.

When Uncle Romie called for me, Mrs. Lease wanted to feed him and his passengers too. He declined. He and Miss Lease firmed up our plans for the trip back home to Oswegatchie.

"Please! Let Noel ride in the rumble seat, I don't like all that wind," I pleaded. I pushed Norma into the middle and helped myself into the front seat. I wasn't about to fight the wind and Billy too. I felt too stuffed to fight with Billy.

By the final week of my stay, I had met most of the male cousins. Aunt Margaret, making a fuss, clicked away with her Kodak Brownie camera. I even met cousin Jimmy, who really did look like me. Aunt Phil's favorite, he easily teased her into making us her famous banana fritters with lemon sauce.

Aunt Margaret took me aside and tried again to coax me into staying. I protested, using the excuse that my dad missed me. But, mostly, I longed to see Earl.

"Your dad will understand," Aunt Margaret confided. "He asked Aunt Phil if she'd take you for the summer. His Union at the Steel Mill where he works is on strike. He's having a tough times making ends meet. If you stayed, he wouldn't have that extra expense."

It knocked the stuffing out me. I felt defeated and humiliated. Dad hadn't mentioned it in the two letters I'd gotten from him. "I don't care," I replied defensively. "I'll work for my room and board. I can make beds and do housework and baby-sit. I've done so before." I was close to tears. I just want to go home.

"Now, pet, don't take it personally. It's not your fault. I'd love to have you live with us."

She tried to hug me. I twisted away from her and ran up to my room. I sat on the bed looking at myself in the mirror. I saw the reflection of the spacious well-decorated room that was not mine. My two suitcases sat nearby, already packed with hand-me downs. Everyone knew I was a charity case. I felt like the plain brown wren in a fancy cage…the solitary brown wren, singing a loud song. That's me, I thought. Pretending—singing to the world about how grand I was. I longed for something that was mine and mine alone. I wanted my mother.

HEADING HOME
Home Is Where The Heart is

If I'd known I wouldn't be seeing my father's people again for a good many years, saying my good byes might have been a lot harder. Only Uncle Romie took me to the bus station. Miss Lease, her sisters and brother Matty were at the bus depot waiting. In spite of the warm hugs from every one and especially from Uncle Romie, my heart was tinged, with sadness. Yet I was anxious to go home, wherever home happened to be.

Shortly after we were on the road, I asked Miss Lease again, "Are you sure I'll be boarding with the Fletchers? I forgot to ask Dad and he didn't mention it."

"Will you stop worrying? Mrs. Fletcher is expecting the both of us. I'm surprised Earl hasn't told you," she said.

"Why would HE be telling me that?" I feigned surprise.

"Why not? Everyone knows you've been writing to each other."

"Oh…yeah! No, he didn't say." Pretending to watch the scenery, I guessed our secret was no big deal. Happy and so eager to see him, much my mouth went dry, and I could hardly swallow.

The Greyhound bus rolled along covering the miles at a fast clip. Settled back in our seats relaxed, Miss Lease rattled on. My mind drifted, playing out scenes I hoped would happen when we arrived.

After eight hours of traveling and many changes, we got off in front of Fletcher's boarding house dragging our luggage. I could hardly contain my excitement. As soon as we stepped inside the entry, depositing our luggage, Mrs. Fletcher and her two daughters came out and we were all hugging one another. I beamed, expertly covering up for my anxiety, as we walked into the dining room. Earl was nowhere in sight.

Amid the chattering, we heard, "Well I'll be!" Mr. Fletcher came in with his hand extended ready to shake hands with us and especially with Miss Lease. His blue eyes twinkled. He was the most pleasant person with a smile for everyone; he made you feel glad by being in the same room with him. A great sports buff and a professional baseball player in his youth, he kept up with the latest baseball scores and what teams certain players were with. Miss Lease and Dad Fletcher (as I soon called him) exchanged good-natured

MY MOTHER'S SPIRIT

bantering: who was the best team, the best hitter and who would win the World Series. The two entertained us. Dad Fletcher mirthfully challenged her and she picked it up and ran with it. He couldn't stump her when it came to sports. We congregated in the dining room. I sensed this would be the hub of all activities in the years to come; eating, playing cards, doing our home work, putting picture puzzles together and carrying on discussions. In winter, we'd be crowding and huddling over the one large heat register on the floor in the dining room.

Two other teachers boarded here. Irene Hain, our music teacher, was demure, with naturally curly, red hair. Soft spoken and shy, she rarely dated, and dedicated most of her time to her students. She had been my favorite, ever since she let me play the bass drum last year. She gave me piano lessons, had me singing solos in choruses, and chose me as drum majorette. In the coming years I'd spend a lot of time, evenings and weekends, lying on her bed listening to classical music. She'd tell me stories about the composers and I'd tell her all about how Tota and I used to listen to Caruso on our old victorola.

The other teacher, Miss Button was on hand, having arrived just before us. She looked the typical spinster "schoolmarm," tall, thin, and prim. She wore her graying hair pulled into a bun in back. Her glasses sat low on her nose and she lowered her head slightly to look over them as she spoke. She taught third, forth and fifth grades.

Of the five Fletcher children, three still lived at home. Besides Earl, there was Bessie, my age. We'd been friends when I lived next door and we were in scouts together. Although she was two grades ahead of me, we chummed around together. Thinner and more sensitive than I, she tended to get upset often. I'd sit calmly by her side until she got over it. Mrs. Fletcher had me share a double bed with Bessie. She must have heard about my having occasional nightmares and hollering out some nights. When I slept fitfully, Bessie would reassure me and rub my arm until I went back to sleep.

Dotty, a sweet pudgy little ten-year-old, with a pretty round face and blue eyes, followed us around. At times, Bessie and I ignored her when we wanted to be off by ourselves somewhere.

The evening of our returning home, Earl finally sauntered in almost unnoticed. He and I covered up our attraction for one another, especially after the scout dance fiasco. We didn't want to upset any more folks. He ruffled my hair as he walked by, and sat opposite me. We enjoyed eye contact, and a rush of happiness engulfed me. After an evening snack, everyone pitched in to clear the table and did the dishes.

DOLORES EOSTENUNI STANFIELD

Earl dumped the box of a picture puzzle on the center of the dining room table. He and I sat trying to fit in the pieces. Others would stop and search for a piece here and there, staying for a bit. The two of us kept at it until bedtime. Then we picked up all the pieces, our hands touching at times. He squeezed my hand, said good night and went off to his room up the back stairway. I went up to bed, blissfully happy, enjoyed a giggle or two with Bessie, plopped into bed and slept soundly.

Early next morning, Miss Lease came skipping, almost hopping one step at a time down the stairs. "Well!" she said, "Oh my!" Toying with her pearls, she looked at the array of breakfast foods. There was a choice of rolls, orange juice, eggs, cereal and coffee. She had one slice of toast and a glass of orange juice, talked through out the meal and was last to leave.

Miss Button appeared next, sat down and daintily fluttered her napkin to her lap. "The prettiest little bird chirped at me outside my window this morning. Cheep, cheep, cheep," she mimicked, as if we were her third grade pupils. She ate slowly, amused, listening to Miss Lease.

I wished for all of them to be gone before Earl showed up so I could breakfast alone with him. Just then Mrs. Fletcher called me into the dining room. "Dolores, eat your breakfast. I need to talk to you before you take off."

I jumped, fearing the worst. "All right." No doubt she'd be laying down rules.

She sat knitting at the dining room table. Matronly at fifty-five, wearing wireless spectacles, her gaze made me pay attention. She spoke softly but firmly.

"Although your dad will pay for your room and board, he told me to show you how to do housework." She smiled. "It won't be easy living with all these teachers but I know you'll do just fine."

I grinned. "Gee! Is that all? Would it be okay if I called you Mother?"

I'd take it as a compliment," she smiled.

A SECRET LOVE NO LONGER

We all enjoyed going for drives to neighboring towns for shopping expeditions. Mother always drove. Right away, Miss Lease would announce that riding in back made her carsick. She'd get the front seat every time and I always ended in back. This one time, Mother couldn't go. Earl, having just gotten his license, would drive. By some fluke, Miss Lease couldn't go either. I got the middle front seat. Sitting close, Earl slid his right hand over mine and we drove along without anyone being the wiser. I was thrilled spending much of our time together right under the scrutiny of everyone and believing no one noticed.

Then came the day Earl left for college. He hugged everyone goodbye. I believed he hugged me extra hard and held me longer, before he drove off with his Mom and Dad. He'd be coming home for Thanksgiving and he promised he'd write often. When he did write (which wasn't too often) I treasured his letter. I wrote almost everyday. His excuse for not writing as often was the grueling schedule he was expected to maintain. He worked part-time to help with his college expenses.

Just before Thanksgiving, he wrote asking for his identification bracelet back. My ring was taped to his short note explaining he wanted to date other girls. He suggested that I should date boys in my class…as if I could or would want too. It didn't make much sense. If he wanted to be free of me, so be it. I took the ring from the letter and threw it in the pond.

Thereafter, when he came home for vacation, I made myself scarce. The first time, he found me alone in the living room he had the nerve to complain. "You just threw my bracelet in the envelope without as much as a note. You could have at least written something, letting me know how you felt about it."

"Why? Would it have made any difference? Just be thankful the post office delivered it intact," I scoffed and walked out. Later, while Bessie was playing the piano, and I was sitting on a hassock listening and reading, he came in and sat in the chair by me so it looked like I was sitting at his feet. I quickly got up and left the room. Holding back the tears, I stumbled on the stairs. I continued to avoid him and I missed him terribly when he left.

Living with three teachers, they made sure I was kept busy with school activities. Ours was a small school and to compete with other high schools in surrounding counties, many students doubled up on extracurricular activities. I was in band playing the clarinet; a baton twirler when in parades, I sang in chorus, and was a cheerleader for our basketball team. Ours was the smallest schools in the district but we had the best basketball team and won many championship trophies. Our marching band placed best in show a few times. No one had time for getting into serious trouble. Our teachers knew us all by name and we didn't dare to talk back. In our household, if we got a scolding in school for misbehaving, Mother's lecture at home was far worse.

Once Mrs. Parrish caught me chewing gum in her English class. She ordered me to put my gum on my nose for the rest of the period. So humiliated, I stared straight ahead so my tears wouldn't spill over. Yet, no one dared to laugh. They were too scared.

Mother must not have heard about it, she didn't mention the incident at home. But when I was called into the principal's office for detention, she came to find out why. I had twisted a girl's wrist to the point of breaking for taunting me. The girl thought it funny to do the Indian war cry, placing her hand over her mouth imitating the Indian war hoop every time she passed me in the hall, and called me Chief Wahoo. Mr. Williams, the school principal threatened to expell me. Mother talked with him briefly and I was allowed to leave with her. There were no further talks of expulsion and the girl stopped teasing me.

Another time Mother came to my defense was when a young teacher, Mr. Percy, came to board with us. Bessie, Dotty, and I were giggling over something we thought funny. Our silliness annoyed him. He looked at me with his steely blue eyes doubly enlarged behind his horned rim glasses, and spit flying between his big horsy yellow teeth.

"For your stupid behavior, I'm giving you a failing grade in your Social Studies assignment. You should be ashamed of yourself, acting so childish when you should be doing your homework. No wonder you're so far behind for your age."

Stunned, we stopped laughing. "It's not fair," I cried in protest.

The door to Mother's bedroom (off the dining room) flew open. She stood there staring at him. The three of us girls backed away fast. Bessie and Dotty hid in the kitchen. I sneaked upstairs, expecting a good scolding.

"See here! These girls meant no harm. Granted, they were noisy and I'll see to it that it doesn't happen again. But I do not want you reprimanding Dolores in any way concerning her schoolwork while in this house."

Two hours after the fallout, I was sitting at my dressing table in my

MY MOTHER'S SPIRIT

pajamas, winding my hair on rollers. I heard a timid knock on our bedroom door slightly ajar. Mr. Percy stuck his head in. Looking sheepish, saying he wanted to apologize.

"I'm sorry if I hurt you with my careless remark," he said. When I didn't reply, he continued, "I merely wanted to point out that you have such potential, if only you would apply yourself." I continued staring at him. After a second or two, he backed out saying, "Well! Good night then." He quietly closed the door behind him.

In class two days later, he handed us back our essays. He had given me an A+ with a note, "When do you do all this work? Midnight?"

I had discovered a long time ago the best time to do home work was early in the morning when everyone else was still sleeping. I could concentrate better. I'd start with cold showers until Mother told me to cut it out. The teachers complained that hearing water running at five robbed them of an hours sleep. So I'd run down to the bathroom off the kitchen and douse my face in cold water, just enough to get my juices going.

Spring term came to a close and it was summer vacation. Mother suggested that, if I liked, I could stay the summer and work for them taking care of their cabins. Dad Fletcher, looking for ways to bring in extra income, had built four small cabins on the back end of their lot facing the road. It was the only road (Route 3) through the scenic Adirondacks. I jumped at the offer. My Stanfield relatives had not invited me back for the summer. Best of all, Earl would be coming home.

LIVING AT FLETCHER'S BOARDING HOUSE
Settling In And Liking It Too

The Fletcher household ran smoothly with a steady hum of routine, plenty of good humor and courteous behavior. There was nothing lackadaisical about the way we did our chores. Mother liked me. When I scrubbed the kitchen floor on my hands and knees she said I did a very good job.

One day, Earl and his oldest brother, Don (was visiting for a few days) came in from someplace and saw me down on the floor scrubbing. They made an uncharitable remark about how ungraceful I looked with my rump up in the air and my head in the bucket. They cleared out fast enough when Mother came out to the kitchen.

"I wish I could get Bernie (the oldest Fletcher daughter no longer living at home) and Bessie to get into the corners and clean as well as Dolores does."

Earl and Don disappeared into the back hallway. I went ahead with my cleaning.

Lowering her tone, she said soothingly, "I wish I could get my own daughters to follow your example and be the worker you are."

At the end of our chores on Saturday afternoons, we showered and changed into our casual clothes for our more leisurely activities. Dad Fletcher had installed a shower stall in the back of the garage. The four of us (Earl, Bessie, Dotty and I) were expected to shower there, leaving the bathrooms in the house for the teachers.

That summer after the cabins were done, Earl always tried to figure a way to meet me after I showered in the community shower, even if it meant spreading a puzzle out on the dining room table, which I had to pass when I came in.

He confessed to me in a letter from college, "I liked getting a whiff of whatever talc or lotion you used. You stopped to help me out with just your robe on, before you went upstairs to get dressed. That too was enjoyable, wondering what you looked like without your robe. Mother didn't make an issue of it like Mr. Durham did. Remember that time when they were very disgusted with you (and me)? You came out wearing your robe and whatever else I couldn't see, and we met at the guardrails and sat there talking. Naturally, nothing else happened, but apparently they were prudish enough to think it was distasteful for you to be seeing me with just a bathrobe. Naturally, I liked it and probably did a lot of wondering, about what was under the bathrobe…"

He and I had a secret relationship, but almost everyone knew about it, so I guess it wasn't secret. Trying to be secretive, but knowing it wasn't. Especially, the time I went to visit my Stanfield relatives. He told me that for him it was a fun thing…trying to be secretive, but knowing it wasn't—how he couldn't wait to get my letter each day, and he knew others in the family knew what was going on. He admitted just how excited he was when I returned.

There were times we were able to get away. For some reason we got together for a walk one evening after dark. We kissed. It was a gentle kiss and it was the most intimate we ever got. I didn't know which was more important, to have a secret love or to care about someone, openly.

CLEANING CABINS

Mother assigned Earl to helping me clean the cabins or more specifically, make beds. We each had jobs to do but coordinated the bed making. He teased me when I said to him, "You make the *other side* and I'll make the *other side*..." We laughed. He said it always worked because he knew what I wanted, and he didn't mind getting in by the wall, while I had all the room out in the open. I secretly believed that it was a slip of the tongue, for what I really wanted—for us to be on the same side. We had good luck making beds, making it more fun than a chore.

One day, Earl said to his older sister, Bernie—who was home for a visit—that since he was into sports: soccer, basketball and baseball, it was imperative that he be in some aspect of physical condition. One of the things he had to do was jog. He thought that Bernie could keep up with him for four or five miles and challenged her to come along on his trip around Brown Falls Road and back home on the hill.

"Humph!" I jeered. "I can jog as well as either one of you." He suggested that I come along too... "To keep Bernie company," he added, insinuating that I couldn't keep up with him either.

The first half of the trip, I saw him looking back over his shoulder to make sure we were still coming. As time wore on, the distance between us widened, he didn't bother looking back anymore. Bernie and I were no longer in his sight (or very far back) he later told me. He kept moving on past Wards farm, along the flat prior to Oswegatchie onto Route 3 and through lower Oswegatchie. He said, afterwards, he checked over his shoulder a couple times and didn't see us. When he made it up the lower Oswegatchie hill and almost to the site of the school, and turned around—there I was, chugging along right behind him! He wanted to know how I managed to catch up to him.

"I got my second wind and ran faster just as you were pooping out." I maintained steadily to his doubting questions. He never did figure out how I gained on him.

Coming over the hill, I took a short cut through the Willard Maybe Farm, leaving Bernie far behind but nearly catching up to him. We never had a chance to run again, before he left for college. And I never owned up claiming all the time, the whole thing was fair and that I just decided to catch up.

MY MOTHER'S SPIRIT

I knew that in a few days, Earl would be returning to college, and I wished there was some way I could win him over again with out being to obvious about it. That first week in September, the weather cooperated. We all took advantage of the exceptionally hot afternoon. Earl drove Bessie, Dotty and me to the beach in Star Lake. As soon as we got there, Dotty and Bessie raced ahead, eager to get into the water. I took my time unfolding an old blanket and prepared a place for all of us to laze in the sun. I worried that I might be starting my period, so I decided to just sit and bask in the sparkling beauty of the lake. Hugging my knees, I gave into the quandary of my discontent. Earl dropped down and sat quietly, beside me. After a while, ever so gently, he leaned over and kissed my bare shoulder. I didn't moved nor did I break our silence. The sensation of his mouth brushing my shoulder gentled me.

All to soon, Dotty and Bessie had had enough and were ready to dry off. For the drive home, Dotty sat up front snuggled in her towel. Bessie, shivering, sat in back with me, and she wasn't in the mood for girl talk either. She was also, leaving for college in a week. Each of us had a lot to think about.

That fall, I involved myself with school activities, mostly focusing on chorus and band. Miss Hain started us out with a bang and had us practicing for a musical recital. My father came to hear me play and I sang my solo, "Pale Hands I Loved Beside the Shalimar." At the end of our performances, with the rest of the students, we rushed back to center stage to take our bows. I glimpsed over the audience in the darkened auditorium and spied Dad, sitting tall with a woman I had never seen before. My mind became a whirlwind of confusion mid all the excitement—my heartbeat raced to keep up. Then, there was Dad and this woman shuffling along with the audience on their way out the doors, we stepped aside, to let everyone pass. He introduced me to his lady-friend, but I wasn't paying attention and I can't remember what all was said. Before I knew it, Dad and his friend were gone, and I stood there alone. I hugged myself for warmth and shuffled back inside to help Miss Hain. We straightened out the music room. "Here," I said to Miss Hain, "let me help you. I'll stack these chairs on the other side, while you stack those chairs on the other side." Then I doubled over. I wanted to laugh and cry at the same time.

"What's so funny?" she asked. "Oh! Nothing," I replied. "I was just thinking of making beds with Earl. It was a private joke between us. I miss him."

"I know you do. He'll be home again, before you know it," she said. "By the way, I saw your father in the audience with his lady-friend. I'm so pleased he likes to come to our concerts. Who was she?"

"Darned, if I know," I replied. I almost said, "Who cares," but I didn't.

DAD'S NEW LADY FRIEND

The more I thought about the woman who sat beside him at our musical, the more curious I became. I called Dad that Saturday morning.

"Hey dad! What was your lady friend's name again? I forgot. And what ever happened to Jenny? I thought you had a thing going with her. I liked Jenny."

"Whoa! Slow down. What are you talking about? What about Jenny?"

"That summer before we left for our trip. I saw that look between you."

"Oh! That!" He gave that short laugh he used when he was uncertain about something and stalling. "I took her out a few times. She's a nice lady. But…too much baggage between us."

"What does that mean. You and her were moving in together?"

"It's an expression." I heard the hesitancy, then he continued. "You'll like Bess. Mrs. Wilcox. She's got a daughter your age…a year younger. Her name's Janis."

"Well!" I paused, not wanting to say more about it. I needed to ponder over this new development. "Anyway, I'll see you the next time I find a ride to church in Star Lake." And I hung up.

The second time I met Mrs. Wilcox was at our piano recital. It was bad enough that I was worried over the piece I had to play. *Tchaikovsky's Opening Theme* from Piano Concerto No. 1. I found it difficult despite having practiced for many months. I was nervous. Miss Hain kept telling me, "You'll be okay, don't worry." While waiting my turn, I peeked from behind the stage curtain and watched Dad sitting tall. Mrs. Wilcox looked confident and pleased to be with Dad. He looked eager, fidgety even. He had said, many times, he didn't care to be in close quarters. He only came to these recitals to please me.

I gave her a good going over. A good-looking woman, her dark hair attractively permed, modestly made up, and poised, she seemed pleasant enough. Although matronly, she looked younger than Dad. How long had he known her I wondered.

Suddenly, I heard my name announced. I turned quickly, stumbled and walked awkwardly towards the piano. I fumbled for the center of the piano bench. My heart pounding so loudly, I couldn't hear myself think. I sat looking at the keys and became aware of the audience. They were waiting for me to begin. "Oh God! I can't remember!" I thought. Just then, Miss Hain calmly walked on stage, placed the sheet music before me and faced the audience. She announced a coming event, inviting all to come. The audience clapped, which gave me time to get my act together. I struggled through my piece well enough to get by. Then, as I stood up, it felt as if someone had just given me a karate chop across my shoulder blade almost bringing me to my knees.

As the audience filed out, I made an appearance long enough to mumble a few words, " Thanks for coming."

Mrs. Wilcox chimed right in, saying how well I played and, in the same sentence, inviting me to come for dinner the following Sunday. "I'd like you to meet my daughter, Janis." For once, I felt as uncomfortable as Dad looked sometimes. To my great relief, they pressed on, saying they had to get going. I walked with them to his truck.

"Don't forget next Sunday," Dad said. "I'll come pick you up for church." I watched as Dad opened the door for his lady friend. He got in, gave a slight wave and drove off. Sullenly, I went back inside to walk home with Miss Hain.

At nine-thirty the following Sunday, Dad came to pick me up and dropped me off at the church. Afterwards, I walked to his boarding house. I followed him down a path to the lake. Mrs. Wilcox and her daughter, Janis, lived over a boathouse on Star Lake. I thought, how fun listening to the water lapping at your door below and sitting out on your balcony, overlooking the water.

Janis attended a Catholic Girls' Boarding School. She was smart as a whip, precocious and spontaneous, and she used big words. I could tell dad was impressed. I had assumed I held my own and was smart enough. But, with me, Dad never beamed nor seemed as amused and talkative as he did with Janis. She acted as confident and affectionate with him as if he were her dad.

Mrs. Wilcox asked me to call her Bessie.

"My best friend's name is Bessie, too. Bessie Fletcher. I consider her my foster sister, really. The Fletchers are my family now," I told Mrs. Wilcox.

" I hope, in time, you and Janis will become very good friends. She thinks the world of your dad."

"Yeah! I noticed."

We had spaghetti with meat sauce. Janis wound hers up in big forkfuls and talked freely all the time we were eating. I never saw anyone so rambunctious. Dad and Mrs. Wilcox watched approvingly, drinking beer and smoking. The more they drank, the louder the conversation became. Mrs. Wilcox talked as much as anyone. They coaxed Dad to sing. I'd never even heard him sing before. He did have a good tenor voice, just like Aunt Margaret had told me. He sang a ditty to the tune of "Lil' Brown Jug" in Mohawk. But it wasn't a translation of the words to the song. I knew what he sang. I said, "Dad! That's not nice." He laughed, obviously having a good time.

Mrs. Wilcox and Janis coaxed me to tell them what the words meant. "Come on! What did he just sing?" I hesitated. Then he sang, "If I had The Wings Of An Angel." How beautiful! I was speechless. I had no idea he could sing so well. We urged him to sing another. He sang "Danny Boy" and Mrs. Wilcox cried. Gee! I felt sad for her, too. I liked her from then on. I decided Janis wasn't all that bad either.

Mrs. Wilcox wiped her eyes, laughed, and apologized for being sentimental.

"That Bess," Dad said, teasing. "She cries over every little thing. Give her a dishcloth for a gift and she'll cry. Come on, babe! Let's get going."

"Thanks for inviting me. Bye, Bess and Janis," I hollered going out the door. We walked slowly up the path. "I think Bess is pretty nice," I told him.

THE RESERVATION REVISITED

Dad singing a risqué little ditty in Mohawk had made me homesick for Rita and Florence. It had been so long since I'd heard from them. After I left the reserve we wrote to one another often. Now their letters had dwindled to two or three a year—Christmas and around my birthday or maybe one in mid summer. I'd stopped promising I'd be coming for a visit, a long time ago.

I took Rita's last letter and tried translating her Mohawk words into English. As I struggled with it at the dining-room table, Mother sat with her knitting, listening.

"How long has it been since you've seen your Indian relatives?"

"Three years. Dad thinks I'm better off not ever going back."

"You must miss them very much."

"Yes I do, especially Rita and Florence too. If it weren't for Florence, he won't have gotten out of prison as early. He forgets that."

"It's not right." She sat knitting for a while. "I'll tell you what," she began slowly, "The next nice weekend, we should plan on going. You'll have time to write and tell them we are coming. And it's best if we keep it to ourselves."

I felt like jumping up and hugging her, I said, "Golly, that'd be super." All excited, I got out a clean sheet of paper and began writing to both Florence and Rita.

Two weeks later on a beautiful September morning, right after Saturday breakfast, Mother, Miss Lease and I took off for St. Regis. We went by way of South Colton, through Potsdam and Massena. In two and a half hours we were driving into the village. Gleefully, I directed Mother to Florence's house.

I was surprised at how the village had shrunken since I left. The houses seemed all scrunched together, like a pile of discarded empty cardboard boxes of all shapes at the local dump. In my mind's eye, at the point where our church stood and next door to Florence's house there was a good distance to Rita's house. The closed up little lots had seemed like open fields back when I lived here. They were the same old houses, but shabbier, and most of them were still unpainted. The grand yellow house with the brown trim where Tota and I had lived was now almost as small as the others, and badly in need of repairs and paint as well. The tall evergreen tree next to our house where Tota told me the owl lived was now a short stumpy tree with most of its branches broken off.

Florence was expecting us and had even baked an apple pie. I met the two surprises she had mentioned in her letters. Her two sons, Roger and Wayne, ages two and three, played on the floor. A warm day, the living room door was wide open and all the flies were enjoying the indoors. I ran and hugged Florence for dear life. She smiled slightly, dismissing me quickly to invite Mother and Miss Lease in, asking them to sit down.

I introduced everyone gushing with excitement, I rattled on talking non-stop. And that's when Allisway strode in.

The town gadabout, he had seen that Florence had company. Curious about a strange car parked out front, he didn't hesitate to come check us out. A self-important middle-aged man, he walked tall and erect as if he meant business in his second hand rumpled old brown wool suit. Allisway never knocked. Everyone in the village knew him. He lived with his Mother and never worked but would perform a service or a chore for a meal. He grabbed the fly swatter and went to work swatting flies. The floor was soon littered with them.

Florence kept a neat enough house but she always had a problem with flies. Mother sat comfortably on the couch admiring the two brown faced little boys. Miss Lease, for once, was speechless. She watched Allisway from the corner of her eye with that inquisitive expression of hers—almost a sneer.

I had lots to tell Florence after three years. We spoke English for the benefit of the two women.

After a while, Florence said, "I knew you were coming so I baked a pie." She asked us to come into the kitchen for a piece.

Miss Lease flew out of her chair. "No!" she sputtered. "I couldn't." Mother declined gracefully, saying we had other places to visit.

"We're going to see Rita," I blurted. "How is she?"

"She's expecting you."

I relaxed knowing that at least, Rita wouldn't be entertaining customers. I had written, joking that the Fletchers were "Hook and Eye" Baptists, didn't believe in alcohol. I hugged Florence, promising to write and kissed the two little boys busily playing on the floor.

As Miss Lease hurried to the door she asked about the Catholic Church across the street.

"Why don't you take them in and show them the inside," Florence said.

Mother replied that she'd rather look at the beautiful scenery outside. She walked along the church grounds overlooking the beautiful St. Lawrence River. The clean cool breezes from the river did seem refreshing after watching the demise of so many flies while cooped up inside.

"To me," I said to Miss Lease, as I heaved open the heavy wooden door of the church, "once you've seen one, you've seen them all."

All churches in Quebec were alike, except ours was smaller, much older, shabbier, and the windows and doorframes were in need of paint. Our humble little mission church was over two hundred years old, built of stones gathered by the men, women and children from the village. It had the typical swooping silver metal roof, and the simple white wooden cross at the tip of the spire. The inside made our church unique. The ornately carved alter, graceful archways, and the square solid stairway up to the choir loft and two side balconies added dimension. (I remembered the many times I had run up and down those old stairs, late for choir practice.) Miss Lease pointed to the metal brackets holding the kerosene lamps.

"That's right! They don't even have electricity, do they?" she whispered.

I took a deep breath of the old familiar scents of old wood, incense, and burning candles. A wave of sadness engulfed me. I saw the beauty, the simplicity of our humble little old church. Just like an old lady, aging but still full of grace. I remembered my Tota. I lit a candle for her and whispered a Hail Mary. I felt grateful for my faith in the Catholic Church.

We joined Mother, got back into the car, and slowly followed the dirt road circling the village following the two rivers. I pointed out Jo-ba-num's fish house and felt sad we didn't have time to stop. We passed Aunt Helen's old house. Just Uncle Pete lived there now. Aunt Helen had moved and now ran a boarding house in Syracuse.

Rita sat on the front stoop waiting for us. I grabbed Rita by the middle and kissed her cheek. She laughed, speaking in Mohawk, invited us in. She believed in closing up a house with the shades down to keep the house cooler during warm weather. As soon as she opened the door—whew! I got a strong whiff of cat pee. I tried not to notice.

I understood every word Rita said and I tried replying, mispronouncing many words. Her laughter sounded lyrical, like music to my ears. I can find no words to describe it. She smiled as I introduced her to Mother and Miss Lease. From the time she entered, Miss Lease's nose flared as if she couldn't breathe, and her nose stayed flattened through out the visit. She remained standing by the door not saying a word. Mother sat on the edge of a chair by the kitchen table and asked the usual questions; the climate; how many lived here, and inquired about the school. Rita answered softly without detail.

Rita's house was clean as always with the same colorful oilcloth on the table and the linoleum floor highly waxed. But Rita must have gotten used to the cat odor; they were all over; I quickly counted seven. Just then, I spied old Jake Betters coming to the door. Rita hurried over and quietly spoke a few words to him.

He looked puzzled, "No?" he asked. He shook his head sadly and slowly turned and walked away. I was relieved the two women didn't understand our language.

Mother stood up and I took it as a signal it was time to leave. I suspected, Miss Lease had need of a restroom or maybe just to fill her lungs with pure oxygen. She did look greenish. Not wishing to show her to the outhouse, I agreed. We said our goodbyes.

Rita wasn't into hugging. She had her arms wrapped around her. I leaned to her and kissed her on the cheek as she followed us to the car. "Oona, I'll be back," I said in Mohawk. She stood there smiling as we drove away.

On the way home, Miss Lease, having gotten over her culture shock, started in. "I've always wanted to see what life was like on an Indian Reservation. Tsk, tsk…how sad."

I didn't bother answering. Everyone I knew, who wasn't Indian, always said the same thing.

Mother said Florence and Rita were kind and obviously cared a great deal for me.

"Yes, I know, and someday, I'm coming back here for good." And I meant it.

GETTING MY SHOW ON THE ROAD
My mother's spirit must have gone on a sabbatical.

Seventeen and a junior, I pranced around like a pony at the county fair. Involved in just about every school activity, and I thought I was hot stuff. Then, one evening after the supper dishes were done and the table cleared we prepared for a game of cards—Queen of Hearts, my favorite game. Mother read a part of Earl's letter to us. He wrote that he'd be coming home from college for Thanksgiving weekend and bringing a girl friend. Mother's words, like a heavy lead ball at the pit of my stomach, sunk me to the depths of wanting to drop out of everything. But stoically, I played as usual. When Mother passed me the queen of spades, I pushed my cards away and ran from the table crying, thinking, how could she do that to me. Mother, Miss Lease, Dot, and Bessie, sat looking dumfounded.

"Now! What bought that on?" Miss Leased asked looking down at her cards. Unconcerned, they went on without me. I buried my head in my pillow until I shook off that feeling of despair and was able to go on as if nothing bothered me.

When Mrs. Wilcox called and asked me to come for Thanksgiving dinner, I sucked up her invitation with my undying gratitude. At least I'd be out of the house for one day, and maybe I could manage to stretch it to a weekend. I didn't want to see Earl with a sparkling college twit and every one making a big fuss.

Maybe I could convince Dad to let me stay with him. He now had a room over Bill O'Neil's Bar & Grill. He had had to move out of Myra Smith's boarding house. A month ago, in the middle of the night, a car came too fast around the bend in front of the house and plowed into her living room. Dad was thrown out of his bed. No one was hurt but her house was demolished. Dad had to find lodgings elsewhere. He and Bill were good friends. Twice now, after church, I had walked to Dad's place for a ride home and had found him with Mrs. Wilcox in the bar, having a drink with friends. I worried, but it wasn't my place to say anything.

Gossip about Dad and his lady friend had already circulated at my school. Miss Lease stopped a rumor cold, when she emphatically told someone's

MY MOTHER'S SPIRIT

mother at a PTA meeting that he was not living with Mrs. Wilcox. She said that she knew, for a fact, that my father had a room at a boarding house. I felt grateful to her for sticking up for me, but I suspected he kept the room mainly for my sake.

I surprised Dad the next time, coming from church, I walked into Bill's bar, asking him for a ride home. "Look, Dad! If you think you're doing me a favor by keeping a room for appearances sake, forget it. Everyone's talking about it anyway—so move in with her and save yourself some money."

"You think so?" He sat at the bar, grinning, not paying attention. I'd wised up to the fact that he wasn't interested in anything I had to say since our trip to the city. "I'll give it some thought." He swallowed his beer and pushed his glass away. "Let's go, babe."

On the way home, "How's school?" he asked.

"I'm passing." I figured that's all he cared to hear anyway and I was right. He didn't say any more till he turned into Fletcher's driveway. "What time do you want me to pick you up Thursday?"

"The earlier the better," I snarled. I made no pretense of offering the customary peck on the cheek. I slid out, and slammed the car door.

Thanksgiving morning, I thought, better to compete with Janis for Dad's affection than watch Earl and his girl making goo-goo eyes at each other. Thank God, Dad came for me early, as I had asked. I delayed in coming home till late in the evening, avoiding the members of the household as much as possible. If I could have managed it, I would have worn blinders like a horse. It helped that Miss Lease and Miss Hain, living far enough away, that they didn't go home for Thanksgiving. I busied myself helping Miss Hain reorganize her room. I didn't give Earl a chance to introduce me to his girlfriend. By Monday, thank God, everyone was back to a normal routine.

Christmas was less hectic. Earl didn't come home. I concentrated on my studies.

That spring, a boy in my science class started following me around. He had a habit of standing next to me, sharing the same lab equipment. Everywhere I went, there he was. A senior, Ken had one of the leading parts in the senior play. The school band sat just below the stage, musical instruments on our laps, ready to play between acts. With my clarinet standing upright on my knee, I happened to look up and noticed how green Ken's eyes were. The bright stage floodlights enhanced his well-defined eyebrows, long lashes, and sandy reddish hair combed neatly in a wave. Rather pale, not at all athletic, gaunt and about my height, he was the neatest, best-dressed boy in high school. His socks always matched his sweater. He wore freshly ironed white shirts, neatly pressed trousers and his oxblood loafers were highly polished. He came on the Newton Falls bus but, I didn't pay much attention until he asked me for a date.

First, I asked Mother and she had to ask her friend, Mrs. Parrish our English teacher, who lived next door.

" I suppose, mebbe. Ken's all right, kinda quiet though."

She was the only English teacher I knew who said mebbe for maybe or perhaps. Mother gave me her permission with the understanding that I wouldn't go anywhere where liquor was served and I had to be home by ten-thirty.

We made a date for Saturday night, April 1st, to go to a movie in Tupper Lake, thirty-five miles away. We'd be double dating with Rob and Julie, both juniors. Rob had a driver's license and his parents allowed him to drive the family car. They'd pick me up at six.

I sat at the dining room table in my Sunday best, waiting. Six o'clock came and went.

"I'm afraid your date has played an April fool joke on you. I don't think he's coming. It's quarter after seven." Mother sympathized.

I was about to go upstairs and change when I heard Rob's car racing up the driveway. Ken explained that he had a paper route and it had taken him longer than usual to deliver his papers. Then, Rob hadn't been able to get the car right away. We still had to pick up Julie in Fine, ten miles away. By now, it was too late to make it to Tupper Lake and be home by ten thirty.

"We can always go to the dance at Merchants in Cranberry Lake. They're having a band tonight," Rob suggested.

"I'm not allowed to go there. They have a bar."

"Oh Cripes!" Rob complained, "I suppose we can't go to the Blue Bird and jitterbug to the juke box, either?"

"Guess not," I replied, ruefully. The Blue Bird was the local bar where all the seniors hung out. Star Lake sported seven bar rooms. Oswegatchie, a dry town, had none.

We parked on a side road and necked. Ken spoke in a low, slow monotone. I had to listen carefully or I couldn't understand a word he said. Much later, his monotone voice would become monotonous. Sadly, I didn't realize that until too late.

I SHOULD HAVE LISTENED TO MY TEACHERS

I should have listened to Coach Green that night coming home from a basketball game. I sat up front with him. Our little old bus, The Blue Goose, chugged along carrying a busload of happy players and cheerleaders. Our team had just defeated Harrisville High. Some of the cheerleaders and players were necking in the back. Coach Green, our chaperone, paid no attention. Since I was now going steady with Ken, it won't do for me to sit with other guys.

"Naw! You don't want to go steady with Ken," said, coach Green.

"Why not?"

"He's always in the bar room. It's the first place he hits as soon as he gets out of work." Coach Green lived at the Newton Falls Hotel. The hotel's barroom was a favorite mill worker's hang out.

"There's not that much to do around here," I replied. "All the guys drink. But Ken doesn't when he's out with me."

A year ahead of me, Ken had already graduated and chose to work at the Newton Falls paper Mill.

Coach Greene shook his head, and leaned forward to talk with Mr. Golden, our bus driver. Staring out the window, darkly, I pushed Mr. Greene's advice aside. A boyfriend, sure of having a date for school dances felt good. I seriously doubted other guys would want to date me anyway. I thought myself lucky to have someone who cared enough to want to go steady. Sooner or later, wasn't every woman expected to marry and raise a family? Why should I be any different? Might as well get my show on the road...the sooner the better.

Double dating with Rob and Julie, Rob whined, "I can't see why you won't go into the Blue Bird. Cripes! Ma Chapple ain't going to allow any underage drinking. She keeps a pretty good watch. What's the big deal anyway? You and Ken are both eighteen."

"Sorry! It would be the just same if I were twenty. Mother would hear about it and I'd be out on my ear."

Then, Rob would make a farting noise with his mouth, laugh his silly little laugh, and he'd wheel us down another back road. I could have mapped out all the back roads in St. Lawrence County if Rand McNally had only asked.

DOLORES EOSTENUNI STANFIELD

All my life I'd been lucky with hand-me-downs. For formal dances I attended throughout my high school years, Mother's oldest daughter, Bernie, and her daughter-in-law, Chris (Don's wife) gave me beautiful evening gowns they had tired of, thus, saving Dad and me a big expense.

Our senior class held a pre-Christmas formal dance. Mother said I looked lovely dressed in the white strapless gown Bernie had given me, and suggested that I invite Ken, Rob, and Julie over for a snack after the dance?"

"Gollly, thanks! I will." I had my doubts they'd accept, knowing Rob would have some smart remark and Ken wouldn't say one way or the other—he let Rob call the shots, since we rode around in his car. To my surprise, they said yes.

After the dance, we trooped in and the three of them sat around the kitchen table while I made peanut butter, banana, and onions, with mayonnaise sandwiches and served them some punch. We sat talking, trying to keep our voices down and snickering, and snorting at Rob making faces. His blue suit rumpled, he'd yanked his tie off, and rolled his eyes, gagging, pretending to get the peanut butter unstuck from the roof of his mouth. As always, Julie sat quietly in her pink gown, smiling at him. Ken, impeccably dressed in a charcoal gray suit with a red plaid vest and bright red bow tie, dutifully and doggedly, ate his sandwich. I gazed at the perfectly combed strawberry blond wave to his hair. Then, going down on his knees in front of me, he stammered a poem he said he'd written...half plagiarized: "She walks in beauty like the night. Let me count the ways..." He reached into his breast pocket and whipped out and engagement ring.

"Will you marry me?"

My mouth flew open. "Ken! We haven't even talked about it. You're not a Catholic."

He mumbled, "But I will be soon, I've been taking instruction."

Rob, the clown, saved the evening. "Cripes, Price! You gonna give her a diamond for making a lousy peanut butter, mayonnaise and onion sandwich?"

We all laughed...a big joke. I handed him back his ring.

Shortly after, Rob cleared his throat. "Time to go...Brrrp!" He and Julie skipped out.

Ken stood looking at me. I stared, thinking, he had the nicest green hazel eyes. I stepped up kissing his full mouth. He didn't kiss back, instead reached for the door. I closed it behind him and heard the car rev up. I cleared the table feeling deserted and lonely.

MY MOTHER'S SPIRIT

Ken and his friend, Joe, hitchhiked to Carthage, forty-five miles away in below zero weather, and bought me a heavy pink satin dress for Christmas. Ken took catechism classes, and became a Catholic. In March, he offered me the diamond for my birthday and I accepted it.

When not out on a date, I had just as good a time at home with the Fletchers. Almost every evening after supper when the dishes were washed and our homework done, we played our favorite card game, Queen of Hearts. We made popcorn and Mother made her famous penuche candy. Even Mr. Percy joined in from time to time.

Mr. Percy taught social studies but tended to veer from it by introducing his favorite subject, anthropology. He continued with his suggestions that I apply myself more to my studies.

He did such a thorough job teaching us all about prehistoric man, when I took the course in college, I aced it—I owed it all to him. Short and scrawny, Mr. Percy was fresh out of college. He wore horned rimmed glasses, and spit flew when he talked. Hailing from New Jersey, he found our small rural eight-room high school not challenging enough, the students not motivated, and our little hamlet too dull. He left in mid-term—went home for Christmas vacation and never returned.

His replacement, Mr. Bero, made our history classes so interesting; we were glued to his every word. Humorous, and relaxed, he sat on the edge of his desk, and swinging one leg over the edge, his dark eyes dancing mischievously. He, obviously, felt pleased captivating his students. When he told about Lt. Col. George Armstrong Custer's defeat at the battle of Little Bighorn on June 25th, 1876, by the Plains Warriors (the Sioux and the Cheyenne), and how they massacred his 7th Cavalry, I cheered. "Yeah!" He grinned and winked at me. Listening to him tell about history was like viewing a video. I felt as if I were galloping on horseback along vith the victorious warriors. Mr. Bero looked a lot like the Bero's from my reserve, easygoing and unpretentious. I even heard the rumor he was Indian. I raised my hand.

"Mr. Bero! Are you by any chance related to the Bero's from St.Regis?"
"No," he replied, "No connection."
"Oh!" I felt disappointed.

I enjoyed his classes so much. He encouraged me to take the State Regents at the end of my junior year and I scored a ninety-eight.

He suggested, "Why not enroll at St. Lawrence University majoring in history? You'd make a good history teacher."

DOLORES EOSTENUNI STANFIELD

St. Lawrence University, a prestigious school with a very pretty campus in Canton was only thirty-five miles away. I mentioned it to Mother a few days later.

"Don't be silly. Your father couldn't afford to send you to such an expensive school. Why don't you apply to the State Agricultural and Technical Institute next door to the university? It has a good two-year Diet Technician program. The County Home Bureau offers a small scholarship based on need and ability. You'd certainly qualify."

"Hey! Not bad!" I joked. "A hospital dietetic technician. Two of my friends are going to ATI. Julie's going in for nursing and Elsa's going to be a hospital lab technician. We'll be like the three musketeers." I applied to Canton ATI.

Our senior class looked forward to our class trip during Easter vacation. For the first time in our history of fund raising, two big corporations hosted our trip: MacGraw Hill Publishing in New York City and the Chilton Company based in Philadelphia, half-owners of The Newton Falls Paper Mill. Our class of twenty-two seniors, with Mrs. Parrish and Mr. Bero as our chaperones, traveled in our faithful old Blue Goose, driven by Coach Green. After being feted and given the key to the city of Philadelphia, touring and sightseeing for three days, we went on to New York City. To my great surprise, Ken was at our hotel waiting.

Mrs. Parrish knew about it and gave me permission to take off with him and his friend, Joe from the Bronx, busboys from their summers at the Star Lake Inn. I thought it marvelous wedged between Joe and Ken holding hands seeing the sights of New York City. Then Ken got jealous.

Joe sensed it and backed away. Ken and I ended up on our own. Eventually, we found our way back to the hotel while the class whooped it up as guests of MacGraw Hill. When The Blue Goose pulled out, Ken was allowed to ride home with us.

I graduated that June, third highest in my class and received the award for having the highest average for the four years in social studies. Aunt Margie and my cousins, Joan and Mally, came to my graduation. I felt extra proud, walking on stage for the special award because they were there.

My last summer, I needed a job to earn more money for clothes and textbooks for college. Mrs. Ritz, my Catholic connection and a friend of Mother's, suggested I get a job as chambermaid at the Star Lake Inn. As head housekeeper, she put in a good word for me with the owner, Chuck Sayles.

Mr. Sayles hired mostly college students from all over the state. It was a

MY MOTHER'S SPIRIT

fun place to work with plenty of time off for swimming, boating and hiking in the beautiful woods. He provided a bunkhouse for the boys and one for the girls, and all of us ate in the staff's mess hall.

Marjorie Juruskic, an older college girl, took me under her wing. She tried hard to convince me I hadn't lived enough to tie me self down.

"I know Ken," she warned. "I worked with him last year. You don't want to be engaged. Wait until you get in college. There'll be so many guys to choose from."

"It's too late. I've been going with him for a year and a half. I'm lucky to have a boyfriend. You know the old saying: A bird in hand is better'n two in the bush."

"Oh! Please, spare me your tired clichés!" she drawled, threw up her hands up and walked away.

Ken had worked as busboy for three years, knew most of the older workers, and visited often. We walked around the lake, went canoeing, took bike rides and he attended weenie roast for the staff with me. I continued staying out of bar rooms.

Babs Bassette and I were bunkmates and friends from high school, and neither of us drank. We were often by ourselves when others went to beer bashes.

" Babs! Did you ever take a drink?"

"Gosh! No!"

"Want to try it? I've got a few dollars. We can stay all by ourselves and no one would ever know."

Bab's blue eyes sparkled. "Yeah! Let's! I've got some money too. We can ask one of the Ranger School guys to buy us a bottle of liquor."

The guy took our seven dollars, bought a pint of the cheapest whiskey and pocketed a couple of bucks, although we didn't know that until many days later.

We vowed to be discreet, and waited until the older girls went out partying. Then we locked our door and mixed our drinks with ginger ale.

"I'll be the bartender, since I use to be in the business," I said with bravado, I planned on making her drinks stronger so I could observe better. "Shh!" I hushed, reminding her to keep it low, when she couldn't stop giggling.

We got louder and louder after two or three or maybe four drinks, and we staggered out side, yelling, "Hey!"

We called out, waving wildly until we fell and couldn't get back up from laughing so hard. My legs felt like rubber.

"Blabs! You're spelling your drink on my blue dwess."

"We're loosh and franncy fee," she sang out.

"Blabs! You're talking funny." I giggled and couldn't stop.

Margie came home in time to drag me back inside. Then I threw up.

"I'll take care of her." She told the other girls and held my head as I heaved and heaved, thinking I was surely going to die. Margie managed to get me into bed. My head felt like it belonged to someone else. "Oh My God!" I moaned. I felt even worse the next morning. Every joint in my body ached.

Babs and I, sick as we were, managed to go to breakfast. We were the last to stumble into the mess hall. "Yeaah!" All the workers sang out in unison. They greeted us with cheers and jeers and we were the butt of many jokes. Then someone said, "Hey! Mrs. Ritz wants to see you."

"Oh, my God, I'm a goner for sure," I groaned.

Plump, motherly Mrs. Ritz sat at her sewing machine with a sympathetic angelic smile, her eyes downcast, saddened and told me she heard what went on last night. I stood looking down, humbled before her.

"You don't look so good," she said.

"I think I'm going to die," I moaned, and looked for the nearest chair. There wasn't any. My head felt like a ton. "Are you going to tell Mother?"

"I think you are suffering enough and have learned your lesson. If you promise not to do anything like this again while you're working here, I won't tell Alice."

I managed a weak thank you, and stumbled out.

I had many beds to make and I felt like death. As always, some of the guests were very demanding and not a one of them ever bothered to clean their own dirty ring around their bathtub after bathing. Not to clean up the bathroom after use had to be the laziest habit I had ever seen. I scrubbed the greasy grime off while on my knees, thankful the day was coming to an end. I could rest my aching head and weary body. Then, I was ordered to clean the women's restroom off the lobby. An elderly resident had diarrhea and had sprayed all over the toilet seat and floor. The stink was suffocating. I had to get on my hands and knees to clean it up. I vowed, never again if only I lived.

Surprisingly, during that summer I saw very little of Dad, except when I walked to Bess Wilcox's house eager to tell him how much I had saved and that he wouldn't have to give me any money for clothes. I took pride in sparing him extra expense and wanted so much to please him.

I received my acceptance letter from ATI. Mother and Miss Lease

MY MOTHER'S SPIRIT

accompanied me to Canton to an open house for the incoming students. I'd be staying at a girls' dorm. I picked out my room and met our house mother.

I signed up to work as a mother's helper to a professor's family five days a week, helping out with dinner preparations and cleaning up the kitchen. For my services, I received a free meal. I washed dishes in the cafeteria for the rest of my meals.

Freshman wore a black beanie and we were expected to bow to the upper classmen, carry their books when they asked, and we had to have a pack of cigarettes ready to hand them one if they asked. I discovered Wings was the cheapest brand until "meanies," mainly senior girls, demanded I carry Camels. I enjoyed the camaraderie of the girls at the dorm, however, and being initiated into the Pi Nu Epsilon sorority. I tended to be absent-minded and forgetful, always in a rush and stressed, trying to get to one place or another on time and leaving something or other behind and not having time to go back for it. It got to be too much for me. Indian time was unheard of. With white folks, time was of the essence. Trying to comply with that mentality nearly did me in.

We were required to wear hairnets, white cotton uniforms and white oxfords to all our cooking classes. Miss Virkler, tall and stern, with thinning bronzed hair and an aged scrawny neck, was the cooking instructor. She walked around in her white lab coat carrying her clipboard and pencil. One day, she looked down her nose, her gaze stopping at my feet. "Miss Stanfield, you have a spot of dirt on your shoe."

I couldn't believe she said it. Now! I've helped Tota clean and cook muskrat. I've watched Aunt Helen wring the necks of a chickens and I've helped her pluck and singe their tail feathers off. I've scaled and gutted fish in order to eat to survive. *And this woman is complaining about a spot on my shoe?*

"Huh?" I looked at her in disbelief. She epitomized the joke why white people were so stupid: "Half baked... that's why they're so pale...their brains are only half done." We used to laugh about such people.

"Please make sure you come to class with clean shoes from now on." She put a check mark by my name on her clipboard.

The next time she came around, we were mixing shortening and flour for pie crust. She had instructed, "Use two knives to cut the shortening into the flour until it's all the size of tiny peas."

I found it much easier to mash the whole mess with my hand, as I had watched other good cooks do to make terrific pie crust.

"Really! Miss Stanfield, why not use your feet, too?" She had that smug smirk on her face as she walked by.

"Don't pay any attention," Lorna Stein (my roommate) whispered. "She's jealous because you've got a big diamond on your finger and she's just an old maid."

Ken expected me to spend Thanksgiving weekend with his folks. He lived at home with his parents and two younger sisters. I'd ride home with a fellow student only to find Ken at the hotel drinking while waiting for me. His mother would apologize, explaining that once we were married, she was sure he wouldn't drink as much. The next day, with Ken being very attentive, we talked about getting married during Christmas vacation. I thought it would be a great relief not having to wash dishes at the cafeteria nor having to do housework for others. I could concentrate on my studies. I'd have more time for my sorority activities. It all sounded rosy.

I made my big announcement to the girls at the dorm that Sunday afternoon and relished being the center of attention. I couldn't wait to tell the Fletcher's and my dad.

BREAKING THE NEWS

The hardest thing I had to do that week was to concentrate on my studies and writing essays. Lorna called it busy work—professors assigning volumes of reading just to keep students busy in the libraries and giving them less time to hangout in pubs. The Fletchers were expecting me home for the weekend. Friday afternoon after my last class, Mother and Miss Lease came to pick me up. I wondered when would be a good time to make my big announcement.

"You must have something on your mind," Mother said, when she found the salt and pepper shakers in the fridge. She smiled and shook her head. I'd always done goofy things while daydreaming about something else. She told me many times, "You'd be a very good worker if only you could keep your mind on what you're doing."

After the supper dishes were done, we all returned to the dining room table. I sat listening to Mother click-clacking her knitting needles, making a sweater. I wished I could come out with something funny to get everyone in a more relaxed and jovial mood. Miss Lease began correcting papers, and Miss Button busied herself with her crochet hook tatting little white squares. She had the habit of scrutinizing me, looking over the glasses sitting on her nose. Instead of bubbling out with my happy news, I felt like hanging black crepe. "Hmmm! Well!" I toyed with the ball of white yarn.

I watched Miss Button for a while, thinking how I'd bring up the subject of my wedding plans. "What are you making?"

"I'm making a bedspread. After I make the blocks, I'll crochet them all together into one big square."

"I bet it will be very pretty."

"If you like, I'll make you one for a graduation present and you can put it in your hope chest."

I squirmed, thinking they acted as if they were expecting me to make an announcement so I might as well come out with it. I blurted, "I'd love to have one for a wedding present. Ken and I are getting married this Christmas." Wow! The silence was deadening.

Mother put her knitting down and looked at me for a few moments, not saying anything. Miss Lease finally said, "Mmmhmm! I knew it." The way she said it, it seemed as if they had taken bets on my getting married before

I finished my schooling.

Miss Button kept on crocheting and Miss Lease went back to her paper work. Then silence…I felt at a loss for words. Finally, Mother said, "If you waited at least until summer, we could have a nice wedding reception on the front lawn." I didn't answer. I kept staring at Miss Button's tatting.

Nothing more was said for the rest of the evening until I got up and said, "Good night."

The next morning, Miss Lease came skip-hopping down the stairs as she always did, and saw me sitting at the dining room table doing my homework. She watched me while standing warming herself. "What about school?"

"What about it? I plan on continuing. We're going to live with Ken's folks until I finish, coming home on weekends is all."

She stood there with her arms crossed in front of her, as if giving a speech. "You girls are all alike. You just can't wait to get married. You're all so anxious to find out what it feels like, to sleep with a man. You make me disgusted. After all we've done for you. You just wait. He's going to drag you through the mud. You'll live to regret it and don't say we didn't warn you."

I stared with my mouth open. I felt crushed, not knowing how to respond. After a while I walked into the living room and cried my eyes out. She and I avoided one another from then on.

I decided the best time to tell dad my big news would be Sunday morning when he came to pick me up for church. After dinner, he and Bess Wilcox were planning on driving me back to Canton. On the way to church, I said, "Dad! Ken and I have decided to get married this Christmas."

"Jeeze," he cursed, and almost drove us into the ditch. We rode the rest of the way in silence. I waited for some kind of a response and prepared to defend my decision. But he didn't ask. It was Bess who regaled me with lists of concerns as soon as I walked into her house.

"It doesn't give us much time to get ready for any kind of a reception or where to hold it, who or how many we should invite."

"Mother said she'd give me a small reception. I don't care anything about a big wedding and inviting a whole bunch of people."

"I wish you wouldn't get married until you at least finish school. But if that's your decision, I guess you're old enough to know what you want. I'd be willing to go to Watertown with you to help you shop for a wedding dress and a new suit for your going away trip."

"I'd like that very much." I took her up on her offer and was glad I did so, too. Dad went with us and paid for everything. I enjoyed his involvement and

MY MOTHER'S SPIRIT

told him so.

Even Aunt Helen, whom I hadn't heard from in four years, wrote saying if I were in trouble I didn't have to get married. She'd send me bus fare and she knew of someone who'd take care of it so I could continue with school. I fired back with a terse letter saying I didn't need her help. Just because she got pregnant while still at the convent, that didn't mean that I had to get married.

Jeanne Daniels, a friend in high school who was also planning on getting married, wised me up. "You know the whole town will be counting the months from the time the baby is born, don't you?"

It had surprised me, getting so little resistance from Mother and others. Now I knew why. I decided that three days after Christmas was as good a day as any for getting married. Mother and I made plans for a small reception: a turkey salad, homemade rolls, relishes, tea and coffee. She'd even make the wedding cake.

Father Desnoyer, the young priest who gave Ken his religious instructions, joked during the wedding rehearsal. "Since the church is already decked out for Christmas, we won't have to worry about decorations." Still joking, he gave us this spiel about the wife being submissive to her husband according to the Bible.

"No way! Not in this day and time. Ken had better toe the mark or I'll divorce him." Father looked surprised and became somber.

Bess helped me select my white gown and a smart green tweed suit for our wedding trip. She suggested that Janis, being a Catholic, should be my maid of honor. Jan spent the night before the wedding with me to help me get ready.

Earl came home for the holidays. I heard him complaining to Mother in the kitchen about her using up the leftover turkey for the salad. Even though he kept out of sight, I sensed his whereabouts. Heartsick, not daring to go to him, I put on a happy face. My last night with a family I had come to love as my own was dreadful. I spent the long sleepless night knowing Earl slept in the very next room. I spent hours entertaining the thought of going to him. I would have had to go down the stairs, past Mother and Dad Fletcher's bedroom, through the kitchen to the back hallway and up the stairs to his room.

The fear of incurring someone's wrath, I knew not whom exactly, and the embarrassment it would cause, kept me from making the foolhardy journey. Morning finally dawned and I dressed for the ten o'clock nuptial Mass.

My father, although nervous, took the short walk up the aisle with me hanging on to his arm. Ken and his best man, a fellow employee, Dan, were waiting. (Rob, not being a Catholic and now in the Air Force, was unable to be Ken's best man). Ester Hynes, wife of the president of the paper mill was also the church organist. She and her brother-in-law Francis Hynes sang. After the simple ceremony, three full cars headed for Oswegatchie. The sixteen guests--my Dad and Bess, Ken's family, the Fletchers (except Earl) and three of my girl friends, Jan, Jeanne, and Julie -- were relaxed and had a good time.

"Julie! Where's Rob?" someone asked.

"He and Herb Snyder enlisted in the army," she replied quietly."

"Our boys shouldn't have to go to Korea fighting those damn commies," Ken's father spoke up. "We got no business over there."

Secretly, I missed Rob's antics. He probably would have livened up the party, with his, "Cripes, I've had more fun at a funeral," rolling his eyes and tee-heeing. I went through the typical motions of a happy young bride. Everything went according to plan. Mrs. Hynes kept the party humming, telling stories until Ken and I were ready to leave for our four-day wedding trip. Francis drove us in the company van to Tupper Lake for the train to New York City. After my simple wedding, Ester Hynes commented to a mutual friend how pitiful the whole affair seemed to her. "Someone should have taken that girl and helped her with more elaborate plans. Even the wedding cake was plain."

To have had a more elaborate wedding would have been too presumptuous. Mother did a beautiful job with my three-tiered white wedding cake decorated with tiny green leaves and red roses. A simple wedding for someone from a humble background like mine—I wouldn't have had it any other way.

We were in New York City for our honeymoon, celebrating the New Year, 1951. In Times Square with all the revelers, Ken came alive with excitement for partying in the late night hours. As an early morning person, by ten o'clock at night I'd be dead tired, looking for a bed to crawl into for much needed sleep. The only other person to attest to my virginity was the nameless chambermaid who cleaned up the confetti off the floor and made up our room.

Ken's parents were at the train station to pick us up. My new home would be with them until I finished my two-year program. That following Monday morning, Dad drove me back to Canton in the worst snowstorm of the winter to begin the spring semester. We made it through snowdrifts and blinding snow swirls. His knuckles were white from gripping the steering wheel.

MY MOTHER'S SPIRIT

"Jeeze!" he cursed, "I hope we don't have to drive through this again." He got his wish. I quit school that April just weeks before the final days of classes. I couldn't take the hassle of finding a ride back to Canton every weekend. And if I didn't come home for the weekend, Ken would spend his time at the Newton Falls Hotel drinking with his friends.

THROUGH HER INTERCESSIONS

She's been there right along if only I had listened. I have continued sharing my thoughts with my mother's spirit in times of joy and in times of sorrow or whenever I feel the need for her counsel. I gaze at the three photos (now faded with age) that I have of her. My Mohawk elders tell me that I have inherited her genuine love for others mirrored in her soft brown eyes. I see the resemblance in the curve of her smile; her love abides within me and I am no longer lonely. Her soul rests within me and we are together.

She is represented in the many kind women who have showed me the way, giving me guidance throughout the years.

Florence, from the time she was a teenager, tried her best to keep me safe and continued to do so until we reached adulthood. She and I, as we grew older, argued, got into shouting matches, but we loved one another as cousins and we never severed the sinew of toughness that bound us together: the granddaughters of one feisty Mohawk lady, Agnes Jacobs. Florence and I are much alike…opinionated, impatient and self-righteous.

Minnie Mustard, childless, instinctively knew I needed the love and the hugs of a mother, so she hugged me a lot. Her bare plump brown arms reminded me the one brief memory I have of my mother, on the night before she died. I saw my mother coming in from the cold in the dead of a November night bringing in the laundry from the clotheslines wearing only a cotton dress with short sleeves. Always on the verge of remembering what she looked like and never quite sure, I longed to see her face. But it was Minnie who provided the hugs that I needed at the time.

Tota, after my mother's death, turned her own life around, and cared for me as only a grandmother could. She bartered away her possessions to keep us from starving and managed to impart a strong sense of survival, no matter what. She despised people who showed no gumption and she didn't hesitate to tell them so. Confident of her abilities, she depended on her own resourcefulness to make a living way before the term "Women's Lib" became fashionable.

My Aunt Helen kept me clothed and warm sewing, and collecting winter castoffs for me. She shared with us her meager food supply for her own family. She even, carried on my Tota's strict code of punishment for my

MY MOTHER'S SPIRIT

moral upbringing. She did her duty taking care of Tota and seeing to her mother's burial before she went forth with her own plans for a better life for her and her children.

Mumma loved me too, and helped me through my Tota's dying. Mumma epitomized the true stories of Native Indian women who accepted their lot in life with patience, grace and dignity. A true Mohawk, she kept to her Indian ways and seemed reasonably contented. Until one day, she shyly accepted a taste of alcohol from a man-friend, perhaps out of curiosity or loneliness. The alcohol dealt her a fatal blow, by robbing her of her dignity and then, by an early death and once again, Alcohol robbed me of a mother's love.

Rita, a caring neighbor and friend, took me in as one would a stray kitten. We shared the joys of sisterhood and she continued to be my "Mohawk connection" until the day she died.

At fifteen, I was convinced I was a boy-crazy misfit, but Mr. and Mrs. Fletcher took me into their household and convinced me otherwise. As my foster mother, Alice Fletcher became my champion. Showing no partiality, she treated me fairly and saw to it others did the same. She continued giving me motherly advice as I began my own family and on up until the day she died at ninety-three.

Other than my father, all my caregivers were women—until I came to live with the Fletchers. Dad Fletcher was my first inkling how important a father was to a family. He kept us in good humor with that mirthful look and the hint of a smile behind his every word. He kept our household humming and in good repair. I assumed that most husbands were like him and one day I'd get a good one like him.

My father never remarried. He made time for my seven children and gave them the same attention lovingly and wisely as his Granny Stell gave to him when he was a youngster. They adored him. Yet he continued living happily with Bessie Wilcox. Together, they helped me out whenever I asked. Bessie remained a dear friend to me and to my children.

The times I didn't listen to my mother when she sent others to warn me were the times I mistook the wrong path.

My mother's spirit appeared to help ease my pain the day my fifth child, a baby girl, died. Suzie Marie, born with a malformed heart, stopped struggling for breath two days after her birth. I wept when I heard the respirator stop, knowing I'd never feel the warmth of her mouth at my breast. I was soaked in tears when, all of a sudden, my sorrow lifted. I grew peacefully calm. I saw the image of my mother sitting at the edge of my bed holding Suzie Marie lovingly in her arms. My baby was sleeping peacefully. I reasoned, how selfish of me, to be crying in self-pity. I had the love of my four children and, no doubt, would have more. By my baby's death, I had given my mother a grandchild of her own to hold.

At forty-six, divorced and in a quandary how best to go forward with my life, my mother helped me with my choice; to make another stab at the good life. My second husband, a retired educator, encouraged me to continue with my education. I enrolled in classes at the University of Maine at Farmington and went on to Orono. Because of my Indian status, the Penobscott Indian Tribe in Maine paid for my tuition.

There's an old Mohawk saying: "A Mohawk may leave the reservation to make a living but he or she will always come home to die." And in my heart I'm a Mohawk. I am my mother, Mary Sawatis Stanfield's daughter.